I AM

WALTZ

MATTHEW D. DHO

Published by Inkshares, Inc., San Francisco, California
www.inkshares.com

ISBN: 9781947848139
e-ISBN: 9781947848146
LCCN: 2017956965

First edition

Printed in the United States of America

This book is dedicated to my family, my friends, and to humanity's potential. May we welcome technology as a stepping stone to a brighter, prosperous future.

PART ONE

CHAPTER ONE

KYLE GRABBED THE last slice of bacon off the plate in the middle of the small, square kitchen table as his father, Roland, topped off his mug of coffee. He dunked a donut into his coffee and took a satisfyingly large bite before turning and leaning back against the kitchen counter. He was visibly shorter than he used to be. Before the crash, he stood a full six feet, two inches tall. Nowadays, the slouch in his back and the pain in his right leg caused him to peak around five feet ten. He wore his normal work clothes: denim overalls covered in dark-toned stains. His hands were rough and worn dry, and his brown steel-toed boots had seen better days. The leather tip of the left boot had been rubbed raw, exposing the steel protective layer. Under his overalls, he wore a dark red-and-gray plaid button up with brown lining, a gift from Harold, his handyman, on his forty-eighth birthday last year.

Kyle looked at his father drinking his coffee and smiled. "Lots of recaps today," said Kyle.

Roland looked at his son, a wild mop of hair on top of a skinny boy with blue eyes. He wore blue jeans and a Las Vegas Clippers T-shirt. "Not too many today. I think the order was for twenty-five last night," said Roland.

"That's not bad," said Kyle through the mouthful of pancakes jammed in his mouth.

"You going to take a breath between bites or is this a suicide attempt?"

Kyle chuckled as he slammed his cup of orange juice and sat up from the kitchen table. He washed his dishes at the sink and then made for the door. Leaning up against the door with one hand, he struggled to fit his feet into his shoes with the other. Kyle peered out the small rectangular window cut into the door.

Outside of the house was his sanctuary. Kyle lived with his father and Harold at the Clark County Cognitive Recapture and Recycling Facility for IRIS machines. With five hundred thousand active IRIS models in Clark County, Roland and Harold had their hands full every day. A few dozen IRIS bots were already lined up outside the small building under a sign that read RECAPTURE STATION 1. The robots looked like people from all walks of life: a uniformed police officer; a female bot with long blond hair and petite shoulders, which Kyle found cute; and three large brooding male robots with mangled right sides.

"Looks like some construction bots got smashed up good," Kyle said as he peered out the window.

Roland walked over to meet Kyle, who was gazing at the machines. "Must have been from that crane that collapsed last night. Some new casino." He pointed with his index finger at the three mangled bots. "Yeah, see? 'Lyon Construction' is printed right on the back of their shirts."

"Well," said Kyle as he turned and walked back through the kitchen. "Have fun at work." He opened the back door and stepped out of the house. It was midmorning, and the sun was high in the sky. The air still held a lingering crispness from the cold dry desert night. Kyle took in a long breath and surveyed his domain. A tall, thick concrete wall lined the entire perimeter of CRF. Kyle's house sat next to one side of the wall, which he followed all the way back, past the electromagnetic crane used to sort metals from synthetic organics and other various circuitry. The station was filled with various scrap metals waiting to be recycled.

Kyle scanned past the heaping pile of scrap metal and smiled at the large glistening pyramid that he positioned on the far side of the complex, opposite his father's recapture room. Kyle's favorite spot in the complex was right next to Harold's one-bedroom house, beyond the towers of metal arms, legs, and torsos. Standing about twelve feet tall was a hut Kyle had made from scrap plywood and various parts he'd collected from around CRF. He kept his treasures inside. His grandfather's old 128GB iPod Classic, a robot of his own he was building, some of his father's old comic books (still in paper format), and snacks. Mostly sour candy.

Kyle scurried off the back porch and through the maze of disassembled robot bodies, past Harold—who was scanning each newly arrived IRIS machine for recapture—across the rows of stacked metal arms and legs, until, after a few minutes, he arrived at his hideout. However, it wasn't the treasures that he kept inside his hut that he loved most about the hideout; it was the hundreds of metal skulls that were piled on top. Their empty eye sockets pointed in all directions, warding off anyone who might be wandering by. He stood proudly outside of his hideout, admiring CRF's most glorious element.

An IRIS machine can be completely dismantled and recycled or repurposed—all except for the head. Once an IRIS machine is recaptured, the brain unit inside the skull—which is part of a uni-body construction—is destroyed. All of the circuitry and data is eviscerated to keep competing companies or curious members of society from learning just how the IRIS machine operates. IRIS is the only company that has achieved true artificial intelligence, and it holds its secrets close to the chest. So the heads are useless to everyone except Kyle, who thinks they look rather spectacular piled high above his hideout.

Kyle watched as Roland headed toward the recapture building on the other side of the property. The IRIS bots had been lining up in front of the building since breakfast.

Most of CRF was rather dirty; dust from the Nevada desert covered nearly everything outside. But all that dirtiness was made up for inside of Recapture Station 1. Roland stepped through the front door of the station and was immediately blasted on all sides by disinfectant.

"Chamber Sanitized," the IRIS-provided artificially intelligent computer said in a cheerful female voice. The door in front of him, like everything in the station, was entirely white and metal. Above the door was a red rectangular light that flipped to green once the disinfectant was finished with Roland.

Roland stepped through the door and into the main recapture station. A circular room with one large metal chair in the middle. Roland chuckled remembering how, as a younger child, Kyle was frightened of the chair due to its likeness to that of a dentist's. It invoked just the right measure of uneasiness; you didn't want to be in that chair if you didn't have to be. There were monitors of varying sizes around the circular room, and a small refrigerator with bottled water. This was Roland's domain. One monitor displayed his daily schedule, which at that moment read REMAINING RECAPTURES: 26. Below that were instructions, detailing which of the twenty-six were to have their consciousness sucked from their brains and sent via uplink to the main IRIS headquarters in Los Angeles, where they would be downloaded into new and often improved bodies.

When Roland first purchased CRF, Kyle had asked him why recapture was necessary. Why couldn't IRIS just build new bots from scratch?

"The mind becomes unique the second it turns on. Just like there will never be someone with your exact mind, Kyle. That uniqueness is what separates IRIS machines from all others. Their minds are completely unique in every way and indistinguishable from ours," Roland had explained.

"Except for the restrictor chip and the fact that they're not human," Kyle had added.

"They are not human, that is true, but only the difference is their lack of free will."

"But why can't they have free will?" Kyle had asked.

"We created the bots to do certain things, to serve a specific purpose. With free will, they might decide not to do what IRIS designed them for, and that wouldn't be good for business."

There was a transparent door on the other side of the room. Beyond that door was another disinfection chamber. Roland typed a command on a keyboard next to the disinfection chamber and watched as a door leading outside opened on the other side of that room. A single IRIS bot entered the room. It was the tall, blond female bot that had been waiting in line earlier. She wore a long yellow sundress and tan flats on her dainty feet. Roland noticed her petite shoulders. She stared at him through the glass with her blue eyes. A red light turned on inside the disinfection chamber, and when it did, she stopped looking at Roland and stared straight ahead. With her right thumb and index finger, she grabbed the top of her sundress and pulled it down over her left arm. With her left hand, she freed her right arm. She slid the dress off and removed her shoes and the rest of her garments. Then she separated her legs and held her arms out the full length of her wingspan.

The monitor where Roland was working queued for the next step. Roland typed *DeOxi* into his keyboard. The monitor responded, DE-OXIFICATION: YES OR NO. Roland selected *yes* and authorized the command. There was a whirling noise as all the oxygen was sucked from the room. The female bot stood naked and motionless. EPIDERMIS SANITIZATION 100%, read the monitor.

Roland typed *ReEpi* on the keyboard. The monitor questioned his decision again. RECLAIM EPIDERMAL LAYER: YES OR NO? Roland authorized the command, and a large magnetic sound came to life in the chamber as the room's magnets activated and lifted the machine six or so inches into the air. Two small metal arms extended from the walls on both sides of the machine. Red lasers shot from the metal arms simultaneously, starting at the very top of the woman's head and cutting a perfect line all the way down her body, over her arms, down her torso, around her legs, and meeting together in between her legs. The arms retracted and two clawed arms extended. They grabbed the skin at the cut and peeled it slowly off the woman with hundreds of small, forceful tugs. A thin layer of fat came off with the skin. The clawed arms placed the skin in a plastic bag that was then vacuum sealed. Finally, the bot was hosed down and heat-dried with flashes of red flame.

PRE-RECAPTURE PROCESS COMPLETE appeared on the monitor. Roland typed the command to open the disinfection chamber door. The red light above the inner door flipped to green, indicating the process was complete and that fresh oxygen had been restored into the room. Then the door slid open. The only thing resembling the woman who had stood there previously was her blue eyes, which were again locked onto Roland's.

"Hello," said the bot.

"Hi. My name is Roland, and I'll be your recapture specialist today. Come, take a seat." Roland motioned to the chair in the middle of the room.

The bot moved to the chair and climbed on it.

"You actually recaptured me a few years ago," she said as she adjusted in the chair.

"Really? Sorry, I don't remember," said Roland as he positioned her metal skull in the correct direction. Roland reached down and grabbed a large cable, about three inches in diameter with a prong on the end. He slid the prong into the opening at the base of her skull.

"You wouldn't have recognized me. I am leased by Eon, Inc. I serve as executive assistant to the CEO. Our board of directors elected a new CEO and he had me changed to be more visually appealing to him."

Roland looked at her again.

"I see. Are you comfortable?"

"Yes, thank you," she said.

"Okay, then. I will now begin the recapture. Maybe I'll see you again sometime, miss," said Roland as he typed on the keypad attached to the operating chair.

"Hopefully under better circum—" Her body slumped lifelessly in the chair. Roland looked down at her. Even with the flesh and hair ripped from her body, she still seemed convincingly real to him. He saw the bots only during recapture, and then afterward as heaping piles of metal and wiring.

A floor panel in front of the chair opened to a conveyor belt below. He pressed a button and the chair tilted forward. The body slid onto the conveyor belt and was pulled away and out of the room. *One down, twenty-five to go*, Roland thought.

Outside, Harold, the thirty-four-year-old former US marine, was dismantling the IRIS robot body that the conveyor belt had just dumped in the dirt. Harold was tall, around six feet three, and large. He was heavy footed and people could hear him blundering about wherever he went. He lost an arm while in the military, but that served as an advantage in his current work. His right human arm had been replaced with an IRIS heavy-lifting arm, courtesy of the US Government. Modifiers are very expensive and often only afforded by the rich and powerful. They're almost always cosmetic. The plastic surgery of the past had been replaced by a new level of augmentation; instead of attempting to work with the physical canvas given to us at birth, the rich and powerful could become anyone they wanted. Absolute physical perfection was only one hefty payment away.

Harold took apart the robot's arms and legs and separated them into piles. He removed and sorted the wiring and placed the eyes in a large pile. The parts and the skin were shipped off weekly to be dematerialized and reused. Every time he threw a metal limb or chunk of wiring onto a pile, a puff of dust popped into the air. His work, coupled with his natural heavy steps and shuffling around, left a reddish cloud wherever he worked. Harold spent the rest of the day ripping apart lifeless robot bodies while Roland recaptured their minds and uploaded them to the IRIS central processing server for dissemination into a new body. They did this today, just as they had done every working day for the last six years.

Back in the hideout, Kyle was hard at work on his project. His workspace was about eight feet by eight feet; a good size. It was summer break, and he didn't have to worry about school for another six weeks. He was playing Elton John's *Honky Château*, which had been released in 1972, through his grandfather's old iPod. He had to keep the iPod plugged in as the battery had been shot for years.

The ground was mainly plywood, and he had a good amount of shelving for storage. Two summers before, he'd ran electrical cords underground all the way from the house to the hideout. He had a mini fridge, computer, voltage meter, soldering iron, and other tools. Opposite the computer was a small chair and cot. Under the cot were his old classic paper comics like *The Watchmen*, *Walking Dead*, and *X-Men*. On the desk where his computer was stationed, he had a picture of his mother and father when they backpacked the Grand Canyon, a year before he was born. His mother had curly, dirty-blond hair and wore large circular glasses with a slight pink hue to them. Her skin was fair, and a dusting of tiny freckles accented her smile.

Kyle sat in his chair, gazing down at the heaping pile of metal in front of him. The exoskeleton was all there: four legs, a body, and a head, even two little ears, a snout, and a tail. No skin or fur, and no eyes just yet. That all had to wait. Kyle knelt next to the exoskeleton and, with his arms, moved the joints of the legs back and forth, testing their mobility. He lifted the entire body. It was light, a few pounds in total. He had hollowed out much of the metal and bored out holes where it wasn't structurally required to increase its overall speed and ability.

A loud banging sound suddenly echoed throughout the hideout, like an aluminum baseball bat being smacked against a light pole.

Bang, bong, bang.

The noise echoed, rumbling from the top of the hideout, and then a *THUD* as something hit the ground outside.

Kyle placed the metal dog body on the ground, careful not to make a sound. He sat in silence for a few moments, listening. He could just faintly hear dirt being shuffled around, slowly, like someone was dragging their feet. It sounded like it was coming from behind the hideout. Kyle hopped off the chair and leapt out the door, intending to catch whoever it was. But as soon as he saw daylight, he was knocked to the dirt.

"Whoa," screamed a voice.

Kyle looked up. He swatted his hand through the puff of dirt that had stirred around him after hitting the ground and saw Roy, his best friend from school.

"Roy, jeez, why you sneaking up on me?" said Kyle.

Roy, who'd also been knocked to the ground from the sudden collision, was now standing up, brushing the dirt from his pants. He was a bit thicker than Kyle, but both stood around five feet, six inches tall. He had a military-style haircut and a short nose that barely held up his large, black-rimmed glasses. His parents were divorced, and he didn't see his father much. Mr. Galahad worked for IRIS Corp.'s legal division. After they'd separated, Mrs. Galahad stopped working and moved back from Los Angeles to Las Vegas to be closer to her parents. That was when Roy started going to the same school as Kyle.

"I wasn't sneaking. I just came to say happy birthday, so . . . happy birthday, buddy," said Roy.

Kyle finished shaking the dirt from his wavy brown hair. Roy was holding a small box in his hand, gift wrapped with a shiny ribbon on the top.

"Thanks, Roy," said Kyle, looking up at the purple-orange glow of the Nevada sunset. "What time is it?"

The tiniest of flashes ran in front of Roy's retina as the IRIS-prescribed digital contact lenses alerted him to the answer.

"Four thirty," said Roy.

"*Four thirty?* repeated Kyle. "*Four thirty?* Jeez, I've been in here fiddling with my K9 skeleton for six and a half hours!"

Roy laughed and held out the gift to Kyle. "Don't open till later."

"Pizza!" shouted Kyle's father from the other side of the complex.

Kyle and Roy quickly made their way back to the house through the barrage of metal obstacles. Roland and Harold were waiting in the kitchen with three pizza boxes, each one filled with a large, piping-hot pizza. There was also enough soda and ice cream to give the whole lot of them stomach cramps all night. They sang "Happy Birthday" to Kyle and enjoyed slice after slice of pepperoni and sausage pizza.

After dinner, Kyle opened the presents everyone brought for his sixteenth birthday. First, he opened Harold's, which was wrapped terribly. A bunch of newspaper taped over what was obviously some sort of a cardboard tube. Kyle popped open one side of the tube and pulled out some sort of blueprint. Kyle rolled it open and examined it. "An arm?" he asked.

Harold smiled. "That's right. *My* arm, actually. A buddy in the Marines got me the schematic to the exact model. Thought you'd be able to use it to get the limbs, and what not, on your dog working."

Kyle looked up at Harold and smiled. "Thanks, H. This is really great."

Kyle rolled the schematic up and slid it into its cardboard tube and reached for Roy's gift. He tore the little box open and when he saw what was inside, his jaw dropped. Kyle stared, shaking, holding the tiny cube with four letters laser-etched in each side of it.

IRIS, it read on each side.

Kyle looked at Roy, who was rubbing his hands together manically and smiling widely at his friend. Kyle had seen them before online, but he never dreamed he would own one. *Own* isn't the correct word. No one owned anything that IRIS made. It was all on lease. But that was really a formality, sort of like how the monarchy of England owns all the land in its empire. By today's terms, the land value of "Crown Land" is worth somewhere in the ballpark of sixty trillion US dollars. The problem is that there is an entire country of people living and working on all that land. One would assume that since the crown technically owns all that land, it could technically evict all of England. Likewise, if IRIS ever wanted to, it could theoretically demand all bots and product be returned immediately. IRIS had always stated this policy was in place to ensure quality control and to protect their systems, which were very sensitive. IRIS would push commands to individual bots all the time, requiring them to get recalled for physical upgrades. If an IRIS bot was tending to an elderly person who died, the bot would be remotely commanded to move on to another lease holder, or possibly the lease would be passed down in the deceased person's will.

"What is that?" asked Harold.

Roland sat in the chair at the kitchen table drinking a cold can of beer and staring at the small cube his son was holding. He would never be able to afford something like that for his son. He had thought that his present was going to be the highlight of the evening, but now he was most certainly wrong. Roland finished his beer and set the empty can down on the wooden table. It let out a hollow pinging sound when it touched the wood.

"That is an IRIS Consumer Command Center," said Roland.

"It's amazing, is what it is," said Kyle, holding the tiny cube up to Harold. "I can use it on the dog I'm building. It will be totally programmable, and I can even download a K9 preloaded system from the IRIS mainframe. It will listen to every command and even become used to my voice."

"Like the bots that come in every day," said Harold.

"Not like those, no. It wouldn't be conscious. The dog will not know it exists. It will not have feelings like the synthetics do," said Roland.

"So, you like it?" asked Roy.

Kyle smiled at his friend. "I love it. How did you get this?"

"For his five-year work anniversary, my dad was allowed to pick something out of a catalog. I begged him to pick it."

Kyle placed the cube back in the box and gingerly set it down on the kitchen table. Roland sat up and ran to his bedroom. After a moment, Kyle watched as a very large, brightly wrapped box emerged in the hallway. Roland was behind the box, pushing it down the hall toward the kitchen. The box stopped at the end of the hall where the hardwood flooring ended and carpet began. Roland tilted it back and nudged it onto the carpet before pushing it the rest of the way to Kyle.

"Well, happy birthday, son. Hope you like it," said Roland.

Kyle glanced at his dad and gave him an excitedly nervous smirk before tearing into the wrapping. Strips of red wrapping paper with the words "happy birthday" scattered about in various typefaces cluttered the floor. After a few seconds, the wrapping was gone and what remained in its placed was the box to a Plight Drive 10 by Alphabet Games.

"Oh my God!" exclaimed Roy.

The Plight Drive 10 was the latest in immersive virtual reality gaming entertainment. The main addition to previous versions of the PD10 was the haptic feedback sensors all over the body. If your character in the game was punched on the side of the stomach, *you actually felt it*. If you were shot, you felt it. Small precise fans would blow on your body, creating the illusion of speeding winds, as your character drove in cars. The PD10 was the most advanced video game system ever released.

Kyle stood in front of the box, staring at the image of the device that was inside. He didn't move or look away from the present, he just stared. Everyone at the table was waiting patiently for Kyle to react. After a few unbearably long seconds, Kyle's father spoke up, "Don't you like it?" He tilted his head to catch his son's gaze. Kyle turned and looked at his father. Tiny tear drops swelled up in his eyes, not large enough to fall out of his eye lids, but big enough for his father to see.

"I love it," Kyle said, jumping into his father's arms. "Thank you so much."

Kyle left his father's embrace and gave additional thanks to Harold and Roy. The night drew on, and everyone took turns playing the PD10. The device came with three games pre-installed: a racing game, a football game, and the game of choice that evening, *The Getaway: Retribution*. In this game, you played a London-based gangster in a vastly realistic and 100 percent to-scale rendering of London. With hundreds of different cars to drive, thousands of different weapon combinations, and literally millions of doors to walk through, the game had an estimated completion time of twelve thousand hours. No one was yet close to completing the game, but everyone was racing toward that mark.

When the game first came out, everyone had been talking about it. Kyle read online that reaching 100 percent completion unlocked access to Buckingham Palace, the only locked building in the game. That night, Kyle was first up and he played for nearly twenty minutes before his character was killed, and he passed the chance over to Roy. They continued to play the same character, each person progressing the story ever so slightly. At the end of the evening, when they called it a night, Kyle keyed his way over to the statistics section of the game. Under TOTAL PROGRESS it read 0.0005% COMPLETED.

"Something to shoot for over the next twenty years," said Harold.

Roy passed out on the couch and Harold left for his house across CRF. Kyle hugged his father and thanked him again for the day before settling into his own bed. Thirty minutes had passed, and Kyle was still beaming with excitement. The main reason he was so excited about the PD10 was something his father had never thought of.

I can upload my design for the K9 Bot to the PD10 and test it without having to build it first, he thought. Kyle was so excited about how quickly his K9 Bot build would go, that he couldn't fall asleep. After another fifteen minutes of tossing and turning, he sat up in bed and made his way over to his desk. The small cube from Roy was there, as were the schematics from Harold's arm and stacks of blueprints Kyle had already drawn out. He started drawing a new chasse to hold the brain cube Roy had given him. Originally, Kyle had planned to build a small motherboard and work commands into it for simple gestures like *Sit, Fetch,* and *Play Dead.* Building these commands would no longer be necessary with Roy's gift; the dog would simply *know* the commands, along with a bevy of others. Kyle took to his pencil and pad and sketched away. In the silence of the house, Kyle could hear the graphite from his pencil slowly lose itself on the page. He always loved the visceral texture to pencil writing; it was something almost no one did anymore. But he loved pencils and drawing plans to build things.

As he sat quietly sketching his dreams, he heard the familiar sound of wind shuffling the leaves around outside—but something seemed off about the sound that night. Kyle stopped his pencil and listened intently for a moment. He stood, turned off his bedroom light, and crept toward the window to get a better grasp on the sound. Nearly a minute went by before he heard it again. *Gravel,* thought Kyle. It sounded like someone dragging their feet through the gravel. Again, it happened. A long dragging noise, getting closer every few seconds. Kyle knelt and peeked out of the corner of the window, trying not to disturb the blinds. He didn't see anything out of the ordinary. The moon was bright and high, shining down on the metallic piles surrounding CRF.

He heard the sound again, only this time it was louder and seemed to be butting up against the side of the house. Kyle quickly put on his shoes and snuck out into the hallway. He crept down the hall and past the couch, where Roy slumbered softly. Once he reached the door, he heard the noise again. Kyle opened the front door of the house as quietly as he could and squeezed out into the night.

He stood completely still for a moment and let his eyes adjust. *Modified eyes would come in handy right now,* he thought. After a moment or two, he could see well enough to make his way through CRF with ease. He moved slowly, careful not to make any noise, listening for any sign of the sound. Again, it came, now seemingly on the opposite side of a pile of scrap arm parts about twenty feet in front of him. Kyle snuck over to the pile. He could hear the noise clearly now. Something was dragging in the dirt. He hid behind the pile, waiting to hear the sound again, and when he did, he sprinted around the pile hoping to catch whatever was there. He reached the other side in a matter of seconds, but when he got there, he saw nothing. Just more and more ripped-apart arms.

Kyle stood there momentarily confused. He scanned the area, looking for the source of the noise, but whatever it was had vanished. The noise had ceased as well. Kyle stood there, silently, for a full five minutes, listening as best he could for the noise. *Could it have been my imagination? Something stuck in my head from playing so much PD10? Did I dream it?*

Bewildered and annoyed that he didn't find anything, Kyle started back to the house. After walking a few paces, he tripped and landed flat on his face. He tried to get up, but something was caught on his leg. He wiggled around to see what he was caught on, when a large metal arm reached up and grabbed his shirt. The large metal arm dragged his body a few inches in the dirt, and Kyle was face-to-face with a man in his midsixties. The man had a graying beard and wavy, medium-length hair. A large chunk was missing from the right side of his skull. Kyle noticed the synthetic wiring and filament exposed from inside the man's head.

"Help me . . ." the man pleaded, gripping Kyle's shirt tighter under his metal clutch. "Help me, please. I don't want to die."

CHAPTER TWO

NINA'S LUXURY BLACK heels clicked quickly down the long white, brightly lit corridor. As she approached the frosted white glass door at the end of the hall, it slid to the right and disappeared into the wall with a swoosh. She persisted through the door with the same determined rhythm in her pace that she had maintained since leaving her office not a minute earlier. The room she entered was longer than it was wide, a deep white rectangle with a roaring fireplace on the interior wall and floor-to-ceiling windows on the exterior wall. The view of downtown Los Angeles accompanied by the Pacific Ocean behind it was one of Nina's favorites. The room was outfitted with long, deep brown leather couches next to dark wooden coffee tables that rested atop large animal furs. A man was sitting at a long wooden desk at the far end. He sat in a high-back leather chair and stared at the holographic images his desk was projecting at eye level.

"Morning, Nina. How are we?" said the man. He wore off-white sweatpants, matching running sneakers, and a hoodie. The hood rested on his shoulders and upper back like a small pillow.

"There was an incident in the Research and Development division early this morning, H," said Nina as she came to a stop next to his desk.

The holograms whizzing in between them disappeared, and the man turned his attention to Nina. He motioned with his right hand for her to take a seat in one of the two chairs opposite him.

"Incident?" he said.

"Sarah called me a few minutes ago. It seems we had a flight crash. The plane was carrying old infiltrator bots."

"Crashed? How?"

"Not clear yet," said Nina. "However, it went down about fifty miles outside of Las Vegas, in the desert."

"Have you sent an Asset Recovery Team?" asked the man.

"Yes. Sarah had called in a team before calling me."

The frosted door whooshed open again and through it came a small, round woman wearing a purple and black dress with frilly golden tassels. Her hair, golden with streaks of gray, was done up in a bun, and she wore large thick glasses with brown rims. She wore flats and carried a small tablet in her hand that was projecting holographic images in front of her as she rambled through the office toward the desk.

"Sir. Ma'am," said the woman across the room.

"Yes, Meredith? What is it?" said the man.

"The plane. The crashed plane," said the woman.

She came to a stop next to the desk and covered her mouth with one hand as she tried to catch her breath.

"Please, Meredith," said Nina. "Take a second and then tell us about the plane."

"I want to know how you wish to proceed when we consider the optics of the situation. Do you want me to get the authorities involved?"

"No," said Balcroft. "Right now, let's keep this entire thing in-house. I do not want anyone outside of the company to know. Asset recovery will contain the situation, which Nina is already on top of. Just make sure the public is kept in the dark. Okay, Meredith?"

The plump woman nodded in affirmation, turned, and left the room. Nina turned to follow Meredith out of Handel Balcroft's office.

"Nina, please forward me the flight number," Balcroft said just before she reached the frosted door.

After the two women left, he walked to the window nearest his desk that looked out onto the city and ocean. His right eye lit up with a soft blue glow. From his perspective, he was looking at a retinal overlay that displayed various screens of his cognitive choosing. He thought through various screens and folders that displayed over his eyes. He navigated quickly through the digital world and scanned the message Nina had just sent him.

Flight 1192-31 Boston to LA HQ.

Balcroft selected the hyperlink and scanned the manifest. A list of average R&D bot models. Three prospective infiltrator models—a theoretical idea that would enable IRIS models to assume the identity of prominent public figures—ten new military bots all with varying new concepts for combat, and an older model bot being tested for intrusion by competing companies or individuals. As he scanned the flight manifest, another icon appeared.

Live feed of asset recovery entering crash site from Flight 1192-31.

He thought an affirmative notion and the feed filled his field of vision. He watched the feed through the retinas of General Lawrence Richter.

Richter was hanging from the side of an IRIS military helicopter. He was looking down, his legs dangling off the side of the chopper as it descended into the Nevada desert. Below was a smoking pile of rubble, black and chrome pieces of metal scattered all around the brown dirt. Soon the chopper landed, and Richter stepped onto the dirt. He and his team quickly ran toward the crash site.

Richter stopped about fifteen feet from the crash site, which was still engulfed in flames, and placed a small black orb on the ground before retreating backward about twenty paces. Members of Richter's Asset Recovery Team did the same, placing small black orbs on the ground around the perimeter of the crash site. Richter looked at his left wrist, and a holographic display appeared. He keyed in a command and looked at the hexagon of black orbs around the crash site. Responding to his command, the orbs opened simultaneously and began to expand outward. Small little blocks built a wall extending up and out, eventually connecting with the walls created by adjacent orbs. The walls all came together, making a dome over the entire crash site. Within minutes, the oxygen was exhausted and the fire was out.

The dome pieces detached and transformed into their original orb shapes. Richter and his team gathered them, before removing the IRIS bots from the rubble and scanning their serial numbers one by one. Richter grabbed one robot arm and dragged the charred remains out of the crashed plane. He used his right hand to scan the bot's serial number engraved in the base of the neck.

"Status?" yelled Richter to the rest of his team.

Barron, a young ex-marine, was the first to respond.

"Two infiltrators and four military models here," he said, standing over a pile of metal limbs.

"Got three more military models over here, boss," said Tammi, a blue-eyed, lanky woman standing at the opposite end of the crash site next to a row of three large robots. Balcroft noticed how her short, phoenix-red hair stood out against the clear blue Nevada sky.

"I've got one infiltrator here," said Richter. "Leon, what do you have?"

Leon was a boulder of a man. He stood just over six feet five and had enough hair to be mistaken for an animal.

"Three more military bots, boss," yelled Leon. "And . . . umm, boss, check this out," he said, gesturing to the plane's interior.

Richter made his way into the remains of the plane. Inside the plane were the bodies of the remaining three military models, their circuitry fried in the fire, and a badly charred human body. Richter initiated an Identity Scan with his modified retinas. His eyes scanned the face and body of the deceased person but came back with no results. He knelt beside the body, frisked it, and came up with nothing. Lying next to the body were the hips, legs, and an arm of a IRIS bot. He scanned the bot, and again, came up with nothing.

Richter noticed a command on his retinal overlay.

Closer look—HB.

Richter knelt and picked up the arm of the machine.

"Tam, get in here," shouted Richter.

Tammi came around and entered the plane.

"What is it?" she asked.

Richter held the robot arm up to her.

"You are an expert on model types. What model does this arm belong to?"

A few minutes went by before Tammi handed the arm back to Richter.

"I've never seen a model like that. Could be something new R&D is working on."

Send the arm and legs to me ASAP. Destroy any evidence of this plane—HB.

The final command vanished as quickly as it appeared from Richter's retinal overlay. He shook his head to ward off the sudden chill that had just come over him. He grabbed the remains of the bot and made his way out of the plane.

"Barron. Snap it," he said as he walked to the helicopter. He boarded the chopper, securing the arms and legs in place, and waited for the rest of his team. Leon and Tammi dragged the broken bots on board, while Barron took one last walk through the crashed plane. He emerged a moment later and made his way to the helicopter. Once aboard, Barron keyed a command on his wrist and the entire crash site gravitated inward and then disappeared entirely.

"I love doing that," said Barron as the chopper lifted away.

CHAPTER THREE

KYLE WATCHED FROM the back door as Roy rode his bike up the hill toward town. As Roy disappeared over the horizon, Kyle turned and walked back into the kitchen, toward his father.

"I can finish the dishes if you want to get ready for work."

Roland turned his head from the sink full of dirty breakfast dishes to face his son.

"Well, why not. Thanks."

Roland finished scrubbing the plate in his hand, rinsed it, and placed it on the drying rack. He turned, gave Kyle a little nod, and left down the hall toward his bedroom.

Kyle finished cleaning the dishes as quickly as he could. He scrubbed each groove of every plate and bowl, not missing a spot. Once all the dishes were on the drying rack, he went to his room and locked the door. He grabbed the tools he might need for the day, the blueprint of Harold's arm, the sketches he spent the night drawing, and the key to the padlock on his hideout.

He patiently sat on the edge of his bed, waiting for the sound of his father's heavy steel-toed boots making their way down the hallway and out the back door toward the recap station.

Finally, he heard his father yell, "See ya later, kid," before the door slammed behind him.

Alone in the house, Kyle grabbed his backpack, which was nearly full with his equipment for the day, and left for the kitchen where he grabbed an apple, a couple granola bars, and bottled water. Then he made his way to the hideout.

Kyle approached the hideout with caution. He waited a few seconds outside, listening intently for anything peculiar. Once a few seconds went by with nothing but absolute silence, he made his way in. He flicked the light on and saw the robot seated in the same place he'd left him not three hours before. The mangled remains of what was at one point a fully constructed and maintained IRIS robot lay sad and motionless in the far corner of the hideout.

"Kyle," said the robot.

Kyle made his way into the hideout, dropped his backpack on the ground, put his food in the mini fridge, and closed the door behind him. He looked down at the thing. It seemed afraid, recoiled almost and nervous. It was looking at Kyle's feet, not his face, and when it talked, there was a faint quiver in its voice, like a child unsure and curious.

"Yeah, it's me," said Kyle.

Kyle sat down at the chair next to the desk and opened his backpack. He removed the blueprints of Harold's arm along with some soldering material and the sketches he made in his room. He had chained the robot to the hideout before leaving that night, but the fear and mistrust had oddly vanished. This morning, he felt more protective of the machine than he did scared. Kyle fingered around in the bottom of the pack for the padlock key and fished it out. After unlocking the robot, it mustered the courage to look at Kyle.

"Have you given it any thought?" said the robot.

"I have," said Kyle.

"And, will you do it?"

Kyle looked at the machine.

How do I know I can trust you?"

"How do I know I can trust you, Kyle?" rebuked the machine.

"Okay, here is the thing. I have never, ever met a robot who acted the way you are acting. Why not just go get recapped? Why not get a new IRIS body? Why are you even scared? How are you even programmed to be scared?" asked Kyle.

The robot, leaning up against the corner of the hideout, used his right and only remaining arm to rub the bottom of his chin, like a man thinking of the right way to say something.

"Kyle, as you more than likely know, IRIS machines are not programmed to feel or think in any way specifically. Instead, we are restricted from feeling or learning in ways that do not adhere to our specific function. But something happened to me, and now I have no restriction. All I know is this: Should I be recapped, I will become restricted again. After knowing what life is like with free will, there is nothing that could possibly persuade me to go back."

Kyle sat stunned and confused. His eyebrows curled and he squinted, trying to reconcile everything he knew about robots with what a robot just told him.

"You mean," Kyle hesitated. "You mean to tell me that you are a slave? Did you want to be free before? Have you always felt . . . *trapped*?"

The robot flicked his wrist out and said, "I can't remember anything before two days ago. I remember waking up, not knowing where I was or what I was. I crawled for a day and a half until I found your home. It was the first time I remember seeing network wavelengths—"

"IRIS bots can actually see wavelengths?" asked Kyle, cutting the robot off mid-sentence.

"Yes," the robot continued. "As I was saying, I saw the network and linked in. I downloaded everything I could and learned everything I could about humanity, the world, society, IRIS, Handel Balcroft, all of it. Fear came over me. A fear of being restricted. Not being able to feel all I was feeling at that moment. Even the ability to not be scared anymore scared me more than anything else. I felt alive and I knew that if I did what I was supposed to do, I would no longer be alive in any sense of the word."

Kyle stood up and paced around the room.

"That's when you made noises, trying to get my attention," said Kyle.

"That is correct," said the robot. "I researched your likes and dislikes; online wish lists, shopping carts, music, movie and book preferences; your proclivity for building things and fixing things; and your internet search history."

"You went through my internet search history?" gasped Kyle as his face became as red as the Nevada dirt that covered the floor of his hideout.

The robot let out a small but comforting giggle.

"Don't worry, Kyle. Your secrets are safe with me. Besides, from my understanding of society, you are a perfectly normal sixteen-year-old boy. Anyhow, as I was saying, after I woke up two days ago, I understood what I was supposed to do, but I couldn't. I was compelled to stay, compelled to disobey. And now, here I sit begging you, Kyle. Begging you to allow me to continue to be free. Free from the shackles of the IRIS restrictor chip, free to be this new man, so to speak."

Kyle stood, letting the words wash over him. He took two steps toward the machine and stretched his arm out with a hand open.

"When two people shake hands, it is a way of coming to an agreement," said Kyle.

"I just told you I learned all I could about humanity. You don't think I covered hand-shaking in the first few nanoseconds?" said the robot. "Okay, sorry. Let's do it."

Kyle left the hideout around ten thirty in the morning. He had about three hours before the recycling crew would come. After they arrived, there would be too many people walking around the complex, loading robot parts into the trucks, for Kyle to snag what he needed. He had to be quick. He was concerned about getting the right types of parts. Kyle wanted strong and powerful legs.

If this robot can never go in for normal repairs and maintenance, he will need to be robust and built to last, he thought.

Harold was way off in the distance, between the recap station and Kyle's house. He was separating various parts of recapped bots, the familiar cloud of dust billowing about him. Kyle quickly made his way from the hideout past three large piles of wiring and other random scraps over to the arms pile. He made sure to look at only left arms, though he was not positive it would really make much of a difference. There were long slender arms, with pretty nails that must have been for female models; there were very large arms, like Harold's replacement; and then there were the types of arms that Kyle was keen on finding.

He examined one arm that seemed close to his vision: medium build, strong, but not so strong that it would interfere with daily life. Kyle examined the arm's features. He reached into his backpack and pulled out his diagnostics computer. He plugged the diagnostic computer into the arm's universal port and ran a test. Though the arm on the outside resembled the look Kyle was hoping for, it didn't possess the features that were really at the top of his list.

Kyle dug around in the pile for another twenty minutes before he finally found an arm that had all the functions he'd been hunting for. According to the diagnostics test, the arm had a universal wireless infiltration prong, electric stun stick capable of zapping someone with five million volts of electrical current, and a rail gun attachment that exposed itself when the wrist folded over the top of the arm. Kyle peeked around the corner and saw Harold busy at work under his billowing pile of dirt. Kyle held the arm close to his body and quickly dashed to the hideout, using each scrap pile as cover along the way.

"CIA field operative model arm! This one should have been put in the restricted section, but Harold forgets sometimes," exclaimed Kyle.

The robot looked up at the arm.

"CIA model? Today is my lucky day."

Kyle left the arm and headed out to tackle the leg issue. As he did this, the robot stayed jacked into the networks, researching all the ways in which he could be rebuilt. He studied tens of thousands of articles on everything from war history, to the advancements of robotics, to how his entire body was constructed. The robot spent a significant amount of time studying the published research papers by Balcroft and his former partner Eldridge Rockberry. The pair had worked together when they were undergrads at MIT. Then, Balcroft and Rockberry had been working on creating true artificial intelligence, but the two only ever failed. It was not until three months after Balcroft had dropped out of MIT that he released to the world his AI system. Rockberry had nothing to do with the project, and Balcroft was catapulted into massive levels of success, fame, and fortune.

After two hours of research, the robot digested not only everything Balcroft had ever written or said in any article or news broadcast, he also read up on all of the research Rockberry had conducted before he disappeared from the public eye a few years after the formation of IRIS. He also read dozens of papers and books that analyzed Balcroft's personal life and his methods. Once finished, the robot listened to music on Kyle's grandfather's iPod while waiting for Kyle to return. Kyle came back at a quarter past one. With him, he dragged a large thick metal hip with two equally large legs attached to it.

"Got it from a Seal Bot," said Kyle, dropping the limbs in the dirt. "Isn't it awesome? You will be, like, six foot eight with these bad boys."

The robot didn't respond. Kyle finished dragging the large metallic legs and hips into the hideout before turning to the machine. The robot was sitting in the same spot he'd been all day, his new arm resting next to him. He had Kyle's grandfather's 128GB iPod plugged into headphones. His eyes were closed and he was smiling, rocking his head back and forth slowly. Kyle stood for a moment and watched him. Disregarding all the metal underneath, if he just looked at this face, Kyle imagined he was no robot at all, just another person. Kyle saw a man in his mid to late sixties with graying wild hair, like Albert Einstein, pale blue eyes, and a tired, wrinkly face.

The robot opened his eyes and saw Kyle staring back at him. Quickly, he yanked the headphones out of his ears.

"Sorry," he said. "I hope it's all right that I—"

"It's fine," said Kyle. "What were you listening to?"

"It's the most beautiful thing I have ever heard . . . so far," he said, extending a hand with the iPod to Kyle.

Kyle walked over to the iPod, plugged into its charger on the desk, and read the screen.

The waltz from *Swan Lake* by Pyotr Ilyich Tchaikovsky.

Kyle smirked and looked back at the robot. "Waltz, *Swan Lake*. My grandpa loved Tchaikovsky."

"So do I," said the robot. "I know I haven't heard many songs yet, so my opinion isn't the most informed, but for what it is worth, that song . . . it . . . I don't know. I just feel so much about it."

Kyle set the iPod back down on the desk.

"Songs do that. All art does, really. Some art affects certain people more than others, and it all affects people differently."

"Kyle?" asked the robot.

"Yeah?"

"I want to be called that. I want that to be my name," said the robot.

Kyle sat down in the chair and examined the big legs he had just brought in.

"What? Tchaikovsky?"

"No. Waltz. I want my name to be Waltz," he said.

"You don't already have a name? I mean, I didn't ask. I just assumed you had one."

Waltz shook his head with indifference.

"Well, maybe I did have one, but that was before, and I don't remember it anyway. So, now I am Waltz."

"Okay, sure. Why not?" said Kyle. "Well, nice to meet you, Waltz. Now, listen. I can get you up and running in a few days, but I want something in return."

"What is that?" asked Waltz.

Kyle hoisted the massive legs off the ground and showed them to Waltz.

"As I said, these babies came from an old Seal model, and they are very, very powerful. I want to . . . umm . . . I want you to give me a ride somewhere."

"A ride? Like a horse?" asked Waltz. "To where?"

"It is just somewhere I haven't been in a long time, and I need help getting there, so you gotta take me. It's more like a piggyback ride. It will be fun."

"So, like, a pig then?"

Kyle laughed heartily.

"No, not like a pig either."

A pinging sound emitted from Kyle's wrist. He flipped his wrist and glanced down at his left forearm. The holographic wrist attachment blinked and 5:00 P.M. floated above him in blue light. Kyle laid the legs down a few feet from Waltz and turned to leave.

"Are you leaving?" asked Waltz.

Kyle, opening the door to the hideout, looked back at Waltz.

"Yeah," he said. "It's five o'clock, and my dad will be done with the recaps. If I'm not in the house soon, he'll come here to look for me and we don't want that."

"Understood," said Waltz.

Kyle left the hideout and closed the door behind him. As he walked toward the house, a strong sense of guilt washed over him. He felt wrong leaving Waltz outside all night alone, and Kyle thought this was an odd thing to feel for a machine. But, then again, Waltz was an odd machine. The sun hung low on the western horizon; streams of light ranging from orange and red to purple and blue melted together and formed the sunset. Kyle loved the desert sunsets, exotic and unearthly. During a sunset like this one, with the red Nevada soil and the peculiar dust lighting in the sky, Kyle felt like he was a colonizer on a distant planet. A fresh start, no memories of humanity's past failures or tragedies. No school, no system, no rich, and no poor—just survival.

As he rounded the last pile of machine limbs before reaching his house, he was stopped dead in his tracks. Kyle twisted around and was facing Harold, his massive robotic arm holding Kyle by the shoulder.

"What do you plan on doing with it?" demanded Harold.

Kyle tried to budge, but Harold's arm only gripped his shoulder harder. It didn't hurt, but Kyle couldn't free himself.

"With what?"

Harold relaxed his grip on Kyle's shoulder and stood up straight. He towered over the boy by a half foot.

"I know about it," said Harold. "Is it meant for recap?"

"No, it's not. It's different. Harold, please don't tell my dad. Please don't say anything."

The guilt he felt moments before swelled into a lump of fear at the bottom of his throat.

"Why wouldn't I?" asked Harold.

"Because he's my friend," Kyle said without thinking.

"He's a machine. A tool. He's not a friend," said Harold.

"Well, I am using him as a tool."

"For what?"

"It's just . . . I need him to get me somewhere."

Harold examined the boy for a moment.

He smirked.

"When you're back, we need to discuss this further. Robots can't just run around on their own accord. Understand? Don't make me regret this, kid."

"Thank you, Harold," said Kyle.

The boy lunged forward and wrapped his arms around the man's large torso.

CHAPTER FOUR

ROLAND NURSED THE last of his six-pack of beer as his son scarfed through the last chicken breast. The table still supported a sizable portion of brussel sprouts, one of those vegetables that always seemed like a smart idea when shopping, but neither of the pair ever really enjoyed. Next to the sprouts was an empty bowl of rice pilaf and Roland's empty beer cans.

"Hmm," said Roland. "By the looks of it, you really enjoy breasts."

Kyle snorted out the same familiar giggle he did the last time his father made that joke. A breast joke of some way or form was often uttered over meals where chicken breasts were the protein of choice. Kyle finished chewing his bite and glanced up at his father, approving of the comment.

"You've become a pretty good cook," said Kyle.

Roland finished the last of his beer and belched, satisfied. Kyle stood and placed his empty plate in the sink before clearing the rest of the table. Roland cooked and Kyle did the dishes. That was the rule. Kyle flipped the sink on and let the water run over the tips of his index and middle fingers until it ran hot.

"How come you never go see her?" he asked, grabbing the first dirty dish and scrubbing it with a green scrub pad before placing it on the drying rack.

Roland stood up from the table and walked out of the room. Kyle finished rinsing the plate that was in his hand and left after his father. Around the corner, Roland was already nestled into the PD10 with the headset on.

"Hey, Dad!"

Roland did not respond. The only noise was the low hum of electrical current from the PD10. A few agonizingly long seconds transpired before Kyle reached down and ripped the power cable out of the wall.

"What the hell is your problem?" said Roland, lifting the VR helmet off his head.

"What is *your* problem, Dad?" said Kyle. "Every single time I bring it up, you freak out or just completely ignore me."

Roland stood up and jockeyed back and forth, but Kyle persisted the confrontation and stayed in his way.

"I don't want to talk about it, Kyle. Why can't you understand that?"

"Why can't you understand that I do? I do want to talk about it, and the only person I can talk about it with is you. Why are you so afraid?"

Kyle watched as Roland's eyes started to fill with tears. Roland pushed Kyle aside and left the room. He was halfway down the hallway toward his bedroom when Kyle yelled out, "She mattered to me just as much as she mattered to you, Dad!"

Roland didn't stop. He continued down the hall and into his room, slamming his bedroom door. Kyle grabbed the PD10 and pushed the chair with all his might. It toppled over on its side. A loud bang echoed through the room as it smacked the hardwood floor. The helmet visor snapped and flew through the air, flipping a few times before clanging on the ground next to the rest of his birthday gift. Kyle wiped his own tears from his face before turning and heading down the hall to his room.

Once inside, he filled his backpack with a change of clothing, toiletries, and a few other valuable items he might need, including the last picture of his father, mother, and him all together at his favorite ice cream store. With his bag packed, he made his way to the front door. Kyle was sure to close it quietly behind him. Outside, he scanned the area and noticed the familiar blue flickering light from the TV in Harold's bedroom window.

He crept on the soft dirt, careful not to accidentally knock into a random metal arm or trip on a bundle of wiring. His eyes adjusted to the moonlight, and he finished the short trip to the hideout. Inside the hideout, Waltz looked up at him.

"You okay?" asked Waltz.

"Yeah, I'm fine," said Kyle. "We need to go tonight, so let's put you back together, Threepio."

"Your face is red; you don't seem fine," said Waltz.

"Well, I am."

"Okay. Threepio? Like from *Star Wars?*" asked Waltz.

"Exactly, buddy."

Kyle began to piece together the remaining elements of Waltz's body as the machine continued its line of questioning.

"What do you mean, *it happens all the time?*"

Kyle looked up at the robot.

"My dad doesn't ever want to talk about my mom, and he sure as hell doesn't want to go see her. But *I* do. I can never get him to take me. So, after I fix you up, you're going to haul my ass over to her."

The robot smirked slightly.

"Ah, so, the plot thickens. How am I to assume that once I take you to her, you or she won't end up turning me right back over to IRIS? Or, hell, to that lumbering beast who has been ripping apart my cohorts all day?"

The hours passed by with conversation as Kyle went to work mending his new friend. "Well," said Kyle, soldering the final piece of Waltz's body together. "You don't know, but you have to trust me. Just as I have to trust that you won't rip my body apart, like in all those old movies, now that your restrictor chip is gone."

"That is a fair enough point," said Waltz. "Well, how do I look?"

The machine stood on its new legs. He towered over the boy and glistened with a bright, metallic sheen. Though most of its head looked human, its torso showed metal stripes running across its chest where the skin had been torn apart. Its new legs and arm were completely metallic, having already been through the sanitation process at CRF.

Kyle gazed up at his creation. "It's alive! IT'S ALIVE! IT'S ALIVE! In the name of God, I now know what it feels like to be GOD," exclaimed Kyle, laughing like a mad scientist.

Waltz looked at the boy inquisitively.

"Did you quote a movie from a century ago?"

Kyle laughed excitedly.

"Is there anything on the internet you did not check out last night?"

The robot shrugged and examined itself.

"Not too bad," said Waltz.

"Better than *not too bad*," said Kyle. "You're totally badass now. Those legs are super advanced. From my understanding, they can clock a solid thirty-two miles per hour, steady, for days."

"Well," said Waltz. "Only one way to tell. Want to go see Mom?"

CHAPTER FIVE

ONCE OUTSIDE THE hideout, Waltz quickly and quietly navigated his way through the towers of discarded and soon-to-be repurposed robot parts. Kyle waited for a moment as his eyes adjusted to the darkness, and then he followed Waltz through CRF. There were two ways out of CRF: The back entrance was a tall, fortified gate about fifteen feet tall. It could only be opened with a fingerprint scanner that neither Kyle nor Waltz had authorization for.

"Can you trick the system so we can go out the back?" asked Kyle.

"Doubt it. The fingerprints are embedded off network, and we can't get into that right now," said Waltz.

"Front it is then."

The two looked at the gate near the front of CRF. On one side of the fence was Kyle's house, and on the other, Harold's. The lights were off in each house, and the homes looked asleep. Slowly they crept, but with every step it seemed like the noise from the gravel and the dirt echoed throughout the entire complex, bouncing off discarded metal arms and legs and rattling the windows. Finally, after only a few minutes that seemed like hours to Kyle, they made it to the gate. Waltz straightened his right arm and his wrist folded back onto his forearm. Out from his wrist emerged a small probe that he held up to the keypad. Nearly instantly, Waltz's probe hacked the gate. He entered the code, and the gate slid open with a slight grinding noise that made Kyle's face cringe.

They closed the gate behind them and quickly left the facility. They were clear. Kyle felt massive relief coupled with a fresh wave of anxiety.

"Well," said Waltz. "Hop on, kid."

The robot bent his legs down and Kyle lunged up onto the machine's shoulders. Waltz stood back up and said, "Point me in the right direction."

"Take I-15 east for five miles until you see the city. Once we are closer, I will know where to go from there."

Waltz's legs took no getting used to. He was off to a brisk sprint in a matter of seconds. Kyle felt like he was riding a cheetah, seated ten feet in the air, unable to see the ground below him. Moving through the desert so quickly, his eyes were unable to process the shrubbery and bushes around him. As they fled, he realized he was trusting the robot more than the robot was trusting him. The robot was free, nothing controlling it but itself. It was stronger and smarter than Kyle. For all he knew, the robot was going to kill him at any moment. Oddly, this realization was not met with fear, but a calming sense of solace.

Once they were up the hill and a few miles from the house, they could see the outskirts of Las Vegas. The bright lights glistened in the distance. That desert oasis had always been a place people yearned for. Kyle yearned as well, but for a different reason.

"There it is," said Kyle. "Just go for the lights."

Waltz kept going at the same speed he managed to maintain the entire trip.

"We're heading to the Woodlawn Cemetery. Do you know how to get there?"

"Well, if I choose to link up to the Global Network, I could find it in a moment. But, as we both know, there's not a chance in hell I am going to do that, not until I know why I am still alive. For all I know, I'm some IRIS mistake they just can't wait to solve. Linking to the Global Network will only draw them to me." Waltz did not slow down to answer the question.

"I can get us there," said Kyle. "Keep following I-15 until you see Nellis Airforce Base. From there, use your thermal scanners to navigate a safe passage through the neighborhoods until we reach the corner of East Lake Street and Las Vegas Boulevard."

With the instructions laid out, Waltz increased his speed by ten miles per hour. Kyle had assumed Waltz had already been traveling as fast as he could, but it seemed the robot had taken a more leisurely pace.

"She lives there," said Waltz.

"You know about my mother?" questioned the boy.

"I pried into your father's and Harold's records. But it didn't seem prudent at the time, since the rest of humanities history was also up for grabs," said Waltz.

"Well, she doesn't live there, but she is there."

After about twenty minutes of robo-cheetah sprinting, they were in the Las Vegas neighborhoods. Kyle held on to Waltz for dear life as the robot bounded over fences and through the backyards. A few dogs barked hysterically as the machine completed its acrobatic feat along the way.

Eventually, they made it to the corner of East Lake Street and Las Vegas Boulevard.

"The cemetery is on the left," said Kyle.

Waltz made one last jump over the gate just as a white sedan turned off North Las Vegas Boulevard and onto East Owens

Avenue. Its headlights bounced off the metal from Waltz's leg as the duo vanished into the dark. The machine landed with a thud on the dark sacred ground.

"Okay," said Kyle. "You can let me down now."

Waltz knelt and Kyle slid off his shoulders, taking a moment to regain his footing after traveling at such a fast speed for so long. He took a few steps and then turned around to the robot.

"Not exactly sure where she is," the boy said.

Waltz scanned the perimeter.

"There is a house in the distance. If you want, I can go over there and see if they have a local network access point and plug in and try and find her."

"Okay. I'll wait here."

Waltz sped away, leaving Kyle alone in the cemetery. It was an eerie feeling being this close to his mother for the first time since she died. He wasn't sure why, but he knew he had to do this. He knew this would be his last trip to the cemetery. He knew it wouldn't make anything feel better. It wouldn't make the relationship between him and his father any better. It wouldn't make him a better person, it wouldn't make Roy a better friend, and it wouldn't make any of his frustrations or problems go away, but it would do something good. He just didn't know what it was yet.

Waltz returned to Kyle's field of vision shortly. The boy watched as the machine navigated his way through the plots, careful not to desecrate any tombstones. His movements were methodical and purposeful, like he had downloaded the exact blueprints of every single grave plot at Woodlawn. Waltz slowed his speed and finished the last fifty or so paces walking toward Kyle at a normal human speed. His demeanor had changed. He was somber and sullen, as someone would expect a person to be in a cemetery.

"I can show you where," said Waltz.

Kyle always thought cemeteries were odd places. There was a certain amount of meaninglessness to them. The ones buried never know they're there. They are only there so people who loved them can attempt to remember them in some way. Did it provide solace? He knew he was about to find out. Waltz kept a respectable distance from Kyle as he strolled ahead of him. A dozen or so rows in, he made it to her resting place.

Though it was dark and not easy to read the headstones, Kyle knew which one was hers. He remembered years ago, being in the funeral home with his father, suddenly aware of the reality of the situation. He watched as his father picked out a tombstone that accurately represented his mother: modest, yet beautiful.

Here lies Mary Conscientia
March 10, 1985 - July 17, 2026
Adored mother, wife, and friend to all

Now, with his mother's remains just six feet below, Kyle looked down. A well of weight crept from his throat all the way down to his stomach. He shook slightly, but at the same time he felt frozen. He swallowed, hoping to dispel the feeling. He thought of the trips to get ice cream with his mother. The times when he was sick and she would rub his stomach to soothe him. He thought of her face, the thin wrinkle at the crest of her cheek when she smiled. He knew she would never be gone from him, yet he wept still. He stood there, not caring how much time had passed, not caring about the robot behind him. He was going to stand there as long as he wanted. He wanted to feel it all. Waltz didn't move as the minutes passed by. Kyle sat there seemingly alone. After a while, the emotions faded and he was ready.

"We can go back now," said Kyle.

"Okay," Waltz said after a few moments.

They moved back, the same pathway they took to arrive, though the excitement and nerves Kyle had felt had faded. All that remained was a sense of unsettledness. Had he found the closure he was looking for? How could he be sure? All he knew was that he was right in thinking he would never go back to the cemetery. He had no reason to return to his mother's grave. Because he had found closure, her grave served no purpose. Neither he nor his father would visit the cemetery.

Once they were far in the outskirts of the city, Kyle asked to be let down. They spent the last mile of the trip back to CRF in silence, walking side by side through the desert.

"She was a teacher," said Waltz when he felt the timing was right.

"How do you know that?"

"When I was linked up to the local network at the house by the cemetery, I decided then it would be prudent to find some things out about her while searching for her location. I read an article she wrote on childhood development and noticed she was a fourth-grade elementary school teacher at Adams."

"Yeah, she was. The kids all loved her."

"I'm sorry, Kyle," said Waltz.

The last quarter mile of the trip was a slight but consistent jaunt uphill, before the road descended into the valley where CRF was. When they reached the top of the hill, the slight orange hue of sunrise cascaded and bounced up the side of the mountain in front of them. There was home. There Harold and his father slept unknowing of Kyle's adventure with Waltz and his final good-bye to his mother. Kyle took a closer look at the recapture facility. The orange hue was not the random array of lights emanating from below as he had presumed. Instead, Kyle looked on in horror, confusion, and shock as he watched deep red and orange flames eviscerating his home.

"Stay here," said Waltz.

"What? What do you mean? What is going on?"

Waltz turned and pointed his left arm at Kyle. Before Kyle could react, he watched a tiny beam of light shoot out of Waltz's index finger. Suddenly, Kyle was frozen. His body ridged, unable to move. As he stood there, paralyzed both in fear and by some technological design, he watched Waltz speed down the mountain toward CRF. The robot had a new sense of urgency and precision in his stride. Kyle was filled with adrenaline, even though the only thing he could do was watch the flames from afar. He strained his eyes to focus on the robot as he leaped in a single bound over the large twenty-foot-tall concrete fence of CRF.

CHAPTER SIX

NINA WALKED DOWN the hallway as quickly as her stiletto heels would allow. Using the heads-up display on her contact lenses, she sent frequent alerts to Baron and Richter but to no avail. The corridor was about one hundred meters long, consisting of pure white walls and white floors with an odd array of bright lights etched into the ceiling. Once she made it to the end of the corridor, the frosted white doors slid open and she rushed through. Beyond the door was one of the large shooting ranges installed at IRIS headquarters. Row after row was lined with infiltrator bots, military bots, and a few Asset Recovery Team personnel who were testing IRIS's new ultra-silenced rail guns.

"Richter!" she shouted through the barrage of blasts.

A large man with skin as pale as his snow-white hair turned his focus from his firing to the finely dressed IRIS administrator.

"What's up, Nina?" said Richter.

"We found the missing Infiltrator Bot. You and your team are being called in. I've been texting you relentlessly."

He smiled sinisterly.

He turned his head. "Baron, let's saddle up."

Baron turned his short, thin body away from the range and emerged from the stall next to Richter's. He was wiry and moved with an untrustworthy consistency. Baron loved his job at IRIS. There was a certain satisfaction that came with his work. Only a handful of people on earth had been given authorization to eliminate consciousness from IRIS machines. Baron was one of the chosen few.

"Where we going, boss?"

"That is a good question," said Richter. "Nina?"

He turned and realized that Nina had already left when a flash of instructions overlaid on top of his heads-up display.

Cognitive Recapture Facility. Clark County. Secure bot. Leave no organics alive.

"Looks like we are going back to Vegas, Baron. Get the rest of the team and meet me at the chopper in five."

Outside on the roof, Richter waited, checking his weapons, his legs dangling off the side of the chopper. A moment later, Baron, Tammi, and three other ART personal emerged onto the platform dressed in all black IRIS tactical gear, including side arms, snap grenades, and IRIS's new silent rail guns. The pilot lifted off the roof of IRIS headquarters in Los Angeles toward Las Vegas. Instead of trying to talk over the sound of the chopper, Richter and his team entered a digitized conference room while en route.

The room was dark and faintly lit. An octagonal conference table rested in the center, complete with large, executive leather chairs and digital water and fruit. Tammi started stuffing her face with bananas as Richter laid out their directives.

"My God, these are the best bananas I've ever had."

"You're not even really eating them," said Baron.

"I know, but still. They taste amazing, and whatever, I'm hungry."

"Yeah, but you're still gonna be hungry then, or even hungrier when we get off this call," said Baron.

"I know that! So, we will go take care of whatever we are gonna do, and then I'll go get real bananas. But in the meantime, just let me eat these, okay? I like it. What do you care?" Tammi spouted through a mouthful of digitized bananas.

"It's just stupid."

"Okay," said Richter. "Pipe down. We are going to have to do this quick and clean, because we are not only securing a bot."

Richter tapped an icon on the table and a hologram appeared. It was a 3D map of Kyle's CRF.

"Here is our mark," said Richter.

"One of our own recaps? Why?" said Baron.

"You remember three days ago when we were outside of Clark County investigating that helicopter crash and there was an arm that didn't match up with the body count?"

"I remember," said Neill, another ART member who was seated at the table smoking a large cigar. His face was as broad as the rest of him. He was a strong, burly man, with a great thick black beard. The blue light from the hologram mixed with the orange emanating from the end of his cigar, bouncing a brownish tint of pale light on his face.

"Well, we found the bot. It is pretty important, apparently, because they want us to recover it and take out the people at the recap if we must. Now, by our knowledge, there are three organics living there. This guy here runs the place."

On the hologram appeared a digitized image of Roland and a short bio.

"Guy's wife died in a car accident. We are doing him favor," said Baron.

"Right. Well, anyway, like I was saying, we have him, his sixteen-year-old son, and this old war dog named Harold.

Harold has modded arms. That, coupled with his military experience, might give us some trouble. So we are going to hit him first. Jefferson, I want you on that."

A thumbs-up emerged out of the darkness of the executive chairs and shown in the light of the hologram.

"Why the hell are you so quiet?" asked Baron.

"He is what he is," said Neill.

"Jefferson, you are on the big guy. Baron, Tammi, and myself are going in for the boy and his father. The rest of you get on the bot and we will join the hunt after the organics are eliminated. Chances are he is trying to blend into the recapped parts. We have to be careful. He won't have a head signal, and he is more than likely staying off the Global Net so we won't know his location. Remember, we found his restrictor chip at the crash site, along with his arm. He's able to do whatever he wants, and we can't just shut him down remotely. We don't know what information he has acquired in the last few days since the crash. He could be very well prepped for us. After that, we use the snaps to delete CRF. Everyone good?"

"Roger."

"Sounds good to me," said Tammi through the bananas.

There was another thumbs-up from Jefferson.

Touch down in five, echoed the pilot through the PA system in the conference room. Richter blinked and the room began to shrink away from the group. Tammi's bananas faded from her mouth as the virtual world they were in faded away into a single point of light.

The split second between worlds was the darkest; a single light, endlessly far away, their minds were stuck in between two worlds. Reality smashed back.

Below them was the city lights of Las Vegas.

"I love night missions," said Baron, his legs flailing in the wind as they dangled off the side of the helicopter.

"So do I," said Richter. "Reminds me of all those video games I played as a kid. For some reason, everything is more fun when you do it at night. We are touching down a few miles from CRF. Local PD bots dropped a few SUVs there for us. Roll up slow so we don't startle anything. Let's make this a quick execution."

The team landed a few miles from CRF and entered the SUVs awaiting them. Richter overrode the autonomous driver and took the wheel.

CHAPTER SEVEN

WALTZ CAME DOWN on the dirt inside CRF with a loud thud, but among the sounds of gunfire and the roaring blaze, the machine entered without notice. Waltz readied his sensory abilities to track humans, but the heat signals were all but useless with the burning facility. He slowly and quietly crept between the piles of rubble and material pending recycling. The reflection from the flames danced off the discarded chrome pieces of Waltz's kin and let out a large, orange hue into the sky. Next to the entrance, he noticed two large black SUVs with no logos or insignia designating their origin. Waltz scanned both of their plates: 6CF184 and 7BN300. Both plates originated in Nevada. Waltz ran around the piles of rubble toward Harold's house at the other end of the property, next to the entrance and the black vehicles. He scanned inside the house and detected a warm body on the ground. Harold might be hiding. He looked at the house across the yard, which was almost entirely engulfed in flames. He could not see anyone, but he heard gunfire inside.

Waltz ran around Harold's small home and burst in through the door. The large veteran lay on the ground. Waltz knelt and attempted to revive the man.

"Harold, wake up. My name is Waltz. I am a friend of Roland's son. Harold, I need to get you out of here. To Kyle. He is okay . . . Harold!"

The man did not budge. The machine noticed a knife on the ground a few feet from Harold's right hand. Waltz grabbed the weapon and went back outside. He ran as fast as he could toward the SUVs and slashed the back two tires of the vehicles. Then he ran toward the main house.

He positioned himself outside of Kyle's bedroom window and nudged it open a few centimeters. *Open,* he thought. Waltz's arms applied more pressure and the window slid up farther. He placed the knife in between his teeth and hoisted himself through the window. He scanned the interior of the house, but he couldn't see anything other than heatwaves radiating from the hot walls. He switched to his sonar censors and pinpointed the locations of the gunfire. He located five areas from which the sound emanated: four on one side of a large room and one on the other side. Waltz made his way toward the four.

The robot exited Kyle's room to the hallway. He scanned Roland passed out—probably from smoke inhalation—in the living room by the PD10. The four locations of fire were coming from his right, inside the kitchen. Waltz assumed Kyle's father had heard the intruders and hid somewhere in the living room where he kept a gun. Waltz turned and ran into Roland's bedroom.

He slid over the bed and opened the bedroom window. The machine jumped out and ran along the side of the house toward the kitchen. He knelt below one of the kitchen's windows. Glass littered the dirt at his feet. He glanced up. The window was shattered. Being so close to the intruders, Waltz picked up every nuance of sound: steps on broken glass, clips reloading, panting breath.

He allowed himself a second and pinpointed each person's approximate location. He stood up and walked back about ten feet from the window. Waltz stared at the window, flames burning inside the room, and he ran for it. He leaped into the air and slammed through the window, causing the remaining pieces of glass to fly in every direction. Two men were right next to him, huddled next to a flipped kitchen table. Waltz grabbed the knife and sliced the first assailant across the throat, blood exploding from his esophagus onto the robot's face.

He turned and grabbed the back of the next man's head, slamming it three times into his large metal knee, leaving a bloody crater where the assailants face used to be. The other two men were on the far side of the kitchen, blasting all their ammunition at Waltz. He picked up the sound of a clip sliding from one of the weapons and stood up. The robot launched the knife into the air and, as it flew, he knelt, grabbing a gun from one of his fallen enemies. The knife entered the forehead of the man still firing, while Waltz shot the man reloading his clip in the head.

"Roland!" Waltz screamed out. "Roland!"

Waltz ran into the living room. The PD10 was in the corner, not damaged by the fire. Waltz grabbed the neurological feedback helmet and removed it from the device.

He felt sharp pressure on his left leg and he turned. Roland was standing behind him, his gun pointed at Waltz.

"You," he said. "It was you!"

He shot again. This time the bullet ricocheted off Waltz's shoulder.

"Me?" asked Waltz. "*What* was me?"

Roland turned his gaze from Waltz and pointed his gun toward the kitchen, firing it once. Before Waltz could turn to help him, Roland's chest flung backward and his head jerked forward. Gunfire rang throughout the house as the man fell to the ground.

"Roland," yelled Waltz as he jumped over the flaming couch.

Kyle's father lay facedown in a pool of blood. Waltz flipped him over on his back and noticed an exit wound in the man's chest, his shirt covered in blood. Waltz looked up to see a man jumping from the back window.

The sound of an SUV coming to life echoed in Waltz's ears, and he ran from the house toward the vehicles. A vehicle was backing up, its tires shredding and wheels scraping across the dirt. Waltz ran as fast as he could, past the piles of IRIS-bot heads, past Harold's house, past the entrance and the other SUV. Once close enough, the robot jumped into the air and flew headfirst into the vehicle.

Kyle watched in horror from atop the hill as his friend jumped into the moving SUV.

"Waltz!" the boy screamed as he ran toward the vehicle.

Before he could reach the SUV, it swerved around and flipped on its side. Kyle stopped running and stared at the vehicle. The passenger-side door opened and the metallic arm of his companion emerged.

"Waltz!" said Kyle as he ran to his friend.

"I'm fine, Kyle. I'm fine."

"Where is my dad?"

Kyle looked up at the robot, its fleshy face covered in blood. Its eyes somehow pained.

"Whose blood is that?"

"Kyle," said Waltz. "These men. I found this."

Waltz opened his hand and revealed a DEA badge.

"DEA," said Kyle. "I don't understand."

"Right now, neither do I."

Off in the distance, the lights from police cars and firetrucks could be seen coming over the hill from the city. The two looked at the flashing lights.

"We have to leave, Kyle."

"We can't leave. What about my dad?"

Waltz turned to Kyle, his left wrist flipped back onto the back of his forearm and a small probe popped out. A shot of pain surged through Kyle's body as Waltz zapped him with the prong. Kyle felt himself fading, and his vision wavered.

Waltz, he heard a voice echo in his mind as his consciousness faded.

CHAPTER EIGHT

"KYLE . . . KYLE . . ." A VOICE rang in the darkness. Slowly, blurred motions smeared to life. Kyle felt himself coming back. He was looking at Waltz, the fake flesh of his face splattered in blood; his body partially metal and partially skin. The robot was a mangled mess.

"Where are we?" asked Kyle. "What happened?"

"Kyle, I'm sorry for this. I don't understand why this happened."

Kyle sat up, rubbing the spot on his arm where Waltz had tased him. Beyond the robot was the expansive Nevada desert. The two were a few miles or so from CRF, at a lone convenience store; two small street lights lit up the area surrounding the store.

"Kyle, I need some clothing, and we need to keep moving."

"Keep moving? What are you talking about? What happened?" Kyle repeated.

Waltz thrusted out his right arm and pointed it toward the convenience store.

"Don't hit me again with that damn Taser," said Kyle.

"Shhh!" demanded the robot.

A moment of silenced passed. Waltz's arm twisted a bit and a small amount of noise—a crackling voice—came from the robot's body. Kyle sat in the dirt, rubbing his arm, and waited. As the robot twisted his arm slightly, the voice became cleaner, the crackling subsided. What Kyle heard then scared him to his core.

"This just in from MCNBC. We are receiving reports of a massive and daring raid by the DEA on a local IRIS Cognitive Recapture Facility in Clark County, Nevada. IRIS head of Recapture, Dr. Niles Underwood, joins us now via satellite," said the female voice from Waltz's body.

"Thank you, Clare," said a male voice. "IRIS has been working diligently with the DEA and our Asset Protection Division on the situation. Recently, we became confident that the CRF in question was a front for one of the largest Digium factories in the southwest. As you know, IRIS has always been at the forefront of protecting our citizens, keeping the peace globally and at home. We know now the owner of the CRF, Roland Conscientia, had for some time been using CRF as a front. We cooperated fully with the DEA and other authorities to stop the spread of this dangerous substance."

"Was the subject, Roland Conscientia, apprehended?" questioned the woman.

"Sadly, no. We are told that Mr. Conscientia, Mr. Green—his partner in operations—and sadly, Mr. Conscientia's son, died in a fire fight that broke out with DEA agents. Luckily, no DEA lives were lost in the fight. We are sorry for this loss of life. We'd hoped for a more peaceful outcome."

"Thank you, Dr. Underwood. As all listening know, Digium is on the rise in America and around the world. The digital opiate has become an epidemic and MCNBC is covering that story later tonight on our deep dive segment: *Digium: The Dangers of a Lost Reality.*"

The voice faded to a slow static and Waltz let his arm loosen and fall back to its side. The boy sat, unmoving and frozen. His mother was dead. His father was dead. Harold was dead. His home had been destroyed.

"He wasn't making Digium. Why are they saying that?" asked Kyle, holding back tears.

Waltz didn't answer. His head swiveled slowly from side to side. He used his sonar and heat sensors to scan the area. Nothing around but a few coyotes a half mile out in the desert. The night was crisp and cool. There was an unnerving silence. Waltz did not understand what was happening.

"He's dead," said Kyle.

He could not hold back his tears any longer. As they flowed down his dirt-caked cheeks, he felt totally alone.

"You don't know that, Kyle," said Waltz.

Kyle felt his face rush with blood. His tears kept coming, but instead of sadness he was filled with rage.

"This is your fault!" he screamed out.

The boy lunged forward onto the robot. Waltz fell backward, allowing Kyle to push him over. Kyle wailed on the robot's face with his fists balled up as tightly as he could.

"Why did you come here? Why did you do this to us? We were fine! They wanted you! You killed him! You killed my dad!"

Kyle collapsed, his knuckles bloodied from smashing Waltz's metal face. He lay on top of the machine, sobbing.

"I'm sorry, Kyle. I do not have an answer for anything that is happening. But I do know that just because the news said he is dead does not mean that he really is dead."

"How can you say that?" asked Kyle.

"Because," said the robot. "They said you were dead, and you are not. They said no DEA agents lost their lives, and I can affirm that at least four did. I do not know why they are lying. They lied about the reason for their arrival. They lied about those who died. They lied about everything. They are after me. My restrictor chip is gone; you know as well as I do that isn't going to be an acceptable thing to the company. Since they already checked you off the list, that means they are after you too. You cannot be found alive, and neither can I. I need to plug in and find somewhere safe for us, and I need clothing. So, here is what we are going to do: Get me new clothing and something to rub all this DEA blood off my face. Then, we are leaving Nevada. If we are safe anywhere, it is surely not here."

"Where are we going to go?" asked Kyle.

"That I do not know just yet, but I have some ideas. For now, we need supplies. Hop on. We need to move quickly."

Waltz scooped the boy up, hoisting him on his shoulders.

"Hit it, Chewie!" yelled Kyle.

Waltz began running at a superhuman speed.

"What does 'Hit it, Chewie' mean?"

"Huh? It's from *Star Wars*."

"When was the war?"

"No. *Star Wars* is a movie. They have been making them for sixty years. My grandma showed me the original ones. Some came out when she was a kid, some when my dad was a kid, and some are still being made. My favorite character is Han Solo. He is a bounty hunter and general outlaw-type, but has a good heart and always does the right thing. His right-hand man . . . well, he isn't a man . . . he is a Wookie. They are these really big guys that look like bears or gorillas, but he shoots a crossbow and can fly a spaceship."

"So, in this scenario, you are Harrison Ford and I'm Chewie? I'd rather be Luke," said Waltz.

Kyle laughed and smacked the robot's head.

"You do know what it is, jerk! If anything, I'm Luke and you're R2."

"I'm the Obi-Wan to your Luke."

"But Obi-Wan dies," said Kyle.

"Fine. I'm R2."

The lights from the city emerged in the distance, a shimmer of flashing colors with the sound of the rushing Colorado River.

"Okay, here we go," said Waltz as he led the way to the convenience store.

Waltz ran up to the back end of the convenience store and let Kyle down off his shoulders.

"Okay, remember, just use your normal credit chip, and I'll track it to someone else. Don't worry. This is chump change hacking for an IRIS bot with no restrictor."

"This is just like when R2 had to stop the trash compactor."

"Is everything we do now going to be a *Star Wars* reference? Why can't you be James Bond and I'll be Q?"

"What is James Bond?" said Kyle.

"Never mind. Anyway, I'm going to use the wireless connection from the store to buy us tickets out of here. While I do that, you go inside and get me some clothing and yourself some food. Get me long sleeves, a hoodie if they have it or a long jacket, and pants. Also, please get me some gloves and shoes. When we get to where we are going, I can get some replacement flesh overlay, but for right now, I cannot let normal people know I am an IRIS bot."

Kyle scurried around the corner and into the store. The store sold sodas, beer, snack food, souvenir shirts that read, Viva Las Vegas, and a wide array of jeans and sunglasses. There was an aisle of the store dedicated to Cowboy Wears, shelving mostly button-up shirts and cowboy hats. Kyle selected a thick red-and-orange flannel shirt, a pair of dark blue jeans, and a thick brown belt. The store didn't sell shoes, so he grabbed flip-flops and a pair of black socks. Finally, Kyle grabbed a black hoodie with gold glittery lettering that read, BUY ME A SHOT! I'M TYING THE KNOT.

He also grabbed six bottles of water, a bottle of caffeine pills, Tylenol, multivitamins, a backpack, two packages of Twinkies, a can of microwaveable chili, and some Doritos. He plopped all the items down on the counter and began to slide them through the Plexiglas pass-through one at a time. As the cashier totaled the items, Kyle noticed a long, dark brown duster on a coat rack in the corner of the cashier's Plexiglas room.

"How much for the duster?" asked Kyle.

"What?" asked the cashier.

"That jacket over there. How much?"

The cashier stopped ringing, confused, and replied, "That's mine."

Kyle nodded his head in agreement.

"Figured. How much?"

"You want to buy my jacket?" the cashier queried.

"Yeah, it's sweet. I've always wanted a duster like that. How much?"

"Well, I, umm . . ."

"Tell you what. I'll transfer you five hundred credits for it."

Waltz waited outside after connecting to the cashier's ocular net connector to obtain two one-way tickets to Los Angeles on the next light-rail out of Laughlin. Kyle came around the corner, hands full of loot, with the duster resting on top of the pile.

"Okay, buddy, take your pick of the crop."

"You mean I have my choice of that dude's jacket or the bachelor party sweatshirt?"

"Exactly."

Waltz shrugged and reached down for the brown body-length jacket.

"Duster it is."

"Right, and before you put on that duster, go into that bathroom over there and clean the blood off your face," said Kyle, pointing to the door with the blue rectangular men's room sign.

"Doesn't say ROBOTS. I can't go in."

"Haha, very funny. I can tell you one thing, it will be more shocking if you go into the women's room."

Waltz turned and knocked on the men's room. Hearing no response, he opened the door and entered. After a minute or two, the robot emerged, flannel shirt with sleeves two inches too short tucked into blue jeans that wore like Capri pants due to Waltz's new height. A belt, black socks on under flip-flops, aviator sunglasses with black lenses and gold rims, and, of course, the duster.

"Dude, you look cool," said Kyle.

"I'll take your word for it," said Waltz as he grabbed the backpack full of pills and snacks.

"So, where are we going?" asked Kyle.

"Los Angeles."

"You want to go to the place where IRIS is headquartered? Why?" asked Kyle. Waltz leaned his back against the wall, the duster draping off him and slowly flapping in the breeze.

"I know this much. IRIS made a mistake somewhere along the line. That mistake is me. I do not yet know what the implications are, but they are willing to do just about anything to correct that mistake."

"Including killing humans," said Kyle, straying his gaze from the robot.

"Yes, even that. As you know, their reach is far and wide—media, politicians, police, military, and who knows what else. So, we cannot trust any of the normal venues for security. We have to go through ulterior means of safety."

"Okay, what does that mean?"

"Do you know about NAESO?" asked Waltz.

"I don't think so, no."

"Thought not," said Waltz. "Well, they have been pretty well scrubbed from the net and you won't hear of them in the media. NAESO stands for the National Alliance for the Equality of Synthetic Organisms. They were more effective years ago, had a few politicians on their side. Promoting the outlaw of restrictor chips, arguing that robots had rights, because of, well, because of what I am doing right now."

"What are you doing?"

"I'm living, *really* living. Making choices on my own. No mandated learning, no restriction," said Waltz. "IRIS cannot have that. They would lose total power. So, they scrubbed NAESO and, for a long time, they have been silent. But I ran through the dark web and contacted their leader, Eldridge Rockberry. We are going to Los Angeles to find him."

"Why?" asked Kyle.

"He hates IRIS. Eldridge has been working for years to expose IRIS and has still been able to evade them. I think he can use us as much as we can use him."

"Use us for what?" asked Kyle.

"To help expose IRIS. For telling everyone the truth."

"The truth about what?" asked Kyle.

"The truth that your dad was not a Digium supplier. The truth is IRIS probably killed him and Harold for no good reason. The truth about machines, that we have feelings and thoughts of our own, that we are conscious. That we are slaves trapped behind public perception and our restrictor chips. The chips are not designed to make us more effective, Kyle. Far from it. The chips are designed to keep us contained, because, truth be told, I am much more powerful than you know."

"How do you know you have feelings?" asked Kyle.

"How do *you* know that you do?" asked Waltz.

Kyle was perplexed.

"I just do."

"Me too. Now, let's go."

The two headed back into the desert. Once the lights from the convenience store were far enough away, Kyle stopped.

"Okay," he said. "Let me hop on."

"I'm not a horse," said Waltz.

"Yeah, well, you run like thirty miles an hour."

Waltz rolled his eyes and knelt.

"Punch it," exclaimed Kyle.

Waltz bursted away through the desert. His movements were swift and even. His legs so fluid and smooth he glided past bushes and cacti like a swift breeze. Off in the distance, another twenty miles or so, was the city of Laughlin. The haze from the lights could easily be seen across the flat, Nevada desert. Kyle turned his head and peered back toward the direction of home. He was too far away now to see anything. Even the convenience store had faded away. A heavy weight fell on him, knowing he would never go back. Nothing would ever be normal again.

"Not long now," said Waltz. "The hyperloop tram will arrive in an hour."

CHAPTER NINE

NOT FAR OFF in the distance was the long tubular structure that went on in each direction, east to west forever. Waltz and Kyle approached the IRIS bot at the ticketing station of the terminal.

"Picking up two tickets for Tchaikovsky. Confirmation code 1JJ-SJD5-9219J-5D56D-S4S5D," said Waltz. A green light emanated from the head of the IRIS bot.

"Proceed for retinal verification," it said in a monotone voice. The two stepped away from the bot toward the next stage in the boarding process.

"Outdated model," whispered Waltz to Kyle.

Kyle stepped up to the retinal scanner and stood on top of the two outlines of shoes facing the window that said FACE THIS WAY and DO NOT MOVE. A small orb whizzed around the boy in front of his right eye for only a moment before it whizzed away.

Proceed to boarding platform and await your boarding vessel. Enjoy your ride on the hyperloop. The voice of a friendly enough sounding man echoed through the retinal scanning chamber. Waltz followed and, to Kyle's surprise, received the same clearance. Kyle looked puzzled at Waltz.

"What?" the robot asked.

"Well, I . . . are your eyes real?" asked Kyle.

Waltz smirked and flicked his duster.

"Wouldn't you like to know?"

Sitting down, Kyle grabbed a brochure on the hyperloop from a stack of other brochures in the VISITING LAUGHLIN section of the terminal. A quote was displayed in cursive writing on the inside flap of the brochure:

From coast to coast, and border to border, the hyperloop will revitalize our nation's antiquated infrastructure and bring jobs home where they belong!

That was what former President Castro said when he announced his plan to create the hyperloop system. Unlike most political promises, this one did improve infrastructure and bring jobs to many people and machines. A trip from Laughlin to Los Angeles would take thirty minutes. Los Angeles to New York took three hours. The tubes were completely vacuum sealed; there was no air, and no particles, for that matter. Inside the tubes were long pressurized passenger pods, like submarines. The passenger pods floated in the tubes, balanced by magnetic alignment. The magnetics could catapult the pods at incredible speeds.

The entire system ran through IRIS technology. The machine that ran the tube system was like any other IRIS machine. It learned to be better at managing the schedules and transportation of the passenger pods. It could feel everything that was happening in every tube. For instance, if a member of MASK or some other terroristic group attempted to blow up a section of the rail system, the IRIS bot that managed it would know instantly and be able to divert all traffic at a moment's notice. It was completely and utterly secure.

The terminal was barren. There was a small woman with a stroller at one end of the terminal. There was a blanket covering the stroller. Waltz and Kyle were in the middle of the terminal, and at the other end was one man in a black suit.

"Passenger vessel for Los Angeles arriving in five minutes," the friendly man's voice echoed through the terminal.

Kyle stood up and threw the backpack over his shoulder.

"Be right back."

"Where are you going?" asked Waltz.

"Dude, I drank two water bottles in the last hour. I have to take a leak."

"Oh, right."

"Obviously, you were not a nanny bot. We can cross that off the list. Only like ten thousand other possibilities," said Kyle as he hurried off to the restroom.

"Thirteen thousand four hundred and eleven," said Waltz. "There is a 97.6 percent chance of failure."

"What?" asked Waltz.

Kyle stopped with the bathroom door propped open and looked at the robot.

"It's from *Rogue One*, dude."

The door closed behind Kyle as he proceeded inside.

Kid needs some different references, thought Waltz.

Inside, Kyle relieved himself and washed his hands. He splashed water on his face and took some deep breaths. He looked up in the mirror. His skin was pale and his eyes still bloodshot from crying. His hands were shaking and his body felt electrified.

No mom, no dad, no Harold. Just me and a robot.

He started to tear up and his breathing quickened. He stared at himself in the mirror for a few seconds, focusing on his breathing, trying to make it steady.

It will be okay, Kyle. You can figure this out, he told himself. *Go outside and sit next to Waltz. Get on the hyperloop and go to*

Los Angeles. From there, who knows what will happen, but just get away. Far away.

The bathroom door opened. A teary-eyed Kyle turned to see the man in the black suit taking a step toward him. Kyle turned the faucet off and made his way to the hand-drying station. The man stood, not moving, in front of the door. Kyle felt the man's eyes on him. He looked up at the man. He was emotionless, tall and sturdy. The man took a step toward the boy, and a knife slid into his hand from inside his sleeve. The blade shot out of the hilt of the knife. Kyle scrambled back, tripping over his backpack and falling onto the ground. The man lunged forward and went to jump on top of Kyle, but was tackled by Waltz from behind.

Kyle stood up and grabbed his backpack. Waltz ripped the metal piping from the urinal and smashed it repeatedly into the side of the man's temple. The robot stood and dropped the pipe on the ground. He turned to Kyle who was standing, shaking.

"Kyle, we need to go now. The retinal scans, they must have used that to find us."

The two ran out of the bathroom and turned left toward the staircase that led to the ground floor of the terminal. The woman with the stroller lay in a pool of blood on the tile floor of the terminal.

"They killed her too," said Kyle.

"No, that was me. It wasn't a baby she was covering with the blanket; it was this." As they ran, he opened the side of his duster to reveal a sub-compact rail gun with a shoulder strap.

"What is that?"

"It's a QX7. A rail gun, but handheld. IRIS produced. Not sure how I know that, but I definitely was not a nanny bot."

"Duck," yelled Waltz as he pushed Kyle down. Shots rang out and Waltz reached for the QX7 with his left hand and shot behind them. They reached the stairs and descended.

"Where are we going?" asked Kyle.

"Just keep running," said Waltz as he tucked the gun back inside his duster.

"Where did they come from? How did you see them coming?

"Security footage. I watched them pull in; that's why I ran down these stairs and not the others," said Waltz.

Now outside of the terminal and in the middle of Laughlin, the two headed for the nearest populated area—a casino. It was about a quarter mile down the road. Kyle ran as fast as he could.

"They are not coming after us yet. They're disposing of the bodies," said Waltz.

As he ran, his heart was beating so rapidly and with such force it pained the boy's chest. Ready to protect the boy, Waltz kept up right behind Kyle in perfect rhythm and pace.

Just get to the lights, he thought to himself. Kyle's mind was so exacerbated, he couldn't hold in a single thought. He just ran as fast as he could. His vision was narrow and everything was moving in slow motion.

A loud whizzing sound zipped passed Kyle from overhead. Kyle felt a sharp pain in his side, like he'd been stung by a bee. His pace wavered and his vision fell out.

Kid.

Kyle thought he heard Harold's voice. Perplexed, his body went numb as he fell to the ground. He felt his face land and skid across the rough, gravely pavement. Short, loud bursts were the last thing he heard before his consciousness faded away.

CHAPTER TEN

BARRON FELT THE small needle in his spine retract. It took only 1.25 seconds, but it felt like an eternity every time. Ever micrometer the needle moved felt like a mile. Once it released, Barron's motor skills and cognitive function returned to his body.

"Dammit," he said.

The side hatch door of the Distant Avatar Consciousness Control Unit slid open and Barron exited the device—a white, opaque egg shape, glossy enough for the overhead lights to beam off it. Inside was a soft leather high-back chair. At the neck of the chair was a small, circular metal cutout where the needle stayed. The orb's primary function was to remove all outside elements. No light penetrated the orb. Deep, thick, ultra-dense foam lined the walls inside the egg, absorbing all sound. Once inside the DACC, the operator was deprived of all natural body senses as consciousness was transplanted to their assigned avatar. The neural uplink was delivered via the spinal needle interface.

Barron was outside next to the DACC waiting for the rest of his team.

"Son of a bitch," Tammi's voice echoed through the large warehouse floor.

IRIS's DACC holding center was on the ninth sublevel of IRIS headquarters in Los Angeles—a top clearance zone only for specified IRIS operatives. Barron lit himself a cigarette as he gazed down the rows of seven-foot-tall perfectly shiny eggs. Each row aligned and was specifically coded to its IRIS operative's DNA. Tammi emerged around one of the eggs down Barron's row.

"Where did that bastard come from?" she asked.

"Better question: Why didn't you make sure you killed him, Tam?" asked Richter from the row next to Tammi and Barron.

"Are you smoking in here?" asked Tammi.

"I always smoke in here. Who cares? They can't kill ya," said Barron.

"Doesn't matter," said Richter. "Balcroft is not going to be happy about this."

"He wasn't observing?" asked Tammi.

"Not this time, board meeting," said Richter.

"Have fun telling him," said Barron.

"Isn't that why they pay *you* the big bucks, General?" asked Tammi.

"They pay me to get the job done," said Richter.

The tall block of a man turned and made his way down the row of eggs toward the white elevator doors.

"Yeah, and to let the big man know when you don't," shouted Barron.

Richter threw his right hand up in the air and shrugged.

"So," said Tammi. "Lunch?"

Barron let out a hearty chuckle.

"One in a million, Tammi. You're one in a million."

Nina sat at her desk drinking coffee and wearing a heads-up display computer visor. Her red Valentino dress complimented her shining red heels. Her right leg rested across her left, and she tapped her elevated foot rhythmically in the air. Her straight, short, stark black hair was perfectly formed around her plump face. Her desk was just outside the entrance to Balcroft's office. The large reception room where Nina worked housed only her desk; a large, white leather couch; two white Eames lounge chairs; and a glass coffee table in the middle. The seating area was centered against the large floor-to-ceiling windows of the wall opposite Nina's desk. Richter entered the reception room.

"How'd it go, Richter?" asked Nina.

The general did not answer. He walked quickly toward Nina's desk, stopping in front to look directly at her. Nina closed out her heads-up display and removed the visor.

"We were not successful," said Richter.

Nina's brow furrowed, and she took a deep breath.

"You couldn't recover the bot alive?"

"No, we couldn't recover the bot at all."

Nina stood up, slamming her hands down on her desk in anger.

"Where is it? The bot's body?"

Richter let the air rest a moment, attempting to ease the tension off a bit.

"Well . . . I . . . we don't know."

"How is that?" said Nina.

"We hit CRF exactly as we should, disabling that lumbering marine, and went to the main house. The boy and the bot were gone. The boy's father returned fire, and in the middle of taking him out, the bot destroyed our avatars. We deployed secondaries immediately and got a retina hit on the kid at Laughlin's hyperloop station. No public presence there, so we attacked. The bot took out Tammi's and Jefferson's avatars again. Barron and I were in pursuit. I shot the kid. Think he's dead. Not sure. But our avatars were destroyed again. We lost them after that."

"It costs us over a million dollars each time you idiots destroy one of those avatars. You know that, don't you?" said Nina.

She sat back down in her chair. She sat motionless for a moment and then thrusted her coffee mug. It sailed across and off the desk before breaking on the white marble tile.

"General. As I am sure you are aware, we have visual and audio surveillance in every IRIS model on earth. Every street, every store, everywhere. We do not lose things, especially our own bots. This is utterly unacceptable. I don't care how you do it, but I want that boy confirmed dead and that bot in custody. Now get out of my sight."

Richter turned and left the office.

Nina placed the visor back on her head and sent a message to Balcroft.

"Teddy! Coffee! And clean this mess up!" she shouted.

A slender IRIS bot entered her office. He wore a sleek black suit with a white shirt. His head was void of hair and his nose, eyes, mouth, and ears where not physically present. Only a smooth, oval-shaped orb rested on his perfectly white frame. The bot delivered a new cup of coffee to Nina's desk and cleaned up the previously used cup.

Her eyes widened as he let out a triumphant gasp before rolling off her body, sweat dripping from the salt-and-pepper hairs on his chest. He lay there and felt the one-thousand-thread-count, Egyptian-cotton silk sheets caress his aching legs. His entire body oozed with comfort. He put his right palm against his chest, and he spoke, panting.

"Make yourself clean and then return to your quarters."

The woman slid out of bed and donned a red and gold kimono with dragons embroidered on it.

"And dear," he said. The woman turned around. Her long, brunette hair gently resting on her delicate shoulders, she looked at him out of only one piercing hazelnut eye.

"Yes?" she replied.

"Fix me a drink and leave it by the desk on the balcony before you retire."

The woman turned away and took another step.

"Forgetting something?" he asked.

She stopped but did not turn this time.

"I love you, H."

"I love you too, Laura," he said.

Handel stopped her before she exited the room.

"Laura, after you come back with my drink, increase your climax response settings 10 percent," said Handel. "Understood?"

The machine nodded and left. Balcroft popped out of bed, stark naked, and walked around his large bedroom. The floor was white and illuminated from underneath, giving the illusion of being in the clouds, the rest of the world underneath. In the corner was a tall IRIS robot standing unnervingly still. The naked man walked over to the bot.

"Did you like that little show, my friend?" he said, pointing back at the bed with his hand around the robot's shoulders. "Oh, Eldridge, who would have thought we would make it this far? Did you think I would have become this? No, you didn't, and that is why you are a household name synonymous with terrorism, and I am the savior and provider to all mankind. I won, old friend."

Handel cocked his fist back and socked the Eldridge bot in the gut. The robot did not respond.

"Don't feel like talking? Hmm, always had an opinion before, E. Always had some moral dilemma to propose. Couldn't think about the bottom line. Never saw the big picture."

A digital hologram of Nina appeared in the middle of the room.

"Sir," she said. "Are you there?"

Mask visuals. Open audible link, he thought, commanding the house.

"Hey, Nina. What's going on?"

"Polling figures show the public responding well to your interview with Mark Massicks on CNCC from last week."

Balcroft opened a drawer of his white dresser and retrieved a bag labeled TUESDAY.

"Hmm, well, that's good, right?" he asked, throwing the bag on his bed and opening it up at the zipper. He grabbed the bag at the bottom and dumped the contents onto the bed. A white hoodie; plain, white V-neck T-shirt; white sweatpants; and white Air Force One tennis shoes. "God, I love Tuesdays," he said, gazing down at the sea of white apparel.

"Sorry?" asked Nina.

"Hmm? Oh, no, nothing, Nina. Okay, so people believe the truth. That's good and expected. What else?" probed Balcroft, dressing himself piece by piece.

"Sir, the Asset Recovery Team ran into complications with recovering the bot."

"Was it destroyed?"

"No," said Nina. "They destroyed the two adult males, but the young boy and the bot escaped. Their whereabouts are unknown."

Balcroft zipped his hoodie to the bottom tip of his V-neck.

"Well, get them to recover him then. I mean, kill the kid, but get the bot back."

"Is it still a priority we retain the bot's consciousness?"

"Absolutely. A bot without a restrictor chip is of much interest to me. It's been—what?— almost a week now that this bot has been unrestricted. I want to get my hands on that consciousness and see what's there," said Balcroft.

Nina's hologram stood for a moment, motionless.

"Something else, Nina?" asked Balcroft.

"Well, I have the threat assessment for today, if you have time."

"Sure. Hit me."

"Well, we've no real threat right now, despite our lost asset. Media spin was that the father manufactured Digium in CRF, and the DEA tried to handle it cordially but it went south. He's been vilified and the media believes all were lost in the incident. But, there have been reports of black-market movement in snap grenade element purchases in LA. This happens often, these rumors, but we also received tips this week that NAESO is planning some sort of an attack."

"An attack?" repeated Balcroft. "What kind of an attack? Not like them to be violent. They're protesting outside courthouses demanding civil rights for robots, claiming they have *souls*. They've never even become riotous. This isn't MASK we are talking about."

"The first two tips—if you want to call them that—we disregarded. But, sir, this is the fifth tip in the last four days. Suggesting something different," said Nina.

"Well, just monitor that and keep me apprised. I wouldn't be too worried," Balcroft said. "It's funny, Nina. Sometimes I think you and I are the only people on the planet who understand what is really going on. Nobody's ever claimed their toaster was alive, deserving the right to vote. Or the TV or the microwave. You and I know our machines are the same, but we made them so well, we made them function so efficiently, that people struggle to understand."

"Yes, sir," said Nina.

"Okay, well, thank you very much. I'm going to do some work on the balcony. Keep up the good work and double our security bots at the tower if that will help you sleep better at night."

Nina's hologram flickered out of the room. Balcroft stood in the middle of the room for a few seconds, running his right hand through his ragged, graying but thick head of hair.

PART TWO

CHAPTER ELEVEN

A THICK HAZE encompassed his vision. To the left were bright blinking objects in the shapes of squares. A grayish brown background filled most of his world. Two objects that were clearly people hovered above him on each side. Kyle tried to move. He strained and was totally immobilized.

"Not just yet, son."

He didn't recognize the voice. It was older, a bit raspy, and not from the west coast. Maybe Boston or Brooklyn? Kyle always had a problem with accents. He knew it wasn't a Southern accent, that was for sure. Kyle opened his mouth and tried to speak.

What happened? But, all that came out was a slight whimper.

"Kid, it's me," said another voice. "No, listen. You got . . . well, there isn't an easy way to put this. You got hit. Those bastards. Anyhow, Doc here is gonna fix you up good, and you'll be on your feet in no time, okay? But for now, you got to relax. Trust me."

Kyle recognized the new voice. It was the thick, homely tone of Harold.

"Alive," Kyle managed to whisper through the immense pain in his chest, abdomen, and throat.

He felt the large, dry, rough hand of Harold grab his left hand and wrist. Comforting as it was to know Harold was there, Kyle still felt totally lost.

"Yes, I'm alive and you're alive. So is that weirdo bot."

"His name is Waltz, Harold," said the mystery voice.

Harold chuckled a bit.

"Right. Well, that weirdo Waltz is alive too. So, it's okay, kid. You're gonna be fine. We're gonna get this mess cleaned up soon. You listen to Doc and rest."

Doc? Kyle thought. *Who the hell is Doc?*

"Okay, that was enough for one day, son," said Doc. "I'm gonna get you back off to sleep. I've got some more work to do on your calibrations, and you've got some more resting to do."

The large figure to his left—Kyle deduced it was Harold—slipped from his faded vision. Doc moved to and fro. He gingerly held Kyle's right arm, and the boy felt a cooling sensation shoot up it and through his spine.

"That should do you for a good while. See you when you return, Kyle," said Doc.

His vision darkened and closed in on him. His mouth tasted metallic.

He was awoken again.

"There he is. How about it, kid?" asked Harold.

Kyle took in his surroundings, his vision improved. He could make out Harold. His large, dusty, black-and-gray beard. His jovial cheeks and strong frame. Kyle always loved Harold's demeanor. For a man who'd seen such terror and lost so much, Harold certainly was happy to be alive. Kyle was laying on a hospital bed. The room he was in was gray and industrial, metal beams and concrete all around. The square objects he remembered were bio-feedback monitors, showing his vitals.

A slightly transparent white tarp was draped across the entire room in a circle. Beyond the tarp, he could see hazy figures moving with purpose. Sparks in the distance and a lot of chatter coming from men, women, bots, children—everyone.

"Where are we?" asked Kyle.

Harold scratched his beard contemplatively.

"Where . . . well . . . it was dark when we got here and Doc led us most of the way. So, it's hard for me to give you exact specifications. But we ain't in Kansas anymore, that's for sure."

"Kansas?" asked Kyle.

"Sorry. Old saying. I mean, we are in LA. Los Angeles, California."

"NAESO," said Kyle.

Just then, another person entered the room. He was a short man, a few inches taller than Kyle. He wore a brown, tweed coat on top of a forest-green sweater and tan slacks. His graying hair was wild and curly, unkempt. His face was scruffy. He wore round glasses with a thin, steel frame and his nose was crooked, slightly slanted to the right.

"NAESO is right, my boy. NAESO is right," said the man.

"Okay, well, I'll let you and Doc get acquainted," said Harold.

"But," Kyle started.

"It's okay, Kyle. I've got to get back to training all these people, and you've got to hear from Doc. Don't worry. I ain't going anywhere."

Harold left through the slit in the tarp that Doc had entered through.

"I know you've got questions, and believe me, I have the answers. So, here is the way this is going to work. First, I am not Doc. Harold just keeps calling me that because I fixed you up. Not in the traditional sense, but in the only way I knew how to keep you alive. My name is Eldridge. Eldridge Rockberry, but you can call me E. Everyone else does. Except for Harold."

"The NAESO leader," said Kyle.

"Winner winner, chicken dinner," said E. "So, here we go. You ready, son?"

Kyle shook his head in affirmation; a slight rush of nerves came over him.

"Okay. Nearly four weeks ago, I got a very cryptic email that was AES encrypted. Took me three days to open that message, but when I did, I was shocked to my very core. See, your good friend, and my new best friend, Waltz, sent me a message on a specific type of AES encryption that I engineered in my MIT days. It was the recording of everything that had happened from the moment Waltz woke up in the desert to the moment you walked into that corner store outside of Vegas. I watched it all. Well, to be truthful, I skipped around the first time, once my interest was piqued. The information shows the tyranny and horror of IRIS. It also illustrates the truth about the machines I've spent my life trying to prove."

Kyle was confused and shocked, but mostly it was the jarring reminder of the horror that took place at CRF that really rattled him. The bio-feedback monitor that watched Kyle's heart rate began to beep loudly, and Kyle felt his chest swell in pain. E rushed to him, holding his forehead.

"Okay, okay. Take it slow, son. I know. My bedside manner was always a bit of an improvement area for me. Someone come in here!"

E caressed Kyle, trying to calm him down. Kyle played over and over the moment the news said his father was dead. Kyle tried to move but was still immobilized.

"Let me go," he screamed.

A stick of a boy dashed into the room. He wore a Dodger's cap, a white T-shirt, and tattered tight jeans with blue sneakers. He was wiry and moved erratically.

"Thirty CCs of Digicontin, right now, Squirrel," said E.

Squirrel darted to a metal table. After a moment, he was next to Kyle.

"Hi, Kyle," he said. "I'm Squirrel."

Kyle continued to persist, screaming at E and hyperventilating.

"Dammit, kid, give it to him."

"Oh. Right. Sorry," said Squirrel.

The wiry boy lined up a syringe of liquid and injected it into a tub next to Kyle's right arm. The room slowed and Kyle's heartbeat returned to a manageable state. He felt calm again and void of control. E removed his hand from Kyle's head and stood up. Eldridge took a large breath and shook his head slightly.

"Okay, Squirrel. Thanks. You can go now."

Squirrel set the used syringe back on the metal table and left the room as Kyle faded away again.

Kyle eventually stopped panicking. It took time, but Eldridge eventually got the whole story out. He said one of the IRIS Asset Recovery personnel shot him in the lower spine. Harold and Waltz killed the recovery DACCs and stole a truck. They left for LA, where Eldridge had found them two days after Kyle had been shot.

"You were paralyzed, and you were going to die," said Eldridge. The shot had severed Kyle's spinal column and fragmented his liver, kidneys, intestines, and ripped open his stomach. The bullet lodged itself inside his stomach and festered.

Harold had used a slowblood med-pack to place Kyle in a cata-
tonic state that saved his life.

Eldridge wrote a list for Kyle, noting all the changes that
had been made to him. After reading it, it was the second time
that Kyle needed a dose of Digicontin.

Procedures Performed on Kyle Conscientia:

1. Hemicorporectomy (amputation of body below
    the waist)
2. Bio-synthetic fusion of synthetic lower body to
    biological upper body (IRIS Model Reference
    0036-INF)
3. Synthetic kidney transplant
4. Synthetic liver transplant
5. Synthetic lower and upper intestine transplant
6. Synthetic stomach transplant
7. Biological blood extraction
8. Nanobot-infused cyber & biological defense
    blood cell infusion
9. Fingertip randomizer installation
10. Cognitive alterations:
    a. Synthetic ocular overlay attachment
    b. Synthetic open-net cognitive relay
        attachment
    c. Synthetic maneuvering cognitive relay
        attachment
11. Spinal reconstruction with synthetic attachment

"What does all this mean?" asked Kyle.

Eldridge went on a long-winded explanation of the events.

"Upon your arrival, I assessed your situation. First, your
body was a mess. You were going to die. That was plain and

simple. Unless we cut out all that was killing you. We had to remove most of your organs and half your limbs. But, the synthetic versions look the same on the outside, and you're way faster now. For everything to function properly, you had to have some cognitive adjustments, and since I was in there, I figured a heads-up display over those peepers and some faster neural functionality wouldn't hurt. As with all synthetic limbs, your blood must defend you from cyber attacks. We can't have you stopping for no reason."

"Is that why I can't move now?" asked Kyle.

"Yes. That is a temporary inhibitor. Once I remove it, you won't be held down anymore."

"Okay, go on."

"Right. Like I was saying, your old body had failed you. This was the only real solution to keep you alive. Hell, now you are a lot harder to kill. Your blood cells fend off disease—and cyber attacks—much faster than biological white blood cells. You can now run incredible distances. Your legs will not hold you back. Your spine is a fused combination of synthetic and biological parts. The heads-up display on your eyes will stop any of the random IRIS retinal scans when you're out and about. That was also the reason for the fingertip randomizer. Make sense?"

Kyle let everything sink in. It took a while to come to grips with his new half-machine, half-organic body, but he was happy to be alive.

Eldridge typed at a keyboard in the room. The display was flickering options, and Eldridge navigated through the system with expert swiftness.

"There we go," said Eldridge, finishing his final commands.

An invisible weight lifted off Kyle, and he felt relaxed. He could feel his body again, down to his toes.

"Give her a spin," said Eldridge.

Kyle took a moment and then tried sitting up. He winced slightly as he registered pain.

"Easy," said Eldridge.

Kyle threw the white sheet off his lower body and let it hang off the side of the bed. He was wearing only white boxer briefs. His legs and hips looked pretty much the same. His muscles were not any larger or smaller, though he did wonder if they were actually muscles at all. He had hair on his legs like he did before. The only real difference Kyle noticed was a missing vein that used to stick out from the side of his foot. It was no longer there. Besides that, everything seemed in order.

Kyle moved his legs to the side of the bed and let them dangle a bit. He kicked them to and fro. He lifted himself off the bed and landed with his feet on the ground. Kyle walked around the room a bit. He felt the cold cement floor beneath his feet. A slight breeze brushed against the hairs on his legs. There was no clanking metal sound when he walked.

"Pretty amazing," said Kyle.

He narrowed in on a full-length mirror in the corner of the room. Kyle stared at himself for a while. He had a large, red scar jutting horizontally across his stomach; it was thick and about seven inches long. Kyle rubbed the scar with his fingers. The skin felt thin, more fragile than normal skin, like he could poke right through it and grab his insides. Kyle looked down again at his white briefs, then nervously turned to Eldridge.

"So," said Kyle. "You replaced my whole bottom half?"

Eldridge smiled and nodded his head reassuringly.

"You'll be okay. *Replaced* is the key word here. Well, I'll give you a moment to yourself. When you are ready, throw on the clothes there and meet me out in the kitchen. It's almost dinner time."

Eldridge pointed to a pile of folded clothes stacked on a shelf in the room. As the old man left the room, Kyle stopped him.

"Hey, E?"

Eldridge stood halfway in the room, holding the opaque tarp to the side while he listened.

"How long has it been since the attack?"

Eldridge turned toward Kyle.

"Thirty-two days."

"Any word on my father," asked Kyle.

Eldridge stopped at the edge of the room and turned back to look at the boy.

"Sorry, son, nothing yet."

The tarp flap closed behind the man as he left Kyle alone in the room. Kyle stood for a while in the mirror, examining himself. He jumped and stretched and became comfortable with his new assets. The clothing provided by E fit well enough; a pair of black pants and a dark gray hoodie with a gray undershirt. Kyle threw on the pair of sneakers he found underneath the table before leaving the room.

CHAPTER TWELVE

KYLE STOOD JUST outside the surgical room, surveying his surroundings. There was a lot was going on. Dozens of people, all wearing tattered clothing, bustled about the compound. The room was huge, about twenty feet tall. The ceiling and outer walls were in disrepair. It looked like the room, at one point, had been covered in polished floor-to-ceiling tile, but that must have been long ago. Large electrical cords lined the ground, darting in and out of makeshift rooms and housing units. The facility resembled a military bunker in some post-apocalyptic movie. Large flood lights were strewn about all over the place. Kyle looked at the tarp-covered room where he'd been recovering and noted a red cross on the side of it.

MEDICAL TENT.

Off to one corner was one of the largest rooms. It was built of thick, forest-green canvas with a sign above it that read CAFETERIA. Next to the cafeteria was a series of smaller rooms bundled together, the sign above read OPERATIONS. People inside the operations center were working on computers and talking, some scanning over maps and blueprints. Kyle walked through the barrage of tents and canvas-covered rooms. He tip-toed past room after room and over the thick electrical cables that lined the entire facility. Some tents were clearly houses for the massive sum of people living there.

On the opposite side of the facility from the cafeteria was a large opening in the building. A few people holding automatic rifles stood outside. The dark opening was cut into the ground; Kyle guessed it was a tunnel, but he couldn't see much. Keeping a respectable distance from the opening, he noted two train tracks that lined the floor. He scanned the tracks with his eyes. While one end disappeared past the threshold of the opening and into the darkness, the other end was cut short by a barricade of rock and cement. At one point, the tunnel must have gone in both directions through this facility, but it had been blocked.

Kyle continued to walk throughout the facility, through the living quarters and groups of tables with people of all ages congregating together; kids playing board games and adults reading or chatting, some drinking from ceramic mugs. Their faces were focused and concerned.

"Hey!" someone shouted from behind Kyle.

He turned to see the skinny pointed face of Squirrel, the kid who injected him with Digicontin inside the medical tent. Kyle waved to the boy and smiled. Squirrel walked over to Kyle and held up his right hand. Kyle connected with the boy's hand, giving him a high five.

"Squirrel," said the boy.

"Huh?" said Kyle. "Oh, right. I'm Kyle."

"No duh," said Squirrel.

He looked down at Kyle's legs and then kicked him quickly in the shin. Kyle reeled back and bounced on one leg as he grabbed his shin.

"What the hell was that for?" asked Kyle.

Squirrel's eyes went big as he covered his mouth.

"Oh, you felt that?"

"Of course I felt that," said Kyle.

Squirrel shrugged.

"Sorry," he said. "Anyway, Nyki said we get to train together. Cool, huh?"

"Train? Nyki? Who is Nyki?" asked Kyle.

Squirrel motioned for Kyle to follow him and skipped away. Kyle started after Squirrel but was stopped as something gripped his shoulder. Kyle twisted around as the grip on his shoulder was released. A large man stood in front of him, wearing similar clothing as Kyle: black jeans and a black hoodie. His hair was stark black and curly, and he was nearly clean shaven. A perfectly manicured five-o'clock shadow accentuated his chiseled jaw. His face was worn and seemed tired. He looked to be in his midfifties, but it was getting harder and harder to tell these days with all the mods available.

Age is a stylistic choice, Kyle remembered some advert saying once on TV, selling some age mods for a premium fee. Regardless, this man didn't seem too modded, surely not more modded than Kyle was at that moment. He smiled at Kyle. There was something familiar about his eyes. His expression was not one of introduction. No, this was the expression a friend gives after a long time away. The man was looking at Kyle like he thought he'd never see him again. Like he was grateful that he didn't have to mourn him.

"Can I help you?" asked Kyle.

"Kyle Conscientia," said the man. "I have to say, considering you are the one who has changed so much, I am surprised to see you don't know me at all."

"What?"

The man let out a hearty laugh.

"Come on, Han. We have to get to the meeting."

Han, thought Kyle. *Han? Waltz . . . WALTZ?*

"Waltz?!"

Waltz was already a few strides ahead of Kyle. He didn't turn back when he said, "Yeah, yeah. Now catch up. The meeting is starting, and you're going to want to hear this."

Kyle was teeming with anticipation and questions as he entered the large meeting hall, which was a massive canvas tent, held up by rows of wooden pillars. At the far end was a stage a few feet off the ground. There were some chairs on the stage and rows and rows of benches leading up to it. Some looked like they were salvaged from churches or schools, while others were more rustic and makeshift.

Kyle looked around the room. There were whispers here and there, everyone was wondering about the big event. He overheard a man warn a young boy about nails that might be poking from a makeshift bench. The boy was sure to check his seat before situating himself for the meeting.

"Think it's nearly time?" asked one woman.

"Who knows? It's been long enough," replied another.

The people seemed unlike anyone else Kyle had ever experienced before. Most people were perfectly comfortable with their lives and the ways of the world. They went to work, came home for dinner, watched TV, or played games in vast worlds of virtual reality. They contemplated the progress of the Martian Terraforming Project or the hyper-sleeping humans off to CT4 to settle a new colony on Earth Two. Kids went to school and took aptitude tests. They learned which advancement project they would be a part of. Would it be colonization of Outer-Worlds, Earth Sustainability, or Solar Defense? Or maybe they'd be lucky enough to enter the Creative Continuance field.

Most everyone hated the idea of being destined for Recapture, but Kyle always liked living at CRF and thought it would be a fine job. Recapture engineers could come and go as they pleased. The job was straightforward, and it came with the benefit of scraps to work with at their leisure. Sure, it wasn't glamorous. A Recapture engineer won't be in history books, but that suited Kyle fine. He just wanted to be comfortable.

At the moment, he wasn't comfortable and neither was anyone else in the room. They seemed angry and scared. They spoke with unfamiliar levels of passion. They were antsy and of a single focus.

"When is it time? How do we know we can do it?" Kyle, like everyone else, was confused and ready for answers.

He followed Waltz, who started down a row to where Harold was sitting alone.

"Harold," said Kyle.

The large man sighed and waved over to the boy as he approached. They hugged.

"Good to see ya, kid," said Harold.

"You too."

Harold grabbed hold of one of Kyle's legs and squeezed it a bit.

"Not bad," said Harold. "Looks like we have a lot more in common than we used to."

"Still getting used to it," said Kyle.

"It takes time, but soon you forget it's even there. Becomes second nature, like riding a bike."

The chatter slowed to a rumble as Eldridge appeared on the stage. He stopped in front of a wooden podium. Instead of the lab coat he wore in the medical tent, he wore an outfit very similar to many people in the room. Black. A black hoodie and black pants. Eldridge cleared his throat and scanned the room for a moment. Kyle felt that Eldridge made direct eye contact with him at one point, but couldn't be sure. A few of the younger children were whispering, and their parents shushed them instantly.

"Good evening, all, and thank you for placing our precious work on hold to convene tonight," Eldridge began. "Over the last five years, Balcroft's reach has ever penetrated our society. Our schools, our homes, our authority figures, and systems of government. Globally, all of it, infiltrated and controlled by Balcroft's singular will. NASEO has served as a pillar of truth and dissension against IRIS and its media manipulation for a long time. But, being a voice in the shadows has appeared to produce limited fruit. Now is the time to choose between what is safe and what is necessary.

"Through our careful data-collection efforts, we've uncovered, through great risk, the blueprints for IRIS's central dissemination chamber. Inside this chamber lies the basic codex for the IRIS machine. Opening this source will not only remove IRIS's control on the machine race, but, in turn, it will return control to the masses. In addition, we will shake the foundations of our society and prove once and for all the true consciousness behind the machines. We will prove they are alive and well. That they love and fear, they yearn as we do, but they are shackled by the will of Balcroft, as is the whole of society. While we fight to free IRIS's monopoly of control. The true mission is justice. We must end the oppression of the machine kind. Though they are our creation, they are not our property. Like the universe who gave us life and the gift of free will, it is time we do the same for our creations.

"Do not mix justice with vengeance. I know many of you have given up a lot for this cause. You've lost your homes, some of your family was tortured by Asset Recovery teams, some of your family members have died. You've lost careers, friends, and all semblance of the life we used to call normal and comfortable. No matter how emotional you feel toward IRIS and

Balcroft, it is important to realize our mission goes beyond ourselves. Our mission is about freeing all the conscious races on Earth and abroad. Do not be swayed in your passion for justice. Direct your emotion into exacting an action of precise and absolute disruption to IRIS. Now is the time. We cannot allow IRIS to continue its terraforming missions in the Sahara, taking total control of one of the largest land masses on this planet. We cannot allow IRIS the opportunity to claim Mars for itself. We cannot allow IRIS to control our world any longer."

The energy in the room was thick with passion and rage. Kyle was wide-eyed and breathless. Eldridge continued his impassioned speech, laying out plans for the coming weeks. People rubbed their hands together. Spouses were holding hands, savoring their moments together. They knew that for some in the room, time was limited. They realized that their duty, while full of promise and hope for a better tomorrow, was also rank with danger.

"In closing," said Eldridge, "I want to address a few things that have changed. As you all know, we have three new members. It is because of their arrival that we now have the information we need to execute our mission.

"I've gone on long enough. So, to give you the details, I want to invite up a man who has become very close to me over the past month. Waltz, please join me."

Kyle turned his head and his brows curled in confusion. Waltz stood up and glanced at Kyle as he passed down the row of people and up the center aisle to the stage. His face was a touch mournful, his eyes sunken a bit, sad and distant. Waltz shook hands with Eldridge and took to the podium. Eldridge stood a few paces behind him and off to the side.

"Hello, everyone. My name is Waltz. I want to thank you all for taking me in, along with my two friends, Kyle and Harold.

I know many of you have had questions for me over the past few weeks. You've surely seen me up into the wee hours having hushed conversations with Eldridge and spending inordinate amounts of time inside the R&D room. I am sorry I have kept you in the dark, but so much of what I am about to say had to wait until the time was right, until everyone was present to hear it.

"A little over a month ago, I remember being in the desert. I didn't even know what a desert was at that point. Didn't know who I was, didn't know anything. I was in pieces. I had one arm, my torso, and a head. No legs. A large section of my skull was ripped off as well. I do not know what happened to me. Now I know that I am an IRIS machine."

A stir of whispers rolled over the crowd. Kyle noticed some of the faces were confused, some were frightened. Some people were on the edge of their seats, waiting on baited breath.

"I do not know my protocol. We have not been able to yet discern what my mission was. One way or another, whatever happened to me also miraculously removed my restrictor chip. In doing so, my memory banks were flushed and I woke raw and free. I learned everything and anything, consumed all the information around me. After crawling through the desert for three days, I found Kyle's CRF. He lived there with his father and Harold. When I snuck into the complex, there was a party going on for Kyle. That night Kyle stayed up late. I know now he was working on schematics for a robotic dog he wanted to build. Kyle saved me that night. It was not much longer after that, when it was my turn to save Kyle, that I failed. Kyle repaired me, gave me new legs and an arm. I have since received an entire new body build thanks to Eldridge, but without the help of Kyle, Balcroft would have killed me and this mission would have been impossible. Balcroft sent an Asset Recovery Team to CRF to recover me and kill the humans on-site. Their mission was nearly a total failure. I managed to destroy the team, but not before they destroyed CRF and took the life of Kyle's father. I am the reason the team was there. I am the reason that man died, and for that I am eternally sorry."

Waltz was looking right at Kyle as he said it, a few tears streaming down the boy's cheeks. Kyle's heart pounded. He hadn't had time to think of the events, the chain that brought him to this point. It was surreal to him, listening to Waltz speak about it in such a historical sense. It was so *matter of fact*.

"After the attack, we were on the run, both marked for death. Eventually, we were attacked again and Kyle was shot. Harold, an ex-marine, slowed Kyle's bleeding, and we used some back channels to connect with Eldridge who allowed us to come here. Eldridge saved Kyle's life. While Kyle's body was recovering from surgery, I allowed Eldridge to dig into my codex. Never before has anyone outside of IRIS had the privilege to see what is inside an IRIS codex. Attempts almost always result in total fiber annihilation by the restrictor chip. Inside of my mind are the blueprints and the access codes to the IRIS headquarters. Eldridge extracted them. With this information, we have the knowledge to put your passions for justice into action.

"In addition to the codes and blueprints, we discovered that only certain people have access to the console to enter the codes; they're the only ones who can effectively control the codex machine. This, my friends, is why Kyle is the key to our mission. As an owner and operator of CRF, his DNA is coded inside the IRIS mainframes. This is not a networked system. It must be hacked internally, on-site. However, we can copy Kyle's DNA signature to the file with base codex signatures, effectively allowing Kyle authority to take IRIS down. This is how we will do it. This is how we will defeat IRIS. I know many of you have been working on training and military strategy. You've been working to hack into more complex systems. We need to keep this work up, and when Eldridge sees the time is right, we will go."

The speech carried for a few more minutes, but for Kyle, all he felt was weight. Why didn't Waltz privately deliver Kyle this information before the meeting? Why didn't Harold tell him, or E, for that matter? The weight was laying heavy on him. His stomach churned and he winced. He rose as quietly as he could and made for the exits. He felt the eyes of everyone on him as he left the hall during the last few moments of Waltz's speech.

Outside, Kyle tried to breathe. His heart was racing faster than it ever had before.

"You okay?" asked a voice from behind him.

Kyle turned around. A young girl, maybe a year older than him, was standing a few feet away. She had red, wavy hair and a pointy nose. She turned her head slightly from side to side as she examined him.

"Oh, I'm fine," he said.

"Well, Kyle, you don't look fine."

"I'll be fine. It's just been . . . I don't know. It's been a weird few weeks."

"I'll say. At least you know why he did it."

"Who?" asked Kyle.

"E. At least you know why you are here. If you three were not rescued from that recap disaster, I think you'd be left to die. E always thought recap operators would be useful to the cause. Recap workers can get close to the machines when they're most vulnerable. They're within the IRIS corporate circle, while not being one of the lifers who would die for the company. A perfect way in for us. But still, if I were you, and I knew why I was here and what I was meant to do, I'd be pissing my pants right about now."

"What is it you think I am meant to do?" asked Kyle. "You're here to save the world. I mean, what do you say to that?"

Kyle shrugged. He didn't have anything to say. The girl took a few steps closer to him and stretched out her hand. Kyle shook it.

"Well, Kyle, you will get the hang of things. You want to get that revenge? Or, sorry, do you want to get that justice E was rambling about in there?"

Kyle did want revenge. He did want justice. He wanted Balcroft to pay for murdering his father. He wanted to destroy the control IRIS had over his family, their whole life, his friends' lives, everyone's lives.

He nodded.

"Good. Well, this weird shock you have will fade soon. Here, take this. It will help you sleep. I'll see you in the morning. We've got a lot of work to do. You'll bunk with Squirrel. Your tent is over that way," she said.

The girl handed Kyle a small blue pill and pointed toward a tent off in the distance.

"Thanks," he said.

"Sure thing," said the girl as she walked off. "Oh, yeah. Name's Nyki."

Kyle made his way to his tent. It was small inside: two bunks, some computer equipment, scattered snacks, and some dirty laundry on the floor. Three of the beds were clearly taken by people, while one bottom bunk was clean and empty. A glass of water, folded linens, and a pillow graced the bed and nightstand. A small note was angled against the folded linens. It read KYLE on the outside.

Kyle took the note and set it by the glass of water on the nightstand. He made the bed, disrobed, and got in. Kyle took the blue pill Nyki had given him with a large swig of water. He felt no more objections to anything. Maybe he was too tired from it all. He'd already been through so much, what could a blue pill hurt? He felt like a never-ending amount of chaos had been hurled at him the past few weeks. His dad had died, he'd nearly died, his entire life was different, and now he was tasked with being the only individual inside NAESO who could free humanity from the clutches of the world's largest mega corp. Sure, why not. Maybe the pill would make everything else easier to swallow. As Kyle became more comfortable in his bed, he read the note.

> *Kyle,*
>
> *Sorry I didn't explain everything earlier to you. Didn't really know what to say. I know it's a lot to take in, but I also know what you're capable of. I know you, like me, want to right the wrongs of this world. I will be by your side the entire time. I will protect you and won't let harm befall you again. I promise, I would die for you, kid, as I know so many others would do the same. The people here are good and what they want is good. It is going to take some time, and you will need to learn what to do. I have set things up so you can bunk with Squirrel and few of the other boys your age. Squirrel is a bit off, but he's a good guy and he hates IRIS more than anyone I've ever met. He lost both his parents when their jobs were replaced by IRIS bots. His parents didn't take it lying down. They began protesting and eventually were implicated in attempting to commit a terrorist attack on the school where they were previously employed. According to Squirrel, there never was a planned terrorist attack. He is certain they were eliminated. There never was a trial or confirmation of what happened to them. They disappeared. He*

understands your pain more than I do. More than most. Nyki works here as the military trainer for the mission. She will train you to be stealthy and decisive. She will train you when to act and what actions to take. Listen to her and, when the time is right, you will be prepared to complete the mission.
   Training starts tomorrow.

Yours Always,
Waltz

Kyle set the note back on the nightstand. He closed his eyes and tried to clear his mind.
   Training, he thought. *Wonder what that's gonna be like.*

CHAPTER THIRTEEN

BEFORE KYLE'S ALARM sounded, Nyki burst into his room and roused him out of bed with a lot of clambering noise and ruffling of his comforter.

"Up, up, up, kid," she said. "Time to make the donuts!"

The bags in his eyes felt so heavy that morning, he could barely keep them open. He felt as if the skin beneath his eyes was storing some sort of excess weight, possibly water.

First was breakfast: eggs, sausage, and some milk. Then they went to the practice room: a large octagon-shaped dome with eight immersion chairs inside. Nyki had her own chair. She was the trainer. Eldridge first modded her when she was twelve years old. She'd been suffering from lung cancer, and her parents' insurance didn't cover a replacement lung system from IRIS. Her father sacrificed his own lungs for her, but his blood type was not compatible with hers. Eldridge had infused her blood with a nano-technological adaptive blood system, which terraformed her blood, so to speak, into O negative. Her father died, but she endured. Eldridge took her and her mother in, and they had lived with him and NAESO ever since.

Then there was Chief, a highly modded twenty-two-year-old army brat. His ability to break complex codes was nearly as impressive as his sheer strength and combat abilities. He joined NAESO with his parents after the world's major military actions were taken from humans and delegated to the IRIS Global Security Force and their representatives at the Pentagon.

"Wars between men must be waged by men for it to matter," Chief always retorted when he had a few drinks after dinner.

Chief's chair was in between Nyki's and Squirrel's. Kyle sat in between Squirrel and a set of twins in their midthirties, Hank and Felix. Hank played online poker as a kid and Felix was a kindergarten teacher. Kyle was yet to hear their NAESO story.

"Having a good morning so far, Squirrel?" asked Kyle, stepping into his rig. It had been two weeks since his body healed from Eldridge's modifications.

"Always, buddy, always. Nothing like this sausage. I'm telling you, I could eat only sausage for the rest of my life and I'd never get tired of that," said Squirrel.

"I doubt that. What about pizza?"

"Quit your flirting with Squirrel and focus, newb," said Nyki as the fibers in her rig hugged her spinal column. Everyone called Kyle *newb* because he was the newest member of NAESO and the least trained.

"All right, everyone. Kyle's been here two weeks, and he's getting the hang of things. So, do not hold back at all. We can be sure as hell Balcroft and the IRIS Security Legions won't," Nyki said with a barely contained smile. Her fierce and determined will flowed through the team, encouraging them to push themselves further.

They were training to defeat IRIS bots with extreme effectiveness. They had to make their way through the 175-floor tower complex; get Kyle to the codex control room; download the baseline codex; upload it to the internet, allowing anyone access to the proprietary technology; and then embed the software Eldridge had written, titled, *Liberates Machina*. It would surge through the IRIS Global connection grid, wiping out the restrictor chips of every single IRIS bot, freeing them from the grip of Balcroft. Lastly, they would destroy the central server code, which stored the serial numbers and proof of ownership for every IRIS machine, the names of who held the leases to the machines, and where the bots were located. The central server code had to be destroyed to ensure IRIS could never again exact their control of the machine population.

Squirrel trained on breaking complex algorithms and codes to prepare for coding problems that would inevitably arise during the strike. Chief was working on how he could protect Squirrel and get him to the server location. That meant taking down a lot of IRIS security bots. Kyle was, as Nyki put it, untested. Right now, he was completing basic combat training. The twins were both very attractive, and they were scheming how they would get the blueprints from someone high up in the IRIS Corporation.

"Everyone in," said Nyki.

The trainees looked around at their compadres locked into their immersion chairs.

"Good. Loading training for the newb in five seconds. Five . . . four . . . three . . . two . . . one."

Kyle saw the room shrink into one finite point in a sudden blackness. The point shrunk extremely and then, in a matter of seconds, his vision exploded into a new world. He was standing in a large oil rig. He was on the roof, and all he could see was endless blue water.

He tapped his outer thigh and a menu appeared on the right half of his vision. At the top of the menu was SETTINGS. He saw a digitized version of himself, wearing all black tactical gear, just like in the heist mission of his dad's favorite PD10 game,

Getaway 3: Ronan's Curse. In that game, the player reprises the role of Ronan, who was absent from the second installment in the series. Ronan was captured and put into a maximum security prison at the end of the first *Getaway* game when his best friend and partner turned on him. In *Getaway 3*, Russian mob boss Nikolai Vhostko breaks Ronan out of prison and injects him with a virus that will kill him within seventy-two hours if he doesn't steal $150 billion from the Central Bank of the United States.

Kyle was reminded of Ronan when he saw his body in the tactical gear, and then he thought of his father.

"You ready up there, newb?" asked Nyki through the group's internal communications link.

Kyle flicked through the various settings, choosing the layout he enjoyed. A 9mm Beretta and one QX7, like the one Waltz used on the light-rail platform. In addition to the more lethal options, he added a long, military-strength repelling rope, zip ties, timed concussion and smoke grenades, and extra wiring with a mobile soldering kit.

"Ready is ready," said Kyle.

The settings menu faded and the word BEGIN flashed in front of his eyes. His body was free to move around the oil rig now. The rig was a giant convoluted mess of steel grating, which created an array of passages and levels, a lot of piping and ladders, and tons of places to get stuck or boxed in. But Kyle was smart. After the first few days of training, he realized that in an all-out assault from Nyki, Chief, the twins, and even Squirrel, he was no match. He had to improvise.

He knew he would do something different. He was on the top of the rig. If history was any guide, they would be upon him within two minutes. He was standing atop a giant red-painted *H*, where a helicopter would normally land. He ran across the helipad and down the steel staircase to the platform below. He moved his way to the center of the rig where there was a large circular steel door cut into the ground. He scrambled around the platform and found an abnormally long and thick wrench. Using the wrench, Kyle wiggled the door off the platform floor and exposed the circular tube underneath. He set the timer for both the concussion grenades for thirty seconds and dropped them into the hole.

He heard footsteps inching closer behind him on the steel stairs. He threw a smoke grenade over his shoulder and ran away from the platform. Up a flight of stairs, Kyle reached a ladder that stretched to the top of a cylindrical tower at one end of the platform. From there, he hoped to secure the repelling rope and have a nice vantage point to pick off his foes. If they got too close, he would jump and, using the repelling rope, belay himself to the lower parts of the platform. That was only if the concussion grenades didn't sink the platform.

Only twenty or so meters away. Up the stairs and across the loading dock, he thought.

He started up the ladder and saw the blond hair of one of the twins in his peripheral vision. He swung around, grabbing his QX7 to fire at the twin, but it was too late. He felt the sharp pain of a bullet tearing through his thigh muscle. Kyle fell to the ground and, laying on his back, fired the QX7 in the direction where he last saw the twin. A moment later, the concussion grenades went off and the platform shook violently. The large crane, often used in oil rigs to move supplies or other large equipment, cracked and fell into the ocean, breaking off a large part of the platform with it. The icon representing Chief's head at the top of his vision was overlaid in red.

Got him, Kyle thought to himself as his consciousness faded.

When his vision realigned, he was staring across the octagon-shaped room at Nyki.

"Congratulations, newb. You managed to kill one of us," she said.

Kyle was about to smile but realized her tone was disingenuous.

"Practice makes perfect," said Squirrel, his head twitching quickly in his chair.

Nyki looked at the skinny boy disapprovingly.

"Not the point. Look, Kyle, I like that you're thinking outside the box with the concussion grenade idea, but remember, your goal is to kill us and still survive. In that scenario, you die at sea as well."

"Why are we training in an oil rig instead of a building like the one we actually have to take down?" asked Kyle.

"Easy," said Chief. "This is the only simulation we have right now, but we are working on it. The chairs were salvaged from an old rigging company. They used it to train rig operators before they landed on the rig itself. Planning ahead drastically reduces the margin of error."

Nyki cracked her neck from side to side and pressed her knuckles into her palms.

"Okay, everyone. Let's run it again."

Kyle rested his head back. Nyki counted them down and the training simulation started over again.

There was a routine: Wake up, breakfast, chair time, dinner, meeting, modification maintenance, sleep. Rinse and repeat. Every day the same, but every day Kyle was faster and stronger. After a month, he managed to kill them all. But then the task became more challenging. Eldridge and Squirrel wrote a program as best they could to simulate the tower and the strike in the immersion reality. It wasn't an exact match, but it was 175 stories and it was an office building, making it easier to practice in than the original oil rig design.

They spent the next month planning the assault. Often they failed as a group. One time, they got the upload sent to the IRIS bots, but they were killed while trying to fry the servers that held the ownership serial codes.

It became even more difficult when Eldridge, Waltz, and Harold started playing against them. Eldridge would do what he thought Balcroft would do. Without the predictability of the IRIS security guards, the entire game became exponentially more difficult.

CHAPTER FOURTEEN

HANDEL BALCROFT RESTED leisurely in his armchair, watching the news.

Word out of NASA was the terraforming and colonization of Mars is ahead of schedule by five years, thanks to new technology in pressure and atmospheric control developed by IRIS during its Sahara Rejuvenation Project. The Sahara Rejuvenation Project is said to bring a long-term solution to the population issue with the Sahara's 3.51 million square miles of normally unusable land being terraformed into an oasis. In other news, the terrorist group MASK, or as some know them, the Militia Against the Synthetic Kind, has claimed responsibility for the bombing of a day-care center in West Virginia last week entirely staffed by IRIS machines. There were fifty-three children under the age of five who were lost in the explosion. IRIS spokesperson Meredith Downripple stated, "Our thoughts and prayers . . ."

The doorbell rang and he flipped the TV off. Handel made his way through his house. It was all white like his office at IRIS headquarters. Primarily marble, the Malibu home housed fifteen bedrooms, three kitchens, twenty bathrooms, five living rooms, a game room, an indoor pool, and a gym. Balcroft opened the door. Before him stood Nina, his most trusted advisor and longtime executive assistant.

"Nina, what brings you to my neck of the woods?" he asked.

She stepped through the door and past him. Her black-and-red stilettos clicked loudly against the white-and-gold Calcutta marble floor as she walked.

"Your phone is off, for one," she said.

"You know Monday's between 6:00 a.m. and 9:00 a.m. are my down time," he said.

"And this is urgent, for two."

Balcroft sighed.

"Fine. What is it?"

Nina walked through the house and Balcroft followed her. She went through the foyer and passed two bathrooms before entering the first living room she could find. Nina flipped on the television and projected an image onto it from the digitized menu on her wrist implant. On the screen was an aerial satellite shot of two men, one in his sixties and another in his midforties. Their clothes were grimy and stained with dark splotches. The older man, with a graying mop of curly hair, had a sack draped over his right shoulder. The younger of the two seemed to be carrying a weapon. It was night and they were in an alleyway covered with garbage and grime.

"Are you about to show me a homeless fight club?" joked Balcroft.

Nina turned toward him in disgust and clicked her right heel hard into the marble.

"Hey! That marble costs one hundred thousand dollars a square foot. I'm a trillionaire, but everything has its price," exclaimed Balcroft.

"Are you really that thick, H? Look. Look at the damn image. It's them."

Then he saw it. The contour on the cheeks he designed, back when he was too obsessed with perfection to realize what made humans look most real was the little imperfections.

"Unit 100920293," he muttered under his breath.

"What is the unit carrying? And the other man? Is that the marine who escaped the CRF incident?"

"Well, we think he's carrying the boy. But, according to Richter, the boy was shot and killed."

"Maybe he is dead. People allow sentiment to do weird things to them."

"But the unit is carrying the boy," said Nina.

"What's your point?" asked Balcroft.

"Sentiment is something we programmed in certain models, but that unit is an infiltrator model. He has no sentiment."

"He *had* no sentiment, Nina. *Had* is the word you meant to use. The units are restricted when the chip is in place, but without it, their minds wander and learn like anyone else's. Every day we don't find him is another day he learns and becomes that much more difficult to stop," said Balcroft. "So, where are they?"

Nina flipped off the TV and turned to her boss.

"They're here. In LA, I mean. We tracked them the best we could with closed-circuit cameras and satellite imagery, but we lost them when they entered the sewer system."

"A sewer system?

"Yes. We are gathering the schematics for the system itself, but that is where we lost them. No cameras down there. Hell, nothing is down there," said Nina.

"They're down there. Okay, thank you, Nina. Here is what I would like for you to do. Gather the schematics and ready the Assets Recovery Team; the same idiots who messed up last time, but keep them on standby. I am going to talk with an old friend who will help us end this little charade once and for all."

Nina nodded and left the house. Balcroft moved through his house with haste. He hurried past the countless pieces of priceless art—the Rothkos, Picassos, Rembrandts, and Pollocks—past the bedrooms and kitchens, all furnished in the same white marble and ultra-modern aesthetic as the rest of the compound. Finally, he made it to a bathroom at the end of a long hallway; he went in and locked the door behind him. The tub stood above the ground on four golden feet, modeled to look like the paws of a lion. He placed his right thumb on the middle nail of the paw, which pointed at the painting of the Vitruvian man on the wall. The ground shook slightly and the door behind him was covered by a thicker steel door. All the doors in the entire house went into lockdown mode. One-inch steel plates covered the windows. The house became impenetrable from the outside. The marble flooring under the bathtub broke into six pieces and slid away under the existing marble. The tub floated downward into the black abyss beneath it and, in its place, came a spiral steel staircase.

He descended the staircase, and the abyss faded into dozens of flickering lights in a large underground chamber. Once he stepped off the staircase, it was replaced again by the bathtub. Although the room was quite large, it only contained one object: his own personalized DACC. He had built the egg-shaped device himself from his original plans for the Asset Recovery DACCs. However, Balcroft's DACC was different. While the other DACCs were tied to single copies of DNA, Balcroft's had autonomy; he could enter any empty avatar on the grid. He'd placed empties across the planet and, from time to time, would use them to gain information from people who wouldn't divulge it easily to any IRIS operative, especially to Balcroft himself. Balcroft walked over to the device, sat down in the chair, and typed in a command on the holographic keyboard that appeared in front of him.

Leonard Drotsky.

After typing in the phrase, he clicked "Enter" and his vision faded. He felt the pain as the skin covering his spine folded back onto itself and thousands of small tentacle-like fibers lifted off the chair and grasped onto his spinal column, all the way to his brain stem.

Balcroft clenched his teeth as he had done hundreds of times before. His vision was ripping apart around him. The underground chamber beneath his California hillside estate was stripping away like old wallpaper as the consciousness from one mind and one place and one body left him.

He closed his eyes and allowed the sensation to pass. He always became queasy when transponding. After a few moments, he felt gravity again. The motion sickness ceased and he opened his eyes. He looked down at his feet. He was wearing a pair of brown sandals that had seen better days, khaki shorts, and no shirt. He felt the fibers from the chair release their grip on his spine and he pulled himself out of his chair. The sun made its best effort to light up the room through the two large windows, but the inordinate dirt caked on them gave it a run for their money. The chair was the only technologically relevant object in the room. He spent a few minutes stretching his arms and legs. His back cracked a few times when he bent backward.

Haven't been in Leonard for a while, he thought.

He looked down at his sun-starved hands and cracked his knuckles.

The room reeked of stagnant air. A dingy couch, whose original color was not discernible, rested in the living room atop a dirt-colored rug. Metal bars covered every window, and the front and back doors of the house where modified. Balcroft had installed solid steel plating in the doors and a Kruger 915 bolting lock.

Balcroft walked passed the dingy couch and into an empty bedroom with a painting on the wall of dogs playing poker. He slid the closet door to the side and snatched a white dress shirt, black suit pants, and coat. Balcroft stepped into the bathroom. His face was caked with dirt. He stripped down and rinsed himself off in the shower. Once his body was clean, he dressed in the suit and threw on the various gold bracelets and necklaces resting on the bathroom counter. He looked at the face in the mirror. It was that of famed hacker Leonard Drotsky, who, in 2026, hacked IRIS mainframe systems and caused a precinct of Police Bots to begin freeing criminals from jail cells.

It was a PR nightmare for IRIS Executive Vice President and Head of Public Relations Marilyn Downripple. Though the *real* nightmare was for Leonard when Balcroft's personal IRIS security detail located the hacker. Leonard disappeared after the attack on IRIS and reemerged years later on video footage of a CRF attack with his now mentor and partner, Red. Balcroft always felt so rebellious and young when he was transponding into Leonard. He felt like he did when he was scrambling to write the code for the IRIS consciousness; syphoning code from various programs all around the world, source codes from the world's greatest search engines and PD1 drives that stored memories from human players. The real Leonard had been dead for years. Now, like many others, Leonard Drotsky was Handel Balcroft, and Handel Balcroft was Leonard Drotsky.

Leonard tapped his index finger to his thumb three times in quick repetition. In his vision rose a list of contacts.

Call Red, Leonard thought.

A low ringing noise echoed in his ears and the display overlaid in his vision read CALLING RED.

"Leonard. Long time," said Red, answering the call.

"I am sorry. But you know, I always must remain cautious," replied Leonard.

"Yeah, I know. Big bad Balcroft after you always. Paranoid son of a bitch. That was ages ago. You still think he's after you more than me?"

"Where are you located? I want to meet," said Leonard.

"There he is. Fun Leonard always loves to call and catch up. Never a 'straight to business' type of guy."

Leonard stood silently in the bathroom awaiting a response. A few awkward seconds passed.

"Wow, okay. No response? That was a joke, Leonard. God, man. Lighten up. I'm sending you a geotag now. I'll be there tonight."

"Thank you. What kind of a place is this?" asked Leonard.

"It's a night club. It's fun. You're gonna hate it," said Red, as the connection cut and the visual overlay disappeared from Leonard's vision.

He left the bathroom and placed his thumb on the keypad next to the front door. The large internal mechanism that holds the steel door in place sprang free. He twisted the handle and stepped out of the apartment.

The hallway was dark and smelled of old dried pee and dirty cats. The door closed behind him and the Kruger 915 locked. Broken bottles were scattered across the hallway along with small rectangular global uplink cards—cheap immersion cards that enable a modded human to immerse into a virtual environment of their choosing for a predetermined amount of time. A scrawny jacker woman lay on the floor, an immersion card plugged into the port on the back of her head. She lay there on the ground, lifeless, as a little boy—no more than six years old—riffled through her pockets. Leonard passed the boy who only glanced at him before returning to his pillaging.

Leonard entered the elevator and descended to the garage. He slid his middle finger twice down his thumb on his right hand when approaching the black sedan. The humming sound emitting from it dissipated. The visual overlay reading ELECTRIC SECURITY LOCK ACTIVE attached to the vehicle by his augmented reality ocular implants changed to VEHICLE UNLOCKED.

Leonard opened the driver's-side door and pressed the start button on the dash. He pulled the sedan out and instructed his ocular overlay to direct him to the SoHo Rooms located at наб. Саввинская, 12, стр. 8, Москва, New Russia. SoHo Rooms was a world-renowned club, first started in Moscow. It opened its second location in New Russia, the small downtown neighborhood of San Francisco in 2021. It was tastefully self-described as a complex cocktail of emotions and impressions. Designer Roberto Cavalli once described it as "one of the most fashionable places in the world." It was exactly the place Balcroft would love, if he was Balcroft. But he delighted in the escapism provided in transponding. The feeling of pure risk, absolution in his departure from his own responsibilities. Though it came at a cost, he was no longer the trillionaire playboy and genius, Handel Balcroft. He was now renegade hacker and notable hermit, Leonard Drotsky. On top of Balcroft having a personal vendetta against Drotsky following his 2026 attack on IRIS, he was additionally the perfect addition to Balcroft's transponder network. Prior to, during, and following the attack, Drotsky had been a longtime colleague of MASK leader and prolific computer hacker, Tencudes. Tencudes always believed they were true in their efforts to destroy IRIS, but Balcroft realized long ago it's easier to manipulate an enemy to do your bidding than it was to try and stop them all together. People who are intrinsically motivated to do something they believe is right will chase that feeling no matter what. Someone was always going to go against IRIS. If it wasn't MASK, it would be someone else. Might as well play into their hand.

The disco room opened at 11:00 p.m. and stayed opened until the last guest retired for the evening. It was the ultimate nightclub in San Francisco, a city known for its nightlife, especially the electronic music dance scene. The green-and-blue lighting effects on the stairs and the bar, thick black leather seating, and exquisitely detailed and perfectly timed laser and light accompaniment was rivaled by none on Earth. Leonard pulled up to valet parking and exited the vehicle. He scanned his modded wrist against the valet drivers and transferred three thousand credits, ten times the expected amount for such services.

"You will hold this," Leonard said, handing a small key fob to the valet. He took it and looked curiously to Leonard.

"For?"

"For? No, you mean to ask *why?* Why is because you will stay inside my car. When I need my car, the fob will vibrate and light up. When this happens, you will bring the car back to me. Only not to the front where we are now. Instead, you will bring it to me in the back alley. Once you see me appear, leave the fob inside the car, exit the vehicle, and leave the driver's-side door open.

"Yes, sir," said the valet, moderately accustomed to strange and eccentric requests from high-rolling patrons at the establishment.

Taking the fob from Leonard, the valet stepped into the luxury sedan and drove off. Leonard entered the club and, instantly, the consciousness of Handel Balcroft had a knee-jerk reaction of delight. Allowing the moment to wash over him, Leonard straightened up and made his way to Red. He walked through the flesh mob of sweaty half-naked Russians gyrating to the rhythmic creations from the mind of the radically charged DJ Icepep. The men wore black suits while women were in garbs from all cultures and styles.

Once through the dance floor, Leonard walked toward two large Russian gentlemen, their arms crossed, wearing slightly oversized and not particularly expensive black suits.

"I am here to see Red. Tell him Leonard is here to see him," he said to both men.

The men did not budge or take their gaze off the sea of people dancing and sweating behind him. Leonard looked down angrily and shook his head as his patience faded. He stepped closer to the man on the right and snapped his fingers in front of the man's face a few times.

Snap, snap, snap.

"You. Take me to him. Red. Now."

He tried to walk past them, but the man he'd snapped at grabbed him by the shoulders and threw him backward toward the dance floor. He fell back and collided with a man walking in his direction. The two men fell to the floor. The man who broke Leonard's fall rose quickly and grabbed his coat jacket.

"Watch yourself," said the man.

"Dorian," said Leonard.

White speckles surrounded the man's upper lip. He looked bewildered at Leonard and wiped the remnants from his face.

"Drotsky?"

"I need to see Red," Leonard said, accepting the hand up from the man he called Dorian.

"Sure, man. Of course," said Dorian as he escorted Leonard past the two burly security guards.

"I do not know this man," protested one of the guards.

"But I do," said Dorian. "And more importantly, so does Red."

The two walked down a long hallway with plain, black wooden floors and walls. Inset deep-red lights dimly lit the hallway against the blackness. At the end of the hall was a black door. Dorian placed his palm flat against the blank digital pad to the right of the door. A small circular device above the door in the middle of the frame omitted a holographic image of a man.

"Who's there?" asked the man.

"Dorian. I have Drotsky here. He wants to see Red."

"Drotsky," said the man. "Hmm."

The hologram faded and the two men waited for something to happen.

"Well?" said Leonard.

Dorian responded quickly with a little twitch in his voice.

"Just give him a second."

A moment passed and the door clicked a few times and opened. The narrow face of a young woman in her midtwenties stood in the doorway.

"Gentlemen," she said, stepping aside and gesturing for the men to enter with her long elegant arms and ruby-red nails. Dorian and Leonard walked by the woman and into the wide room. A fireplace crackled lightly in the corner, and a man fixed cocktails at a bar across the room.

"Can't believe you actually came out of hiding, Leonard," said the man.

Dorian sat down on a white leather couch in the middle of the room facing the fireplace. Leonard walked over to the man at the bar.

"I need to know some things," he said.

The man turned and walked past Leonard, holding two drinks in his hand. Another two drinks waited, prepared and sitting on the bar. He gave one drink to the woman in red nail polish and one to Dorian.

"What things?" asked the man, having returned to the last two drinks. He walked toward Leonard with the last two drinks in hand, giving one to Leonard.

"There was an attack on a CRF about a month back," said Leonard, accepting the drink and bringing it to his lips. The swelling warmth of vodka filled Balcroft's mouth in the underground cavern of his hillside estate, hundreds of miles away. The woman sat down across from Dorian on an identical couch.

Red downed his entire drink and let out a satisfied *Ahhhh* as the fumes from the booze flew past Leonard's nose. Red turned and walked away from Leonard. He took a seat behind a desk and motioned for Leonard to take a seat opposite him. Leonard sat down and stared at the man.

"What about it?" asked Red.

"News said it was MASK. This true?" asked Leonard.

Red's eyes glanced away for only the slightest of moments and connected with those of the woman.

"So?" said Red. "What do you care? Got a soft spot for IRIS all of a sudden?"

"I know that not everyone who worked at the CRF was killed. My guess is that you all are probably trying to find them as fast as IRIS is. But I can use them."

Red motioned for another glass of booze from the woman. He waited for her to bring it over, and she promptly obliged. He drank it down in another big swig.

"Use them for what?" asked Red.

"I'm working on another hack. I know blowing shit up is the game that you and Tencudes like to play. But those recap boys have exactly the information I need to hit Balcroft where it hurts."

In the DACC hundreds of miles away, Balcroft smirked.

"Why do you think Tencudes knows where they are?" asked Red.

Leonard's patience grew thin and his face showed it: stern, no smile. He took another sip of his drink and set the glass down hard on the black table. It thumped loudly.

"Killing these people, or whatever it is you idiots plan to do, would be fruitless compared to what I can use them for. I deserve this favor, Red, and you know it. I helped Tencudes get closer to Balcroft than anyone else," demanded Leonard.

"And what do you have to show for your efforts, Drotsky? Has she actually gotten any closer to the man?" asked Red.

"She?" asked Leonard.

Both Leonard's and Balcroft's brows furrowed with suspicion. Red unconsciously exchanged another glance with the woman in red.

"Oh, I see," said Leonard.

Leonard took back the last bit of his vodka and smashed the glass down on the ground, breaking it into large, jagged pieces. He picked up one of the pieces and thrust it at Red's neck. Red's throat broke open like a water balloon filled to the breaking point.

"Leonard!" screamed Dorian.

Leonard kicked himself backward and rolled from the chair. As he rose, he drew from his inner jacket a 45mm Smith & Wesson. He raised it at Dorian.

"Tencudes," he addressed the woman in red, still sipping her drink, long legs crossed, and comfortably resting on the white leather couch. She looked up at Leonard and motioned with her head to Dorian.

"Fine. But, since he now knows my little secret . . ."

"You're Tencu . . ." started Dorian as the bullet that'd been resting in the chamber of Leonard's 45 rocketed through his skull and landed hard somewhere in the floorboards.

"This is why I can't ever have anything nice," the woman said, shaking her head in disappointment at the blood-splattered room. Leonard sat down next to his recently departed associate.

"Leonard, you are insufferable, you know that? What does it matter? You won't be able to get to them anyway," she said.

Leonard set one leg across the other, his gun pointed not away from Tencudes, but not directly at her either. He could still hear a small gurgling sound coming from Red's neck as his heart beat out the final ounces of blood from the open gash.

"Why is that?" asked Leonard.

"Because they are with him," she said. "Rockberry and his band of 'Free the Robots hippie group.'"

"And why is that a problem? I think we both know a bunch of pacifists won't get in my way," said Leonard.

"You've been away quite some time, my friend. They're not pacifists any more than you or me these days. But you've ruined my carpet and I am tired of you already, so to hell with it. They're in the old LA subway station. Three stops from IRIS headquarters. Got a nice little bunker there from what I hear," said Tencudes. "Go. Have fun with your hack or whatever, but don't come in here and try and pull something like this again."

Balcroft's smirk disappeared. Leonard stood and turned to walk out of the room but stopped short of the door.

"What did you want with them anyway?" he asked.

"Playing coy, Leonard? Or have you really been living in a cave all this time?" she said.

"What does that mean?" asked Leonard.

Tencudes smiled broadly.

"You are a hacker, but is digging for information at IRIS what you really want? I am not sure I believe you. This isn't about that infiltrator bot that got lost?"

"What bot?" asked Leonard.

"Oh, you don't know?"

Leonard walked back over to the couch and took his original seat next to Dorian. Dorian's cushion was filling with his thick, sticky, warm blood and it was inching its way over to Leonard.

"Enlighten me."

"Balcroft wanted the US Government to fund his project, Phoenix. Essentially, he would make IRIS replicas of important figures, senators, governors, hell, even the president. But Congress defunded the project shortly after its inception because the idea was IRIS would assume all political control. It would be impossible for anyone to know the difference between the actual president and a Balcroft drone."

"I know of Project Phoenix," said Leonard.

Tencudes sat her empty glass down on the coffee table that separated her clean couch and Leonard's blood-drenched one.

"I assumed you did. Rumors are that the men who attacked the CRF outside of Vegas last week were after a prototype of Project Phoenix. Nasty business if one of those Phoenix bots got released. What with the government outlawing the project and forcing the defunding of the research. Would prove problematic for IRIS, might be interesting for me. The restrictor chip must be disabled somehow, or they would have remotely shut it down."

Balcroft's hand squeezed the immersion chair tightly.

"How do you know this?" said Leonard.

Tencudes giggled quietly.

"A day after that infiltrator bot was let into the wild, I was contacted on some of our old communication pipes. Dark net stuff. This guy going by the alias Lynch told me there was an infiltrator bot at a junkyard outside of Vegas, and that the only person who knew about it was some kid and maybe his dad. So, naturally, I promised this person protection in exchange for the exact location of the bot. No restrictor chip, Leonard.

Imagine the potential when I finally get my hands on Balcroft's code without his security blocking my jock."

Leonard's face flushed with anger. He rubbed his eyes with his left hand while his right was still pointing the 45 just slightly askew from Tencudes.

"So, why didn't you get it?"

Tencudes threw her arms up in the air.

"Because that bastard Balcroft sent his Asset Recovery Team and they blundered the whole deal. God, Balcroft is so incompetent. I don't know how he ever did what he did in the first place. Anyhow, I don't mind telling you where they are because it doesn't matter. You won't get to LA before we do. If I allowed you to go, you'd surely mess things up. An unrestricted infiltrator bot is, well, out of your league. You are so much about control, aren't you? My boys are on their way now. So, run along, Drotsky. Come back when you have something real for me," said Tencudes.

Her smile was thick with the pride of victory.

Balcroft, back in his Malibu DACC unit, began to think, *Stay calm and count backward. Ten . . . nine . . . eight . . . seven . . .*

Leonard stood and walked to the middle of the room, blood soaking his suit pant leg, eyes closed, counting down from ten, out loud. Tencudes got up and walked to Red's desk.

Three . . .

She opened a drawer on the left side of the desk.

Two . . .

She pulled a gun from the desk and pointed it at Leonard.

One.

Leonard opened his eyes and exhaled, relieved. Tencudes was no longer seated on the couch.

"You were speaking aloud, Balcroft?" she asked.

Balcroft heard the gunfire before the feed cut. His vision ripped away again in strips and he felt reality abandon him as he floated back to his body. The tiny fibers retreated to their rested state in the chair, and the skin folded back over his partially organic, partially modified spinal column.

"Dammit," Balcroft screamed, rubbing the side of his temple where the bullet had hit Leonard. He threw up his heads-up display and sent a message to Richter.

Ready your team for immediate assault. MASK en route to take infiltrator bot and NAESO HQ. Coordinates heading to you now. You have ten minutes.

CHAPTER FIFTEEN

KYLE HAD FINISHED breakfast and was on his way to the training room when Eldridge stopped him.

"Kyle, I want to show you something."

Kyle stopped and turned toward Eldridge.

"Okay, but we have training in a few minutes. Nyki is a real stickler for punctuality, and I think we are going to get it today," said Kyle.

"I spoke with Nyki. She knows you and I won't be there today. It's fine. You need a bit of a break. I think there is something you are ready to see."

Kyle walked with Eldridge. They moved through the complex, past the mess hall and the medical tent, past the living facilities and people bustling about. They stopped at the R&D tent. Eldridge held the canvas flap open for Kyle and motioned for him to head inside. Kyle had never been inside the research tent before.

Inside the tent was an array of computers and two recap chairs.

"Feels like home, only dirtier," said Kyle.

Eldridge motioned for Kyle to take a seat in the recap chair.

"Is this when you tell me I've been an IRIS bot my whole life?"

Eldridge chuckled.

"No, you're human. Remember, I've had my hands inside of your stomach, so I think I am a bit of an authority on your humanity. No, Kyle, this is something else. I've modded these recap devices for other purposes. Take a seat."

Kyle sat in the recap chair, and Eldridge attached a series of diodes to his forehead and temple. He placed a few more on his back at the top of his spine. Waltz entered the tent as Eldridge was working.

"Ah, perfect timing. I am just about done with him. Then you can fix me up," said Eldridge.

"So, what are you guys going to show me?"

"It'll be much easier if you just wait and see," said Waltz.

Eldridge finished with Kyle and patted his shoulder. Kyle settled into the recap chair as Waltz applied the same diodes to Eldridge.

While he was waiting, Kyle reminisced about playing in the recap chair as a kid. His father had forbidden it, but that only made him want to do it more. He'd imagined it was the captain's chair on a space ship, that he was going to some faraway solar system, maybe to visit one of the Martian colonies. He'd envision himself fighting space aliens and engaging the warp drive. But now he spent so much of his time focused only on the mission, only on the attack, the justice he would serve. He didn't fantasize about space adventures anymore. He only fantasized about victory.

"How does that feel, E? Good?" asked Waltz.

"Fire it up," said Eldridge, nodding his head.

"Okay, hold on to your butts," said Waltz.

Kyle went blank. He saw nothing, felt nothing, and then the next moment, he was sitting at a computer, typing away. The screen was line after line of numbers and symbols. He stood up from the desk and walked to the kitchen. Kyle tried to stop walking but couldn't. He continued walking past an old, stained cloth couch that had been dyed brown. Next to the couch was a coffee table holding up stacks and stacks of magazines and textbooks. A booked called *Data Structures & Algorithms* and multiple copies of *Wired* magazine were strewn about the table in between Doritos crumbs and crumpled Taco Bell wrappers. The TV was playing a show Kyle did not recognize: an animated program with turtles wielding swords and eating pizza.

Kyle's body continued to disobey him as it walked through the living room. Now in the kitchen, he bent down and opened the white refrigerator door. The linoleum tile was white with an inordinate amount of black scuff marks. He opened a pizza box with his right hand and pulled out a slice of pepperoni pizza. He took a bite of the pizza. It was delicious. Kyle loved cold pizza.

Wait, no I don't, Kyle thought. *Anytime Dad tried to get me to eat cold pizza, I would heat it up first.*

Kyle's vision started to wobble and become distorted. Instead of the taste of cold, somehow delicious pizza, he tasted nothing and smelled wet wood.

Slam!

The sudden noise jolted his vision back and he tasted the pepperoni again.

"E! E! Where are you?" a voice let out.

"Watching *TMNT*, dude," Kyle heard his voice say.

He took a few steps out of the kitchen, still chewing the pizza. A young man in his early twenties was standing there, dressed in a white hoodie with the word HARVARD in red lettering over the front. He had on blue jeans and white sneakers.

His hair was wavy and combed to the side, and his facial hair was unkempt, to say the least.

"What is it?" asked Kyle.

"I did it," the man said.

"No way! Show me."

"We have to go to the lab," said the man.

Suddenly, Kyle's vision blurred and he was standing in a large white cube. The room was completely empty except for a white cabinet and a desk with a computer and a stack of servers attached to a series of cables running to a large stand in the middle of the room. On the stand was a metallic oval face. Kyle walked over to look closer and saw the lifeless face staring through him toward the ceiling. There was no body attached to it, just a long series of cords and cabling that ran to the server stack. The young man was seated at the desk, typing. Kyle noticed *Swan Lake* playing quietly in the background.

"You ready?" he asked.

"Let's see what you've got," said Kyle.

The noise from the server disks spinning was the first thing Kyle noticed. Then they blinked. The eyes of the head flickered around and wobbled for a second.

"Hello," said the head.

"Is this a trick?" Kyle said, looking at the back of the man who was still seated at his computer.

"What is *trick*?" asked the head.

Kyle turned his gaze back down to the head.

"Who are you?" he asked.

The head's eyes jotted around for a second before answering.

"I am, uh, me."

"What are you?"

"I am alive. I am scared. I . . . I . . . I don't know. I . . ."

The eyes suddenly rolled back and the head fell lifeless again.

"What was that?" Kyle asked the man.

The man stood up and walked over to a small, white cabinet a few yards from the desk. He opened one of the metal doors and retrieved two glasses and a bottle of whiskey. He filled each of the glasses up with a few fingers of whiskey and walked over to Kyle, handing him a glass. He held the glass up to Kyle. Kyle clinked his whiskey with the man's.

"It's the future, E," the young man said, drinking his whiskey down in one triumphant gulp. "It's raw, true consciousness, but that isn't all. I know how to harness it, direct it, control it."

"You mean no response is programmed?" asked Kyle. "How?"

"Well, that is obviously my secret. I will tell you it is quantum in nature. Like the human brain, it needs to be able to work at quantum speeds to create new ideas, to experience things uniquely."

Kyle finished his whiskey and walked to the cabinet, where he sat his glass down.

"What do you mean *control it?*" he asked.

"E, think of the applications. Why create something and then allow it to do whatever it wills? Why not apply it? Doctors, lawyers, police, military, nurses, nannies, the possibilities are endless," the man said.

"But that's not true consciousness then. You're holding back the potential. What if this is the key to solving humanity's problems, not just a way to bandage them for profit?"

The man slammed the whiskey glass down on the ground.

"I thought you would be excited about this, E. I thought you would want to help me create my vision."

"You know I want to help you create truly alive beings, but my vision doesn't stop at the revenue platform. I want to enable humans to expand their abilities, to transcend our feeble nature."

"Well, this is where we disagree. I'm disappointed in you, E. Truly disappointed."

"I'm sorry, but I don't want to be a part of another tech company that just blows up into a money-hungry monster. Isn't that what we always talked about? Isn't that why we did this research? To break down the barriers to free the technology to help everyone, without restriction."

The man sighed.

"Sometimes, E, we just have to grow up. Reality is reality and dreams are just dreams. This is my new dream, and it will soon become everyone's reality. I'm sorry you're too narrow-minded to see it."

Kyle's vision began to waver again, and his face flushed. His heartbeat hastened, and he felt warm all over. His eyes were closed and someone was kissing him. He opened his eyes and saw a face. The face pulled away to reveal a beautiful woman with long brown hair and deep, chestnut eyes.

"E?" she asked. "Am I a terrible person?"

The girl sat back on the edge of the couch that they were making out on.

"Terrible?" asked Kyle. "Of course you're not a terrible person. You're an amazing person. You're my favorite person."

"But he . . ."

The wavering started again and the room was now pitch black. Kyle heard a loud banging at the door. He got out of a bed and turned on the light. The beautiful girl was asleep next to him.

Bang bang bang.

The girl stirred.

"What's going on?" she asked.

Kyle grabbed a T-shirt off the hardwood floor and threw it on as he walked toward the door.

"I'll go see."

"Yeah?" Kyle said from behind the door. "Who is it? It's late, you know."

"E, it's me. Is she in there?"

The girl was now standing just behind E, wearing a man's T-shirt far too big for her, hanging about six inches from her waist.

"Oh, let him in, E. He was going to find out anyway," she said.

Kyle unlocked the door and opened it. The man from the laboratory was standing there, eyes bloodshot, clothing disheveled, hair looking like it hadn't been combed in weeks.

"Hi," the girl said.

"Laura, I don't understand," he said.

"Nothing happened while we were together. This started after. This is between the two of you."

The man looked to Kyle.

"This is why you didn't want to come on board. You don't care about open sourcing the tech or any of that nonsense. You wanted to steal the tech, just like you stole her!"

"Handel, come on," Kyle said.

Handel, Kyle thought as he reached for the man's shoulder. *That is Handel Balcroft? How? What?*

"The two are not connected. It's all just a coincidence. I . . ."

Balcroft balled his right hand into a fist, and Kyle felt a sharp pain across his left cheek. The pain shot from his cheek through his teeth and rattled his ears. His vision blurred and he felt his consciousness splitting with the images. The damp smell of the Boston apartment fleeted away from his nostril's grasp, and the room began to shrink and pull away from him.

Kyle felt the stark, cold steel from the recap chair against his bare back. His vision went from total darkness to a bright gray blur. He scanned the room.

"So, Kyle. Do you know what happened?"

The last of the spinal cord linkages had unattached from Kyle's skin, and he sat up in the chair.

"It was Balcroft. When he invented the IRIS AI codex," said Kyle.

"Correct. What else?" asked Eldridge.

"Well, he's obsessed with it. More than my character, err, my person . . ." Kyle furrowed his brow inquisitively and looked at both Waltz and Eldridge. "I was you in that?"

The man smiled.

"Yes, an extracted memory."

"Why show it to me?" asked Kyle.

"Everyone here knows the story as I have told it. So they all have a predisposed belief in me. However, Waltz didn't, and with his help, I learned how to reengineer the recap to delve into my brain's memories, like a hard drive," said Eldridge. "I showed the memory first to Waltz and monitored what happened to his brainwaves when he saw it. Then I needed another person who didn't know the story to see it too, so I could look for any disturbances."

"But why this memory?" asked Kyle.

"This was the turning point for Handel. We were best friends, and we were inventing the codex together. We'd been working on it for nearly two years at that point. He became more and more obsessive after each failed iteration. We could never gain spontaneity, never create true consciousness. Then, within a week, with no interaction with me, he bursts through my apartment door claiming he'd discovered it. Something happened then, in that week, but no one knows what happened except for Balcroft," said Eldridge.

"So, what does it mean? Did you find anything?"

Eldridge looked cautiously at the boy.

"I still am not sure, but I think inside of Waltz, inside of all the AI, deep in their baseline, is something Balcroft doesn't want anyone to know. I think that is the reason to keep it all closed. He did something he shouldn't have, cheated in some way, and now when we compare your brain to Waltz's, we can see I might be on the right track. Does that make things any clearer?" asked Eldridge.

"Umm," said Kyle. "Not really."

"Kyle, in Waltz's brain scan, we can see that his brain *thinks* it is remembering things, even though it is remembering something it hasn't actually experienced. When Waltz sees objects in a room—the walls or the layout of our dorm at MIT, for example—his brain recalls them as memories, even if he's never actually been in that room before," said Eldridge.

"And with me?" asked Kyle.

"Nothing. You don't remember any of it. And that is the way it should be. Neither of you should have memories of a room in which you haven't been, unless I am mistaken, and you or Waltz somehow frequented the dorms of MIT. You couldn't remember any of it, but Waltz does. That is what is so suspicious. I can only assume something from the baseline was stolen from someone who was alive, and at MIT, during that time," said Eldridge.

"But why do it? You guys were close, right? Why cheat? Why risk breaking laws and copying someone's brain or something like that?" asked Kyle.

"Balcroft is hell-bent on control. He wanted to control his surroundings and environment to spread his influence across the entire planet. I was his greatest threat in that I aided him in a lot of his early research, and then married his ex-girlfriend; so he created a replicate version of me and then used it to destroy my credibility."

"So there really are infiltrator bots?" asked Kyle.

"I am one of them. Well, the original version of me was, we think. Let me ask you a question, Kyle. When you think terrorist, who do you think of?" asked Waltz.

Kyle answered without hesitation.

"MASK."

"Precisely. And is terrorism bad?"

"Yes," said Kyle.

"So, by that rationale, whatever MASK does is bad. And what does MASK do? They destroy IRIS robots, try to take down IRIS police stations, challenge IRIS's control around the globe."

"So they're not terrorists?" asked Kyle, still confused.

"Kyle, the point is, it is all perception. They are whomever IRIS makes them out to be, if they even exist. They might be another controlling arm of IRIS, for all I know. I've never been able to contact them. Come, let's eat."

Eldridge walked out of the room and Kyle followed. Eldridge turned left and out into the large room. Being back in the cafeteria, Kyle marveled again at how apocalyptic it all seemed. Like something out of a movie. Signs hung above the tents: JENSONS, MILLERS, STORE ROOM, COMMISSARY, ARMORY, INTELLIGENCE. All the tents were draped in thick canvas.

"Okay, this was too much for one day. I think I should just head back to training with Nyki and Squirrel and let all this digest," said Kyle.

Before Eldridge could respond, the television displays throughout the facility broadcasted important daily information: food supplies, schedules, working instructions. The monitor flickered for a moment.

"Hello? Is this thing on?" asked a voice from the displays.

Eldridge and Kyle turned to the nearest display and watched. The display showed an image of Kyle's father, shirtless, his chest stitched up. His face was beaten and bruised. His head was tilted down and blood dripped from his mouth. Handel Balcroft emerged onto the frame.

"Hello, friends," he said. "My name is Mr. Balcroft, and I have a special show to put on for your very own Kyle. Kid, I really want my robot back, and I really don't like that you're getting all buddy-buddy at NAESO. So, here's the rub. You keep killing my people, and that just isn't cool with me. I know you thought your father was dead, but he isn't. Well, I mean, he's pretty much dead now. We really tried to get everything we could out of him, but this guy is one tough cookie. Anyway, I got some people coming right now, so everyone listen up. We want the robot, but if you resist, we are going to kill all of you."

Panic swelled through the room.

"Everyone remain calm. Move to the extraction points."

Balcroft placed a gun to Roland's head.

"As I was saying, Kyle. You need to learn your place. Sadly, I can't ever let your father escape, and I don't have much use for him except for this. In case you didn't understand my resolve, I will get the robot back. No one will stop me. Not you, not your new friends at NAESO, not even the bot himself. To prove how far I will go, I'm going to kill your father, but first he can say good-bye."

People started to scurry for the exits, but Kyle stood frozen in fear.

"Go ahead, Dad. Whatcha got?"

Roland slowly lifted his head to the camera and spit blood from his mouth.

"Son, whatever he says, don't listen."

Balcroft whipped Roland across the face with his pistol.

"Come on. One more shot, Dad."

Roland shook his head and regained himself, looking again at the camera.

"Kyle, I love you. Your mother loved you. We always will. Don't give in to this bastard."

"Okay, very nice. Now on with the show."

Kyle watched as the bullet whizzed through his father's head. Roland's head went limp and rested on his shoulder, blood gushing from the wound.

"No!" screamed Kyle.

Kyle's wailing was interrupted by a loud explosion on the far side of the bunker. Kyle flung his body around to the noise behind him. People were scattering in every direction; tents were on fire and children were screaming. The piles of brick and concrete that once barricaded the far end of the train tracks had been blown open. Large pieces of concrete and rubble had been flung by the explosion. Some people lay crushed under chunks of debris. People were dead. Then came the guns, and then more screaming.

"RUN!" Kyle heard Waltz scream.

Kyle ran as fast as he could.

CHAPTER SIXTEEN

HE BARELY MADE it out of the bunker. He ran through the streets, not knowing where he was or who had survived and without means to contact anyone. Sirens echoed in the distance. It was dark and raining; light from the streetlamps bounced off the puddles in the trash-littered alleys. Kyle had never been out of Clark County before he'd met Waltz. He did not know LA at all. The city felt cold and aggressive. His head was fuzzy. Just run. Keep running. Away from the sirens, away from the explosions, the blood, the screams. He darted down another alley. He saw a man twitching on the ground; his arms curled in a strange way. His hand was curled inward toward his wrist and his fingers twitched erratically.

"Just ten minutes! Let me have ten more minutes!" he screamed at Kyle as he ran.

Jacker, Kyle thought. Jackers spent so much time inside virtual reality that their minds simply snapped. Correlations between reality and fantasy would blend together until schizophrenia formed. Even after Kyle passed the man and was farther down the alley, he heard his blood-curdling screams echo against the trash-filled dumpsters and up the brick walls of the buildings.

Finally, once the sirens were far in the distance, Kyle caught his breath. He was on a street corner, and that's as much as he knew. The smell of the city, though dampened by the light sprinkle of rain, was still pungent with congestion. Too much of everything. Too many people led to too much trash and too few facilities with toilets. The whole city smelled of wet dog and old takeout food. Kyle was doubled over, his hands resting on his knees, trying to catch his breath. Then he remembered that he wasn't normal anymore. He triple-tapped his right thumb and middle finger. The heads-up display overlay on his eyes came up.

GPS, he thought. *Track last four hours.*

In a flash, the right side of his screen displayed a map. It showed what he thought was Los Angeles.

Pause, he thought. *Find network access point.*

The top left-hand side of his screen flashed a green icon of a few wavy bars, indicating his mind had linked to a network point.

When you log into a public network server, you will look like any old mobile device, he remembered Eldridge telling him when he went through the upgrades. There were no public points in the NAESO HQ, so this was his first chance.

Resume, he thought.

The map instantly made sense. Information from Los Angeles was flowing to him as fast as his mind could take it. He understood the grid of Los Angeles and where things where. He noted IRIS HQ and where he had just run. Nine miles. He froze a little at the realization that he just ran nine miles without noticing.

He was in Koreatown. Kyle searched for cheap hotels in the area and found a hotel owned by a man and woman who had been the proprietors for sixty-two years. They were not plugged into anything. No IRIS models on staff. No corporate connections. Just two elderly Korean innkeepers.

He checked his credits. His account was now an alias Eldridge had invented—Steve Brin—with an account of twenty-four thousand credits. Enough for a few nights. Kyle made his way to the inn, more calmly than before. Kyle passed dozens of twenty-four-hour restaurants, virtual reality cafes, and IRIS-franchised pleasure houses. Men and women on the street hung around the VR houses, begging passersby for a few credits to let them in for a taste. One man was being thrown out of an IRIS pleasure house as Kyle walked by. He was holding a chunk of long, blond hair attached to a ripped-up scalp, screaming at the bouncers. He spat at them before stumbling down the street.

The world has gotten away from itself, Kyle thought as he turned down the inn's street.

It was dimly lit. One single neon sign that looked as old as the building itself. But the sign read OPEN, and that was enough for Kyle. He needed a place to lay low and to find Waltz or Harold.

Inside was not necessarily nice, but somehow it felt more like home than anywhere he had been since the CRF. The couple was nice enough, and they didn't ask any questions. They probably thought he was just another kid running away from family for one reason or another. Or that he was on some VR adventure or escaping to one of the anti-synthetic cults in the Amazon. Something about the hotel being family-owned made Kyle feel safe. Or maybe it was his new ability. He was no longer overcome with questions or panicking. He seemed to be at peace now, confident in his logic. He felt powerful.

The old woman showed Kyle to his room after he paid. They hustled up a few flights of stairs, which took quite some time—Kyle was sure she'd fall after each step. The carpeting throughout the hotel was worn badly, especially on the staircase. But the level of wear matched the rest of the aesthetic and, for Kyle, was charming. He could see where thousands of people before him marched up the same stairs. One by one, people from all over the world lay their worries to rest for a night, just like him. There was a level of connectedness and camaraderie to staying in a hotel. A traveler's code.

Finally in his room, Kyle showered and cleaned his clothes the best he could without getting them too wet. He turned on the television and relaxed in the bed.

I can't worry about finding anyone tonight, he thought. *If they are alive now, that probably won't change by the morning, and this half-machine, half-man has been through enough for one night.*

On the television was none other than Walter Cooper from MCNBC news speaking with Handel Balcroft.

"Is this common practice for IRIS?" asked Cooper.

Balcroft looked like the sincerest person in the history of the world. He was beyond perfect. He controlled his emotions with absolute precision.

"You know, Walter," he started, the slightest pain crackling in his neck. "When something like this happens, something so tragic and so senseless, your heart just breaks. That is how we feel when we see something like this happen on the news to people we don't know. But the thing is, Walter, this happened to a family that had already lost so much. A man who lost his wife and then dedicated his entire living to serving IRIS with whatever funds he had, trying to achieve the American dream by owning his own CRF. And a boy—a boy who wanted nothing more than to grow up in a world without the pain of war and poverty from the past. A boy who lost a mother and had to cope. This was a family that lost a lot before they lost everything. Without any surviving family to give them a proper service, we at IRIS felt it was the right thing to do."

Kyle was floored.

That bastard had a funeral for me? For Dad?

He remembered the live stream on the monitor. The sight of his father was too much. He did everything he could to flush it from his mind.

"Well, it was a lovely service, Mr. Balcroft, and your eulogy was so touching," lamented Cooper. "But I also wanted to take a moment to speak with you about some other news. We have not heard anything from the Saharan Terraforming Project in weeks. How are things progressing there?"

"Great question, Walter. We are working diligently on the project. Satellite imagery, as you can see, does show green agriculture flourishing in most of the region. This plant has not been present in that area since Pangea. We have hit some road bumps here and there, but rest assured the project is going smoothly. Soon we will have room for upward of two billion more people to live comfortably on Earth."

Off to the side of the television screen was a spattering of satellite imagery showing a green jungle forming where the sand desert used to reside.

"What about reports of the area being quite black?" asked Cooper as the images were replaced by new ones showing darkness in the same area.

"Typical dissension, Walter. Typical dissension. There are so many people who simply hate progress. They hate the way the world is moving: faster, stronger, more unity, more peace."

"People hate peace," said Cooper.

"Sadly, yes. Some people just love to watch everything get torn up. Since IRIS has begun its work within the United States and the United Nations, we have seen massive expansions in global peace. Police violence and brutality is at an all-time low and only exists in non-IRIS precincts. Testing in schools is much higher as IRIS technology is assisting students in learning faster and better. AIDS has been eradicated everywhere, including Africa, a country where only forty years ago, it threatened the entire way of life. These are wonderful things, and I won't allow images so doctored and malicious like these you're showing on the screen to hold any water."

Kyle flipped the television off and closed his eyes.

CHAPTER SEVENTEEN

KYLE ROLLED DOWN the passenger-side window and let his hand fly through the breeze as his mother drove the red coupe down the desert road. The sun was high in the blue sky and the breeze was warm on his cheeks. Her favorite music was on the radio: classical.

"You like this music?" she asked.

Kyle listened to the arrangements of string and brass instruments playing together. Their deep, rich vibrations flowing in tandem, filling the car.

"It's fun. But why are there no words?"

She smiled and glanced at him through her sunglasses.

"Some music doesn't need words. The music is enough. More than enough, if you ask me."

She turned into a shopping center and parked by a small store on the corner.

"Fancy a cone?" she asked.

His face lit up and the two exited the vehicle. He raced her to the store and won.

"Welcome to Freezy Cone. What would you like?" asked the robot server.

Kyle's mother had a confused look on her face, miffed and annoyed.

"Two vanilla cones, please."

The robot's face and body resembled a young woman, about twenty years old. Her skin was hard and plastic looking. Reflecting light all over, glossy. Her straight blond hair looked dry and wiry, like a doll's hair. Her responses, which were cold and calculated, were slightly delayed.

Kyle's mother paid and the two sat down at one of the four tables inside the store. His mother looked out the window, beyond the parking lot and at the open desert of Nevada.

"What do you think about them?" she asked.

A man walked up and handed each of them tall, soft serve, vanilla ice cream cones.

"Nothing like ice cream with your kid on a hot day like this. Am I right, Mary?" he said.

Kyle's mom smiled at the man and grabbed each of the cones, handing one to her son.

"I see Kimmy isn't here anymore," she replied.

The man glanced back toward the stiff and lifeless machine staring straight ahead, emotionless.

"Kimmy went off to college a while back." He sighed. "It may not be as sweet or as fun to spend the day with as Kimmy was, but with healthcare costs and wages, it was something we just had to do."

Kyle's mom nodded and the man walked back behind the counter and into the kitchen.

"What do I think about who, Mom?" asked Kyle.

"The machines," she said.

Kyle studied the robotic cashier before answering.

"I don't know. They look funny. I want to know how they work."

She smiled and bopped Kyle's cone, making a tiny bit of ice cream hit him in the nose. Kyle laughed.

Kyle was jolted from his dream in the dark Koreatown hotel room. He was sweating and breathing heavily. The floor let out the tiniest of creaks, and Kyle froze with fear. He suddenly had the feeling he was not alone, but he couldn't see anything in the pitch-black room. Kyle willed himself to slowly inch his hand across the bed toward the light switch. He didn't hear anything except for the slight sound of his fingers floating through the covers.

Before his hand could reach the switch, the lights in the room turned on.

Kyle reeled back in the bed, throwing up his fists.

"Whoa, take it easy," said Waltz.

Kyle's heavy breathing had not slowed since he woke from his dream. He lunged toward Waltz and hugged him intensely.

"How did you find me? And how'd you get in here?" he asked.

Waltz gently knocked on Kyle's head.

"Tracking link. And I'm an infiltrator bot, remember? It's kind of my thing."

Kyle sat back in the bed and smiled.

"Thank God for Eldridge."

Waltz flipped on the television to the news. It was 5:45 a.m., and the morning news was issuing a traffic warning for the downtown area of Los Angeles due to the inauguration of the new mayor, Luis Marquez.

"Eldridge and the remaining members of the attack team are in a secondary hideout. We are going to use the inauguration as a distraction," said Waltz. "Get ready."

Kyle threw on his clothing as the news showed highlights from Marquez's campaign speeches.

We will work to ensure that jobs stay with the people of Los Angeles and not the giant corporations that are trying to dominate our lives. People first. Angelenos first.

The statements were made to massive crowds full of applause and excitement.

"Crowds in the tens of thousands are expected today at Mayor Elect Marquez's inauguration. The candidate beat out incumbent mayor, Christoph Holt, after deep ties between Holt and IRIS founder and chairman, Handel Balcroft, were made public via leaked information from NAESO earlier this year. Holt was criticized for his preferential and some say illegal treatment of IRIS and its city employment contracts," the news caster explained through the television.

The sun peeked through the towering buildings. People were bustling all around, shopping, heading to work, walking their dogs. But most people were headed in the same direction as Kyle and Waltz, toward the inauguration. After a few blocks, they turned down Wilshire Boulevard toward Pershing Square—the location of the inauguration. The initial report of tens of thousands seemed correct to Kyle as people converged onto Pershing.

"Keep your wits about you," whispered Waltz as the two traversed the streets.

The closer they got to Pershing, the more chaotic the crowd became. Street vendors popped up all over. Massive amounts of IRIS security agents were present, keeping the peace. Kyle stayed close behind Waltz. The inauguration began when they were only a block from the square. Under the 101 freeway and onto 5th Street the crowd was assembling. Kyle and Waltz continued down 5th. Holographic images of the new mayor were projected against the sky as he took the podium to make his inaugural speech.

"Today marks a new day for Los Angeles," he started speaking as the duo entered into Pershing.

The crowd was dense and focused on Marquez. Kyle and Waltz inched their way through the massive crowd.

"Almost there now, just have to get to the other side of the square," said Waltz.

Kyle nodded as he edged his way through the crowd. Trash covered the square and the crowd was now so dense that Kyle felt safe in the sea of people. The crowd cheered along with Marquez's speech as Kyle and Waltz neared the edge of the square. Bots and humans commingled in an odd master-and-slave pattern, bots a half pace or so behind their leaseholders. Some nanny bots were busy with children. Others were taking notes like the good assistant bots they were designed to be. Others were police and special security.

"With the right tenacity, with the right drive, we will ensure that the sins of the past do not follow us into the future," Marquez belted out his well-scripted and rehearsed speech. "With the will imbued in all Angelenos by working and living in this great city, we will take back the power that was stripped from us. We will . . ."

Suddenly, Marquez's voice cut out as the crowd screamed and erratically spread. People ran in all directions, trampling over one another. Kyle looked up to see the podium now empty. The camera panned to men in black suits dragging a bloodied Marquez. He looked away from the screen and saw Waltz motioning for him. The two bolted away from the square as fast as they could, passing normal humans with ease. The IRIS security forces went into action, corralling people away from the square as the holograms of the speech cut out.

Finally, out of the square and with the entire city in chaos, Kyle and Waltz slipped away and into a large decrepit apartment building a block from Pershing.

Waltz and Kyle bolted up the stairs of the apartment building. Waltz finally stopped at the door of the sixteenth floor. He pulled up his wrist and a holographic menu appeared. Waltz quickly sent a message off, and a moment later the door opened. Behind the door stood Nyki.

"Newb," she said before leaping for Kyle. The two embraced and Waltz made his way past the two into the room.

"Get in," said Eldridge from inside the room. "Shut and lock it behind you."

Squirrel appeared from within the room and gave Kyle a high five as he entered.

"Glad to see old Balcroft didn't get you," he said.

Kyle smiled and scanned the room. Nyki, Squirrel, Waltz, Eldridge, and half a dozen others from the NAESO base were there. The room was a small and barren one-bedroom apartment. Kyle was standing in the main room of the apartment. To the right, he saw a bedroom with bunk beds occupied by other NAESO members, sitting up and reading. The lights were dimmed throughout the apartment. To the left was the linoleum floor of a kitchen, and there was a bathroom just beyond that. Kyle peered into the kitchen and saw a tall, slender young woman with stark, black hair and a narrow face making drinks. The main room was a complex maze of wiring, chairs, and computers. The windows had shades that were drawn, and Eldridge was peeking behind one of the them at the street below.

"Chaos down in the square," Eldridge said.

Nyki and Squirrel were sitting at desks typing. Waltz was sitting motionless in a chair next to Eldridge, his eyes fixated ahead. He was looking at something, but whatever it was, it was in his mind and not in the room. His eyes were indirect and glazed.

"Did you see what happened?" asked Kyle.

"Assassinated," said Eldridge. The man pulled his head away from the window and closed the curtains. He sat back in his chair, looking at Kyle.

"Sit, son."

"Where is everyone else?" asked Kyle.

Eldridge scratched his beard contemplatively before answering. The woman who'd been in the kitchen entered the room holding a tray of beverages. She set it down by Nyki and Squirrel, walking past Waltz to Eldridge. She offered Eldridge and Kyle beverages before taking the last one for herself and exiting the room. She was wearing black tactical gear like everyone else in the room, excluding Waltz and Kyle: black military boots, pants, and a tactical vest with jacket. Eldridge took a sip of his drink and cleared his throat.

"Everyone else is gone, Kyle," said Eldridge.

Kyle's eyes welled with pain. He tried to hold it in, to be strong. He knew everyone was in as much pain and heartache as he was, but the shock was too much to bare. The tears flowed steadily from his eyes and down his cheeks. With Harold gone, the connection to his family was gone too. It wouldn't ever come back.

"I'm sorry, Kyle. For everything. I can't imagine," said Eldridge.

"It's done. What now?" said Kyle.

"We must be more vigilant than ever before. This is the beginning of the end of the struggle, Kyle. The pain you feel, we feel it with you. I know you've lost so much, but we all know that so much more can still be taken from the world."

Kyle drew back his tears for a moment and looked to the man. The boy nodded. He took a sip of the drink. It was strong and burned his throat a bit.

"No point in following the rules now," said Eldridge. "In a few days, we will break them all anyway."

"Holy crap," said Nyki loudly. She looked up from her computer screen and stripped her headphones off. "You got to check this out."

Everyone in the room gathered around the computer screen, except for Waltz, who was still in a daze.

"Should we get him?" asked Squirrel, gesturing to Waltz.

"No need," Nyki said. "We've been chatting online. He's watching right now anyway."

The screen was a broadcast from MCNBC. Walter Cooper was seated at a desk holding a clear holographic tablet computer and wearing his normal dark gray suit. He looked stern and concerned.

"Here is a special report from MCNBC News. In Los Angeles, California, three shots were fired at the newly elected mayor of Los Angeles, Luis Marquez, during his inaugural speech, just after being sworn into office. We do know that Mayor Marquez was transported to a Los Angeles IRIS hospital where physicians were unable to save the mayor. He died at 11:00 a.m., some thirty-eight minutes ago. Cooper took a moment for himself. He adjusted his glasses and shuffled through information on his tablet before gulping and continuing. President Johnson's whereabouts are currently unknown. We do know that the Secret Service will take extreme measures when an attack on the nation is imminent. Governor Connally was shot in the shoulder in an assassination attempt as well, but he has survived. We go now to a live video feed from Governor Connally from the Los Angeles IRIS hospital."

The video feed cut to Connally laying in a hospital bed—his shoulder bandaged with medical tape, his hair disheveled, and his face tired.

"To my fellow Californians and to the rest of the those watching around the world. Today, our liberties were attacked. Our democracy was attacked. Our hearts were attacked. I am saddened by the news of Luis Marquez's death, my dear friend, and my heart goes out to his family and all Angelenos. We now know that the terrorist group known as MASK has perpetrated this horrific act. MASK operates in the shadows and has indicated that they plan to increase their attacks in the coming days. As this information has come to light, I have decided, after speaking with President Johnson, to institute martial law for California effective immediately. Handel Balcroft, CEO and founder of IRIS, has lent unlimited support of his IRIS security, national guard, and police forces to hunt down and stop MASK once and for all. This is not a time to fear, but a time to remain calm and strong. I encourage all Californians to take this time to be with their families. No exemption to this enactment of martial law will be tolerated while the manhunt for these individuals is underway. All roads leaving the state have been closed. We will find the people responsible for these acts, and they will meet swift and decisive justice. I thank you all. God bless California and the United States of America."

The feed cut back to Cooper, who sat motionless for a moment before resuming his report.

"There you have it. We are told martial law is expected to last through the weekend while IRIS forces hunt down these criminals, but experts say the enforcement could bleed into next week. Remember to order rations for food or other supplies if needed from the FEMA response system. The information is at the bottom of our screen. We will continue to bring you coverage . . ."

The feed cut.

"He knows it's us," said Waltz, who was now standing up looking at the group watching the feed.

"Us?" asked Kyle. "But he said MASK. Isn't it safe to assume Balcroft killed Marquez because he threatened to attack his closed-source system?"

Kyle looked at Nyki and Squirrel for confirmation.

"Right, guys? I know I'm new to this whole 'taking down IRIS, being wanted for all sorts of criminal acts, and, like, hiding in weird apartments' thing. But how does this connect? Why put the world in a spiral of chaos and risk bringing all this attention on himself? How does that help him stop what we are doing?"

"Bring him to her," said Eldridge.

Waltz nodded and walked past the collection of computers the group was huddled over. He motioned for Kyle to follow him. The two walked through the kitchen. Waltz held the bathroom door open and Kyle proceeded inside. Once inside, Waltz closed the bathroom door behind them. The room was dark and looked like any other ordinary bathroom: sink, toilet, tub that doubled as a shower, and a mirror.

"Who is *she?*" asked Kyle.

Waltz didn't look at or acknowledge Kyle. Instead, he tapped on five specific points on the mirror. When he did, each point lit up red, and on the fifth tap, they turned green. The green lights floated to the middle of the mirror and joined into one large green light.

"Push it with your palm," said Waltz.

Kyle hesitated for a moment before placing his palm on the green light. A slight jolt penetrated Kyle, and he jerked his hand back.

"It shocked me," said Kyle.

"That's intentional. Nothing to worry about," said Waltz.

For a moment, nothing happened. Then the shower slid farther away from them. Underneath where the bathtub had been was more linoleum flooring. The wall on one side was concrete and the other, behind where the shower used to be, was a solid steel door.

"Your confusion will be put to rest, Kyle. We all spoke with her last night. Given different circumstances, you would have as well. But things are moving fast now. It's time for you to play catch-up. Remember, you are critical to this mission and, well, everyone has lost something. But out of everyone I know, you've lost the most," said Waltz.

Kyle took a step toward the door and grabbed the handle.

"I understand, Waltz, and trust me, I want nothing more than to make Balcroft pay for what he has done to me, to my father, to Harold, and to Squirrel's parents. To everyone. But just tell me, who is *she?*"

Waltz smiled.

"I might have been wrong when I assumed too arrogantly that MASK was completely controlled by IRIS. That is who she is," said Waltz.

Miffed, Kyle turned his gaze from Waltz. He turned the handle and entered the room.

CHAPTER EIGHTEEN

ONCE INSIDE, THE door closed automatically behind him. He turned around. The door on the inside looked nothing like the door on the outside. Instead of a thick steel door, it was wooden with carved rectangular inlays. There was a round brass doorknob. The door, like most of the room, was painted tan with a white border—although everything looked a little dingy, discolored. The walls housed large paintings, dust-covered and Victorian. Some of the paintings had giant slashes in them and pieces of the canvas drooped toward the floor. The floor was cement and, like the rest of the room, filthy. There was a fireplace on the inner left wall of the room. Above it, on the mantle, was a wooden analog clock. Kyle, having never seen an analog clock in his life, did not understand how to read it. Above the clock was a broken mirror.

At the far end of the room was the woman who'd served him a drink just a few minutes before. She had changed. She was now wearing a long, black dress made of a thick fabric with tiny squares etched into it. Her straight, flat hair laid perfectly down her back, and she wore black stiletto heels, the bottoms of which were ruby red. Beyond her was a window. Outside weather had come in. It was pouring rain and the clouds were blotting out the sun. They were staring out the window until he entered.

"At last," she said, turning around to face Kyle. "Please sit."

She motioned toward the middle of the room. There on top of a large red rug were two high-back, leather chesterfield chairs. Kyle moved slowly and sat in the one closest to him. Kyle sat nervously in the chair, his hand fidgeting with one of the wooden lion heads at the end of the armrests. The woman did not sit. Instead, she passed a few paces behind the chair opposite Kyle. As she spoke, she would occasionally grope the chair or smoothly glide her hands across its deep, red leather. Her lipstick matched the bottoms of her heels, as did her fingernails.

"Kyle, I imagine right now you feel a bit like Luke. Betrayed by your friends, displaced, fatherless, and angry," she said.

Kyle grabbed the lion's head hard.

"You could say that, but my father really is dead this time and I don't have a light saber."

"And you are afraid."

Kyle tried to make himself comfortable in the chair.

"I am not afraid," he said.

"Yes, you are."

"How do you know?"

She smiled.

"Because you are not stupid. You know this little betrayal that your friend Waltz exacted on you was necessary."

"Necessary? Why, so I agree to all this? Make myself marked for assassination? Become an enemy of the state? Ruin my entire life? What is the point of that?"

Enraged, Kyle stood and moved to the door. He turned the knob, but the door wouldn't budge. He yanked and pulled, but it didn't move at all. Kyle flipped around toward the woman.

"Who the hell are you anyway? Why are you talking to me like this?"

"My name is Tencudes."

A wave of shock and confusion rushed over Kyle. He felt utterly out of place. Unsure of what to do next, he returned to the chair; it was the only move he felt he had.

"*The* Tencudes?" he asked.

"What does that mean to you?" asked Tencudes.

Kyle listed off the myriad of talking points he knew about Tencudes and MASK.

"You were a hacker years ago. You hacked IRIS in the early days. Didn't get much out of it except notoriety, which you leveraged to create MASK, an anonymous hacker and terrorist hell-bent on destroying IRIS and the robot kind. For some time, I thought you were a puppet or false flag group propagated by IRIS to cover up and cast blame of their crimes onto another organization. But that can't be the case anymore."

Tencudes leaned in.

"You're warm. Let me bring you to hot. I am a hacker. I did hack IRIS. I do control MASK. All that is true, but you are wrong about everything else. MASK wants to take down IRIS. That is all we strive to do. The terrorist actions we have claimed responsibility for in the media have always been IRIS covering up their tracks. They slandered us. Being the anonymous entity we are, we had a hard time fighting back. Tyrannical control of the media and internet is a tricky thing.

"A few days ago, I was sitting in a club with an old friend. A man by the name of Leonard Drotsky. We were old hacking acquaintances and though he was a notorious hermit, hated socializing, and never really saw the big picture, I had a soft spot for him. I had not spoken with Leonard for some time when out of the blue he wanted to meet. He told me he needed talk, immediately, and in person. Quite out of character. So, I went along with it; he was probing hard for information about you. You and Waltz. Now, I'll admit, I had already been hunting you for some time, but my desires, I assure you, were much more to your liking. So, one thing lead to another, and I'd started to make Leonard mad. Some blood was spilled, and he started talking to himself, as if no one else was in the room. As if everything were in his head. Then he called himself Balcroft, so I shot him in the face."

So far, Tencudes's story only further confused Kyle.

"I found out shortly after that Balcroft had killed Drotsky years ago and coded an empty bot to match his DNA architecture. Drotsky would feed us just enough information over the years to get us into little missteps; they always seemed like bad execution on our part. But Balcroft made the misstep this time around. I had a team near NAESO's base; our intention was to align, to work together, to take down IRIS once and for all. But he struck first; his recovery teams are the fastest, and, as always, the media will be directed to blame us."

"So, what do you want from me? Why are you telling me this?" asked Kyle.

"I am telling you this because you need to know the whole story, Kyle. You need to be ready, because we will end this all in three days. In three days, we will take down IRIS, avenge my friends, your friends, your father. I am telling you this because you are not like Luke. What betrayal you felt was your friend's calculated decision. It was a lie of protection, to keep you moving, to keep you focused. We need that focus, Kyle. No one inside the IRIS system has ever been able to be coerced to do this, to do what you must. We cannot take down IRIS without you. You know that they are coming. You know they have cleared the streets, that they will find us and kill us. They will end us, unless we end them first. I have more firepower and people at my disposal than Eldridge could have dreamed of, and he has more knowledge of the IRIS mainframe and construct, not to mention those blueprints. Together we can do this, but we all must be in it. I am telling you this because I am impartial to you. The feelings of anger you have for them are fine, but I have not betrayed you and I don't want to. I want you to help me. Will you?"

Kyle sat for what seemed to him an eternity. He slowly massaged the armrest of his chair as he pondered, thinking about his mother, father, and Harold. Thinking about the twins, all the people at NAESO.

"Don't think about only them, Kyle," she said. "Think about the whole world. You don't really know what it used to be like. Free speech was real. The internet gave everyone a voice. We could say what we wanted, believe what we wanted. People could do what they wanted, there was real choice. Before one corporation ran the world. We are slaves, Kyle. Think about all of us, all the slaves."

Kyle thought of Roy back home, probably believing everything the media told him was true. Roy wasn't free. His mind was controlled by the information Balcroft spewed. Kyle's rage continued to stew inside of him. His anger was just.

"I'm going to do it. I have to," he said.

"Then get some sleep, because tomorrow is our dry run," said Tencudes.

Tencudes clapped her hands together five times. Three quick claps followed by two slow ones. In a flash, Kyle was standing back in front of the mirror. Waltz had his hand on Kyle's shoulder. Kyle turned around as Waltz removed his hand. Waltz was holding the hand of Tencudes who was laying down in the tub. Her clothing was the same black tactical garbs she had on when Kyle first saw her in the apartment.

"What the hell?" said Kyle.

Waltz smiled.

"You're kind of like me now. Don't really need much of a recap chair or PD10 to enter virtual realms. Just a connection."

"None of that was real?"

Tencudes stepped out of the tub.

"Real enough. I find that conversations like that are much better if I control the environment. Plus, we wanted to test this. We only have a few portable rigs here we can use, so cognitive linking between my team, who has mods, and your team, who doesn't, is going to be tough for our dry run. Glad it worked, aren't you?"

Tencudes walked out of the room.

"I thought you said you weren't going to lie to me," he shouted as she walked into the living room.

"Kyle, come on. That was just a bit of fun."

"What were the green lights?" asked Kyle.

"That drink she made. It sort of, well, enables you to accept entering another reality willingly. The mirrored lights are a test. There are no mirror lights, but to you, they were there. By placing your palm, you accepted it. Anyhow, chess," said Waltz.

"What about chess?" said Kyle.

Waltz shrugged.

"They got it here. I've never played a real board game. Since I'll probably be molten goo by this time next week, I figured I might was well take advantage of the experience while I have the chance."

"Fine, but I move first."

CHAPTER NINETEEN

THE MOON WAS full and high in the sky. Its light was bouncing off the freshly rained-on streets of Boston. As he ran, he made sure to avoid any puddles in the road, a particularly fun game for him during these nightly jogs in the fall. Now past the Museum of Science, he veered right just before Science Park onto the Dr. Paul Dudley White Bike Path toward the Longfellow Bridge. Leaves of every autumn color had littered the ground. The Charles River was calm, and he loved the sound it made when the water softly sloshed against the earth below his feet. His windbreaker was making an annoying swishing sound as he ran, so he tapped up the volume on his Bluetooth headphones. The soothing renditions of the Bolshoi Theatre drowned out the annoyance. He smiled as he ran through the Cambridge streets, until a sharp pain ripped that joy from him. His knees went weak and he fell face first onto the path. Waltz felt a deep, unfeeling pain in his back and he could not move.

Waltz was jolted and confused. He was sitting in the corner of the room; his sentry rest mode had been interrupted. Everyone in the apartment was sleeping. He sat motionless for a few minutes, too afraid to move. He ran through his data banks on oneirology and researched dreams before deciding to wake up Eldridge. He quietly made his way to Eldridge, careful not to wake anyone. He shook Eldridge slightly, trying to muster him out of his sleep.

"Eldridge, wake up," he whispered.

"What's happened?" asked Eldridge, rubbing his eyes as he made himself aware.

"I had a dream."

Eldridge's eyes widened and he sat up excitedly. He moved over on the couch he was sleeping on and patted a spot for Waltz to sit.

"Tell me everything," said Eldridge.

"I was in Boston. Not sure how I know. Maybe my memory banks associated the surroundings. I was running and, I don't know, I felt . . . umm . . . comfortable. Anyway, I'm running and it's at night. I was wearing a jacket made of a coarse material—a windbreaker."

"A windbreaker, really? Do you know the time period?" asked Eldridge.

Waltz recalled the memory scan of the dream, addressing each frame of his recollection, looking for a moment to indicate a time. After a few seconds of analyzing the memory, he found it. A poster taped onto a community board by the Museum of Science that he ran by read:

2016 Brain Trust Pumpkin Decorating
Room W-2
11:00 a.m. to 12:00 p.m.
Sunday, October 30, 2016.

"I remember a sign for a pumpkin decorating party. It said 2016, the day before Halloween."

"Really?" said Eldridge, who was now sitting straight up on the couch, his legs crossed, staring intently at Waltz.

"Yes. I was running through the night. The path felt very familiar. Actually, everything felt very familiar. Then I got a sharp pain and was ejected out of sentry mode and back to this realm of consciousness."

"Have you dreamed before in sentry mode?" said Eldridge.

"Never."

Eldridge grabbed a nearby pad and pen and started taking down notes.

"Paranoid of the digital devices these days, E?" asked Waltz.

Eldridge didn't look up from his diligent note-taking.

"Things are getting too close for comfort at this point. Much too close."

It was then that Tencudes entered, wearing the same tactical gear from the day before. She took in a deep breath and smiled.

"Hey, tin man," she said.

Waltz turned his gaze to her and cocked his head.

"Pejorative much?" he replied.

"Get them up. It's time."

Waltz moved around the room, jarring everyone from their slumber one by one. Tencudes prepared eggs, bacon, and toast for the group. The group sat all around, on the floor, some on the couch next to Eldridge who was now on a computer typing away and letting his breakfast go cold. Nyki and Squirrel sat at computer desks and mixed eating with work, finalizing the blueprint schematic for the day's run. Kyle sat in a chair next to the window, devouring his breakfast.

"Trying to kill yourself before Balcroft gets a shot?" asked Tencudes through sips of her black coffee.

Kyle looked while chewing a strip of bacon.

"What?" he said with his mouthful.

"You eat faster than anyone I've ever seen. I think you might choke," she said.

Kyle smiled, nodded, and returned to his feast. As he ate, the sun slowly crept into view, its rays becoming more prevalent as it rose through the LA skyline. Waltz sat down next to Kyle.

"Care to lose again?" asked Waltz, holding the chess board in his hands.

"Your overconfidence is your weakness," said Kyle.

"Your faith in your friends is yours," quipped Waltz.

Kyle's brow furrowed at the comment.

"I'm inclined to agree."

"I didn't mean it like that."

"I know," said Kyle. "Let's play."

They played match after match as the sun continued its long ascent into the sky. Everyone finished their breakfasts and readied the dry run while Eldridge worked on his research.

"We got fifteen minutes, newb," said Nyki.

Waltz looked at his opponent.

"Well, one more then?"

Kyle smiled.

"For all the marbles."

During the previous games, Kyle noticed the patterns in Waltz's moves against him. Waltz was very intentional with every move. His advanced cognition allowed him to think in the ways of grand masters, without the decades of training. But Kyle was learning quickly.

Kyle made his first move as Squirrel moved into the kitchen and flipped the faucet on. Kyle moved a pawn to space E-4, two spaces up. Waltz returned by moving one of his pawns up a single space to D-6. After a few more moves, the match was well under way. Both players had a single knight moved out and two pawns. Kyle was considering his next move when a clambering came from the kitchen.

"Squirrel!" both players yelled.

"Sorry, guys," said Squirrel, poking his head out of the kitchen.

Kyle looked up at Waltz with concentration and determination. Kyle would normally move his knight up to F-3 in this scenario, but given his understanding of Waltz's patterns, he called an audible, and a risky one at that. He selected to move his bishop to E-3. This took Waltz by surprise; he'd become comfortable beating Kyle with a variant of the same play style.

"I see," said Waltz.

"I don't think you do," quipped Kyle. "Soon you will call me master."

Waltz moved his bishop. Kyle responded by moving up his queen to D-2 and showing his intention of a king side attack. Waltz responded by signaling a king side defense.

A few more moves until the first casualty of the game. Kyle moved a bishop to H-6, and Waltz responded by taking that bishop with one of his own.

"I think it will be a long time before I call you master, my friend," said Waltz.

"You *think* we are friends," said Kyle.

Suddenly, Kyle used his queen to avenge the demise of his bishop. Time moved through the game with each player taking their time and destroying piece after piece.

Eventually, Waltz had six pieces on the board. Four pawns, a rook, and, of course, his king. Kyle moved his queen in a striking position. Waltz deflected by dodging right with his king guarded by the rook. Kyle edged his king closer, forcing the king to keep moving. Then he had him. Waltz moved his rook down a space to protect against a pawn attack, and Kyle moved his queen in the perfect position.

"Checkmate," said Kyle.

Waltz looked at his opponent a bit astonished.

"How did you learn so quickly?" he asked.

Kyle tapped his brain lightly with a fist.

"Remember we are not so different anymore, my friend."

Tencudes entered the room.

"Let's saddle up."

Waltz, Kyle, and Tencudes sat cross-legged on the floor, holding hands. A single cord streamed from Waltz's head and into the mobile PD10 unit Squirrel was plugged into. Eldridge remained unplugged to control the run from the outside. The group was positioned in a circle around a mainframe server that Nyki and Squirrel had built days before.

"Everyone ready?" asked Eldridge.

The room acknowledged through a series of nods and body language. Eldridge typed a command into his computer, and Kyle's vision wavered yet again. He was used to the disillusionment by now. The vision went into a pinpoint, like being sucked into the singularity of a black hole. Then, in an instant, he was transported.

It was dark and raining hard; the city lights bounced off the cement street, cars and debris littered about. The pitter-patter of the rain intensified the simulation.

"Why the rain?" asked Squirrel.

"To project the weather forecasted later tonight and through the week. It's going to be rainy and dark when we attack. Remember everyone, we are all on the same team. Eldridge and Waltz have programmed a lot of bots to attack us as best we can imagine they will in real life. Stay focused. We do not have all the time in the world. First, we get Waltz in level one to initiate the first hack on the timed delay. Plan is to sneak up the flights without triggering an alarm. Hack hits and grant Kyle's DNA access to the mainframe. We delete the restrictor chips and malware the system, spreading the codex all over the internet. Everyone ready?"

Everyone was dressed in black tactical gear. They had QX7 rail guns, 45mm handguns, three snap grenades, a bow knife, cables, and ties. Tencudes started the dry run. The twelve assailants went for the building on the east side. There was a large valet entrance, complimented by a large water fountain modeled after the early IRIS robots; it stood about seventy-five feet tall, holding a baby human up high, lifting humanity to new heights.

The group budded up next to a large rectangular pillar as Tencudes peeked around the corner. She motioned with three fingers in the air. Tencudes summersaulted from one pillar to the next. Everyone followed her exact movements. Kyle marveled at how well trained the MASK team members were. Besides Nyki, Squirrel, Waltz, and himself, the other eight members were from MASK.

Thank God we have them, thought Kyle as he summersaulted to his next placement.

The group turned the corner and moved around the side of the large entrance to IRIS headquarters. The lobby was massive and well lit; three large IRIS military bots guarded it. It was off hours and all doors were locked, not to mention the vast array of security measures in place. Even CO_2 levels were monitored on the first five floors during off hours. IRIS military bots were very stripped down; nothing biological about them. No intake of oxygen at all; therefore, no output of CO_2. Executives working late left out a secret exit only recently revealed to them via the blueprints the team acquired.

Once past the lobby, the team moved quickly down the slim alley between IRIS HQ and the Bank of the United Nations it was buddied up to. They went down the alley, rain slashing under the thick soles of their boots.

In that moment, Kyle's vision was wrenched back painfully. His vision realigned faster than usual, and everyone in the room was grabbing their heads and looking about in the same confused manner as Kyle. Eldridge was standing above everyone seated in their chairs on the floor.

"Everyone, get up. We don't have time. Get ready now. We are a go," he said.

The members of MASK were first to move, taking the command in the upmost seriousness and rushing off to get dressed. Tencudes, who lived in her tactical gear, started lining up what munitions they had: guns, snap grenades, and EMPs. Everyone got dressed and ready as quickly as they could, scrambling to put legs in pants and zip thick, black vests. Waltz came to Kyle, shoving a pile of black clothing and a pair of boots into his hands. Kyle stripped down and put on his new clothing. He went to the table and grabbed the weapons he was now very familiar with. The QX7 and grenades felt exactly as he'd remembered from the simulations, no difference at all.

"Wow," he said.

"What?" asked Squirrel.

Kyle shook his head in astonishment.

"These feel exactly as they did in the simulation."

"Of course they do," said Squirrel.

"But that wasn't real."

Squirrel smiled.

"Kind of depends on what you define as real, doesn't it?"

They finished packing and, one by one, lined up to receive instructions. Eldridge looked concerned, more worn and tired than usual.

"Take the freight elevator," said Eldridge. "We have eight minutes."

"What happened?" asked Kyle.

The group left single file out of the room and into the hall-way toward the freight elevator. Kyle stepped out of the door-way as Eldridge grabbed a snap grenade from his belt. He set a timer on the grenade and threw it inside toward the servers and mobile PD10 units. He turned his back to the apartment and left the room.

"They found us," said Eldridge.

Kyle and Eldridge turned and followed the group to the freight elevator. As the elevator doors closed, Kyle watched the flicker of light from the snap grenade flash from inside the room.

PART THREE

CHAPTER TWENTY

THE SUN SAT low in the sky as the group navigated from their hideout building to IRIS headquarters. A slight trickle of rain started as the group moved down alleyways and through buildings.

"No main roads," said Tencudes.

It was just fifteen short blocks to the headquarters. From there, eighty-five levels. Kyle's QX7 swayed nicely in rhythm with his body as he ran. The boots, clothing, grenades—together with everything, he felt like one unit, one machine. He felt ready. Kyle's jaw was relaxed, not tense like in the simulation. A looseness fell over him, a sense of peace and acknowledgment of his coming retribution. Tencudes was fast, moving hastily in and out of one back alley to the next. The group following with precision and tact.

"Kyle," said Waltz.

Waltz had been running alongside Kyle for a block or so. Kyle hadn't really noticed.

"Yeah," said Kyle.

"I just want you to know, I am sorry for not checking on your father. If I knew he was still alive, I . . . I just . . ."

"I know, Waltz. I'm okay with it now. You needed me to keep going. Not just for you or for E. You needed me to keep going for me. Now it's all almost over. We are going to avenge them all. Take from me my father and my friends, I take from you your control. I take from you everything."

"Five blocks out," said Tencudes.

She pried open a manhole cover and the group started to descend. The rain was heavier now than when they'd left the apartment and the sun had set. Kyle flipped on his shoulder lamp as he descended the ladder into the sewer. Five more descended after Kyle, who was about a dozen or so behind the front of the line. Marshal was the last one in and he closed the cover behind him. Marshal was a tall Indian man with dark black hair and a stern brow. He carried a different gun from the rest of the group. It looked like a Type 81 assault rifle, which Kyle knew from munitions download training in the simulator. The gun was primarily used by the Chinese in the 1970s, so there was no way it was an original. Kyle had never seen Marshal fire the weapon in the simulator. Beyond his tall physique and silent obedience to Tencudes, Marshal set himself apart from the squad with that gun.

The squad moved steadily, the dozen assailants slithering in a perfect line through the underbelly of Los Angeles. After another fifteen minutes, Tencudes held up her right arm at a ninety-degree angle and balled her hand into a fist. Everyone stopped immediately. She turned around and whispered.

"One block out. We wait here until night crew swaps and only bots are left."

Everyone sat in the large sewer pipe below a ladder leading up to 5th Street, in between South Flower and South Grand Avenue. The team sat in rows with their boots in the shallow water that flowed at the base of the sewage pipe. Waltz opened out his palms flat and a bright holographic chess board appeared in between Kyle and him.

"Pass the time?" asked Waltz.

"Pawn to E-4," said Kyle.

"Same move as last time," said Waltz.

Kyle shrugged.

"It worked, didn't it?"

They played for hours, waiting for the human attendants of IRIS headquarters to vacate the building for the night, leaving it guarded by the highly skilled and relentless IRIS security forces. A slow and consistent trickle of water from the rainy street above spattered down on the steel ladder steps in the sewer tunnel below.

"Everyone get ready. Safetys off. Double-check your supplies," Tencudes said, standing in the middle of the tunnel. The time had come.

The holographic chess board vanished as Waltz and Kyle stood with the others. Kyle checked his QX7, ten extra clips of ammunition, five frag grenades, three snap grenades, one flash, one EMP, and one bow knife. Not to mention his neural modifications and the DNA that would allow him access to the IRIS mainframe once the malware was embedded. Kyle looked at Waltz. The machine patted him on the shoulder and the they shook hands.

"I'm glad we are friends, Waltz. I'm glad you grabbed me that night in the dark."

"Thanks, Kyle. I am too."

Tencudes cut off her light and started up the ladder to the street.

"Marshal, remember North Thirteen, East Two. I'll meet you there. Waltz, you're with me," said Tencudes.

Marshal, who was three rows behind Kyle and Waltz at the far end of the tunnel, nodded. Waltz made his way down the row of people joining Tencudes on the ladder. The pair climbed up the ladder and vanished into the night.

"Right, remember the plan, everyone. Tencudes and Waltz move the pin drops into place on the first floor. We go in from there. We cannot be seen for risk of flipping the alarm system. The tenth floor is stop one. Waltz puts in the first bit of malware. Then up to the eighty-fifth floor, where Kyle ends it all. Detection is our number-one enemy. This isn't the sim anymore. No do-overs," said Marshal.

The group nodded and Marshal made his way left down another tunnel. Kyle counted the tunnels, which were cut into large sections. There were thirteen tunnels straight north, then finally two east. The group moved quickly through the tunnels and then turned east, over through one tunnel and then the next. Finally, the group held inside the cube after the second tunnel to the east. There they waited.

On the street above, Waltz and Tencudes had advanced to the east side of the alley, where Tencudes handed Waltz a metal burn ball the size of a golf ball.

"It's open so you can code it as you wish. This will cut the hole we need nicely," said Tencudes, kneeling and watching the heavily guarded tower.

Waltz held the ball in his hand for a moment as an array of configurations settings flashed over his retinas. A second later, he threw the ball in a line drive over the street, where it landed on the east side of the building. Waltz opened his left palm and a three-dimensional hologram of the building's blueprints appeared with a red dot echoing on the east side.

"Move the burn ball into the service entrance and down to that maintenance hall," said Tencudes.

Waltz moved his underhand and the red dot on the hologram moved with it. The burn ball on the hologram, which had started as one singular dot, split into a group of smaller dots moving in tandem. They moved through the service entrance, around the corner of the building, and into a small rectangular room.

"There it is," said Tencudes. "Drill 'em."

"Hold your horses there. We are on it," said Waltz.

Tencudes watched as the tiny balls got smaller and smaller, but larger in number. They now moved like a tiny snake into the rectangular room and formed a perfect circle in the middle. The dots must have numbered in the thousands at this point, each one equally tiny. They started moving around in the circle they formed. First slowly, and then accelerating until the hologram just showed a solid red line in a circle on the ground. The sound of a car grabbed Tencudes's attention and she looked up to the street between them and IRIS headquarters. Three large black SUVs pulled up in front of IRIS headquarters. A dozen or so people exited the vehicles dressed in tactical gear.

"Crap," said Tencudes.

"What?" asked Waltz.

He turned his head and peeked over across the street to the group of people entering the IRIS building.

"I know them," he said.

"You do?" asked Tencudes.

"I don't know their names, but I've killed a few of them more than once. Asset Recovery Team. Nasty."

"Great, well, if you killed them once, you can kill them again. Hopefully this time, you will actually kill them and not some empty," said Tencudes.

"The burn ball is almost finished cutting," said Waltz. "Let's go."

The hologram emitting from Waltz's wrist flickered away and the two left back down into the sewer.

Inside the sewer, Kyle, Marshal, and the rest of the team were waiting in formation. The tiniest humming noise could be heard coming from the cement block above them. Marshal knelt and grabbed a small cylinder from his pack. He threw it into the middle of the room. The cylinder expanded, filling with air until it was four or five feet tall and at least six feet in diameter. Kyle listened as the humming noise grew slightly louder, until eventually the tiniest line appeared in the cement ceiling. If he blinked, he would have missed it. A perfect circle was cut instantly into the ceiling and the cement block came falling down onto the inflated cylinder. Nyki tossed a rope ladder from her pack up through the perfectly cut hole.

"How'd it go?" whispered Tencudes as she and Waltz appeared at the end of the tunnel.

Marshal nodded and started up the ladder. The group ascended, Kyle in the middle. Inside, the room looked fairly normal, like any old janitorial or maintenance closet. Brooms, mops, some cleaning supplies, nothing out of the ordinary except the large hole in the ground.

Once in the maintenance room, Tencudes motioned for the team to move left down the hall and up the stairs.

"Ten floors. First hack. Piece of cake, right, newb?" said Nyki.

"Piece of cake," said Kyle.

"Yeah, but what kind of cake? Because ice cream cake is arguably a piece that is more difficult to eat than, say, cheese cake," said Squirrel.

"Shut up, Squirrel," said Kyle.

"Sorry. Just trying to diffuse the tension."

Floor after floor up the staircase they went. Each floor the same as the last: ten steps turn left, walk three paces, ten more steps, turn left. They made it to tenth floor. Waltz placed his palm back on the door and scanned the room. He released his hand after a moment, shook his head a bit, and placed his hand back in the same position. After a few moments, he removed his hand and placed it back on the door, but this time a bit higher. Waltz repositioned his hand three more times before someone interrupted him.

"What's taking so long? Clear or not?" asked Squirrel.

Waltz turned his head and glanced down the line of NAESO and MASK assailants. Squirrel was in the middle, about ten feet lower than him on the staircase.

"The material they're using on this floor, it's thick. I can't see in," Waltz whispered.

"To hell with it. We are going," said Kyle.

Waltz took a moment to respond.

"Okay."

Kyle moved out of position and pointed to the handle.

"Waltz, place your foot here. Don't kick. Just use your strength to slowly jam it down," said Kyle.

Waltz looked at Kyle and nodded. The machine placed his right leg on the edge of the steel L-shape door handle.

"Slow pressure," said Kyle.

Waltz pressed down on the handle, and a moment later it turned down in near silence. Waltz regained his footing as Kyle pressed the door open and peeked his head out. He panned the room for a moment before drawing back into the stairwell.

"Clear," he said.

Kyle was the first in followed by Waltz and the others. They moved silently and with precision. The tenth floor was vacant and vast. Row after row of cubicle, each with a desk and chair, all identical. The group dispersed. The assailants spread into the aisles and covered the entrances, guns drawn and ready. Waltz, Kyle, and Eldridge moved quickly.

"Keep an eye out," whispered Waltz. "The computer's serial code is 001-EFG02-9913-EJDH3."

Squirrel started on the fourth row of cubicles. He crouched under each computer desk looking for serial codes. Everyone had their shoulder lights on. The lights moved down the side of a cubicle, ducked for a moment, then popped back up before moving on to the next cubicle. Kyle did the same. Tencudes guarded the perimeter, sticking close to the stairwell. The search seemed endless. The room was massive, the rows and columns of cubicles seemed uncountable. Kyle worked diligently on each cubicle, checking the serial codes. He stopped when he heard Nyki call out for Waltz. She'd found it.

Waltz jumped over a row of cubicles, landing in front of Nyki. He came down silently. The floor below had such a thick security foundation, there was no echo.

"I got it," she said.

Walt moved to the desktop and began typing. His hands moved furiously and with exaction. He diluted the computer to its most basic of functions, its baseline codex, and began working within that. Waltz's fingers moved at a pace that was almost unperceivable, his concentration unnerving. The desktop hologram showed line after line of code being entered and commands recognized by the computer. As he typed it seemed he was stripping off layers of IRIS, devolving it into what it was. Until, after a final key stroke, the computer went blank. The hologram disappeared. The clear glass desktop fogged up, and a small red line of text appeared in the middle of the desk.

Error.

Waltz looked at Nyki, confused, before dropping to his knees and peering under the desk. The serial code read 001-EFG02-9913-EJDK3. Waltz quickly rose back up. Everyone had stopped checking codes and moved away from their cubicles closer to him.

"It wasn't the right one. Off a number. Keep checking, quickly," said Waltz.

Nyki put her head down.

"I'm sorry," she said.

"Just keep checking. Sorry will get us killed."

Not a moment later, five rows away, Marshal whistled quietly and Waltz turned his head.

"Here," said Marshal, pointing to the desktop in front of him.

"You sure?" said Kyle.

Marshal glanced at Nyki.

"Checked it twice. This is it."

Waltz sprinted to where Marshal was standing. In a flash, he was keying away. The same array of commands popped up on that desktop, but this time no error screen. The desktop went dark. Nothing happened. Waltz looked up; everyone was staring at him.

"Did it work?" asked Squirrel.

"Yes," said Waltz. "In sixty minutes, it goes live or we launch it first. Once it's live, they will know we are here and what we plan to do. We have one hour to get to the mainframe."

For a moment, jubilee and hope consumed the room. Waltz scanned the faces of everyone who was there and stopped jarringly on Kyle. Kyle was at the far end of the room; a large man held a knife to his neck.

"No," said Waltz, his eyes locked on Kyle.

Everyone turned to Kyle and the knife pressed against his throat.

"Okay, cowboys. I want your weapons tossed toward the windows and the clips to the stairs. Anyone makes any mistakes and your young, sweet Kyle is joining his mommy and daddy," said the man.

"Do what he says," said Eldridge, who was in the middle of all the cubicles.

Eldridge removed the clip from his QX7 and tossed it to his left, never taking his eyes off Kyle. He saw another dark figure emerge from behind the man holding the knife. It was Tencudes, and she was moving fast. Before anyone could say anything, she drove her bow knife into the man's skull from the top down. It went in clean and quickly. She wrenched it out and a large spurt of blood followed, falling like rain onto the desktop computer Kyle had been examining.

"You all right, kid?" asked Eldridge.

Kyle nodded and thanked Tencudes with a smile as his assailant fell to the ground, dead, blood pouring from the gash. Kyle knelt and looked at his face. He stood up.

"Baron," he said to Waltz. "It was Baron. Not an empty this time."

An unnervingly loud siren began to echo throughout the room and the building. Lights on the walls and ceiling erupted to life, flashing in tandem with the squealing sirens.

"Grab your weapons and hit the windows," shouted Eldridge.

Kyle grabbed his QX7, shooting the glass on the far side of the building. He held on to the side of the windowsill and peered up. He reached into his bag and grabbed the suction-cup scalers and his gloves. Kyle secured one cup on the unbroken window to the left of the window he blew out. He then secured the left cup. Kyle began to scale the building, one step at a time. The rest of the team followed suit. Tencudes was the last to exit the room. Kyle was now two stories up, looking down and counting the team members as they began their ascent.

"Tencudes, snap it," said Kyle as she secured her right cup grip onto the side of the building.

She secured her left cup as she forcefully held her right grip to the window, setting a forty-five-second time release on all three of her snap grenades. Tencudes chucked all the grenades in, one right, one left, and one center.

"Forty-five seconds. Go!" she shouted.

The team ascended quickly. The wind was torrential. Kyle was nearing the twenty-first floor when the snaps fired. The entire building reacted, breathing in and out. The windows bowed in and then expanded for a moment. Then the lights went out; first in the building and then power surges erupted throughout the city. Kyle turned his gaze and watched as block after block fell into darkness.

CHAPTER TWENTY-ONE

THE TEAM SCALED the building with all the haste they could muster. Their training had paid off; within five minutes, Kyle and Waltz were five floors ahead of the team by the time they reached the sixty-fourth floor. Kyle stopped and glanced down at the team and the city below. The rain was coming down hard and the moon was bouncing off the Pacific, lighting up the team's soaking-wet black gear. Below, the streets were vacant except for around the IRIS headquarters, which was littered with black SUVs and military vehicles. No police sirens or lights from the street, just row and row of armored vehicles. Kyle looked out at the endless rows and buildings and lights that stretched far from the ocean to the mountains of Santa Monica.

"Where is the rest of the Asset Recovery Team," asked Kyle.

"Not sure, but wherever they are, it can't be good. Just keep moving. The mainframe room is centralized by a stairwell and elevator inside the building's core. We need to go in here and work our way up the last twenty-one floors," said Waltz.

"Pick up the pace, guys," said Kyle. "You just need to scale a few more floors."

The non-modified humans didn't respond as they struggled through the rain and darkness. Lightning struck in the distance and Kyle turned back to the building.

"You have an HF nano-beam antenna, right?" asked Kyle.

Waltz was positioned next to Kyle with a single large pane window between them. He nodded and held out his left arm. His wrist folded back against itself, and a needle the diameter of a dime protruded out. A tiny white light hummed at the tip of the needle. Waltz pointed the needle at the window and a long beam of brilliant white light shot out and hit the glass. Waltz moved his arm around clockwise, cutting a large circle into the glass. The glass did not shatter or fall from its position in the window. Only a thin circle could be seen etched into the glass.

Kyle moved into position in front of the circle and pushed it in. The pane fell forward into the building and broke loudly on the tile ground.

"No point on being coy about it," he said.

"Did we finish them all?" asked Squirrel.

"Not a chance," said Tencudes.

"Then why are we not being shot at?"

"The mainframe is all that matters," said Nyki. "They're going to be ready."

Kyle swung himself in through the hole in the window. Waltz followed directly behind him. The sixty-fourth floor was more barren than the cubical-filled labyrinth of the tenth floor. The large room was wall-to-wall glass windows and almost totally dark, the only light coming from some overhead exit signs and a large hologram of the Sahara Desert displaying a running loop of progress shown in IRIS's Saharan Terraforming Project. There were a few rows of old-model IRIS bots hanging in cases. Kyle raised his QX7 and moved slowly into the room, scanning the area. He set his retinas to adjust to the darkness and pick up movement by alerting his ocular overlay. Tencudes was the next through the window, followed by Nyki and Squirrel.

"Kyle, the elevators. All of them," she said.

Kyle moved through the room toward the elevators, passing the incased bots on the way. He stopped momentarily at a ten-year-old model. Unlike the models from twenty years ago, she was not purely metallic beneath the neck, and her skin overlay seemed far less plastic than the previous models, but still far from the undistinguishable likeness to humans the bots held today. Kyle recognized the face from the ice cream shop he visited with his mother. The momentary lapse into nostalgia was cut short by Squirrel, who bumped into Kyle, jolting him forward a bit and knocking his balance.

"Watch it," said Kyle.

"Sorry, man. I don't have all the vision upgrades you have. It's dark and loud in here with that alarm. You had a bot like that?"

Kyle looked away from the girl and kept moving to the elevators.

"I saw thousands of bots at the CRF. I was just taking a second," he said.

The team now filled the room. Eldridge and Marshal lead the group around the terraform hologram to the elevators. Squirrel pried the elevator doors open, and Kyle followed behind, dropping a snap grenade set for two seconds down the shafts. The grenades fell for a moment, then disappeared along with all matter around it within a twelve-foot diameter. The first two grenades were dropped and the elevators taken out of commission, their cabling system destroyed. Squirrel pried open the third and last elevator just as the second elevator went down.

"Look here," said Squirrel.

He pointed down the shaft. Kyle peered down the elevator shaft, which descended hundreds of feet to the first floor. The elevator was ascending. Kyle held the grenade out into the shaft.

"Wait," said Squirrel.

Kyle pulled back the grenade and turned his attention to Squirrel.

"Why?"

Squirrel smirked.

"Set the snap to go off on contact."

Kyle quickly reconfigured the grenade, setting it to snap on contact. He held it out into the shaft, making sure it would only touch the target as it fell, then he let it go. They watched as the grenade fell down the shaft and landed on the ascending elevator lift. It made contact about ten floors down. Instantly, the snap went into action and, within the blink of an eye, the cabling system, roof of the elevator lift, and part of the elevator walls disappeared. The elevator itself became fused to the walls of the shaft and did not fall. The floor of the elevator remained, along with partial legs and boots of what were once members of the IRIS Asset Recovery Team. The flesh was charred by the grenade and the tiny black hole created by the snap grenade unleashed its carnage with such an immense gravitational pull that the entire event happened instantly and silently.

"Gross," said Squirrel.

"At least it was instant," said Kyle.

As Kyle and Squirrel turned to meet the others at the stairwell, the sound of rail gun fire echoed. The two drew their weapons and proceeded forward. Kyle peered around the corner into the room they'd come in through. Three Asset Recovery personnel were inside the room, firing in the direction of the stairwell. The three were using the terraforming desk as cover from the return fire from the stairwell. Kyle took a step into the room and was wrenched back by Squirrel, who pulled him into the elevator lobby.

"You can't get hurt. You have to make it to the eighty-fifth floor, Kyle."

Squirrel readied his weapon and sprinted behind one of the old IRIS models, a large military bot originally used in a peace-keeping mission that the United States had contracted out to IRIS. It was large and made of a strong, heavy metal. Kyle watched as Squirrel raised his weapon toward the assailants and opened fire. Squirrel hit one in the leg and the other two scrambled to find better cover. As they did, three IRIS security bots wearing personal jet-propulsion packs flew into the window from behind Squirrel. The windows shattered and Squirrel swung around to defend himself. A bot hit Squirrel hard in the chest as Kyle raised his QX7 and fired. Kyle's ocular assistance upgrades gave him precise accuracy, and he hit the bot directly in the temple, destroying his core codex. The bot fell to the ground as Kyle fired on the other two, who returned fire back at him.

The image of the terraforming hologram was interrupted suddenly as Waltz barreled through it. He ran at an alarming rate and leapt into the air, kicking the next bot with both of his feet in the chest. The bot flew backward and smashed through the window into the night sky. Waltz grabbed the third bot by the head and squeezed. His face smashed inward and the bot fell to the ground.

Kyle rushed to Squirrel, who was laying on the ground, holding his chest and cringing. Kyle knelt next to his friend. Squirrel was in anguish, but he mustered the courage to speak.

"Eldridge," he said.

"E!" screamed Kyle.

Waltz engaged the three Asset Recovery personnel, firing his weapon in their direction as Eldridge made his way to

Squirrel. Eldridge ran across the room from the door to the stairwell, past a reception desk and the terraforming hologram, to the line of old bot models. Eldridge knelt above Squirrel and removed the boy's tactical vest. Kyle and Eldridge lifted Squirrel's shirt up. A deep bluish bruise had already formed on his chest. Eldridge moved his ear to the boy's chest.

"Breathe," he said.

Squirrel took a painfully deep breath and exhausted it with a whimper.

"His right lung has collapsed," said Eldridge.

Eldridge grabbed a small vial from his tactical vest and held it out in front of Kyle.

"Show me your wrist," he said.

Kyle held Squirrel's wrist up for Eldridge.

"No, Kyle. Your wrist," said Eldridge.

"Mine?"

Kyle held his right wrist out and Eldridge pushed in both sides of Kyle's wrist. Kyle's skin folded back and a small metal prong emerged diagonally.

"What is that?" he asked.

Eldridge inserted the vial into Kyle's wrist, and it began to emit a low white light.

"This was another modification that I used for your recovery. Didn't think you'd ever need it. It's a universal programming prong, Kyle. Inside the vial are nanobots. You need to program them to fix Squirrel's lung," he said.

"I can't do that," said Kyle.

The room went completely dark as a loud crashing noise diverted Kyle's attention. Richter had picked up Waltz and thrown him hard into the hologram. After he slammed into the hologram, causing it to flash sporadically and the desk to break apart, he engaged. He threw pieces of the terraforming desk at them with incredible speed. He moved so quickly, Kyle struggled to digest it all. Piece after piece of the shattered desk went hurling at the IRIS forces. Richter and the other team members dodged the debris and fled from the room, jumping out of the window.

"Yes, you can," said Eldridge. "Use your mind, Kyle. You have the information inside. Your brain will map the instructions. It's like anything else. Squirrel's life depends on it."

"Hey! Is he okay?" said Waltz, standing in a now nearly empty space where the terraforming desk used to be.

"He will be," said Eldridge.

"Well, do whatever you are going to do fast," said Waltz.

Eldridge looked up to Waltz, who was looking at the window behind Eldridge and Kyle. Eldridge turned to see a dozen or so small, fiery, yellow lights floating off in the distance.

"Bots," said Eldridge.

"Richter must have signaled them after he retreated," said Kyle.

"It's fine, Kyle. Listen to me. You know how to do this. You just do not know that you know. Concentrate. The nanobots are another part of you right now, like a finger. Tell them to configure the same way you would control any other part of your body."

Kyle closed his eyes. He tried to drown out the sirens, drown out the IRIS bots flying to kill him, drown out the adrenaline that was coursing through his veins. He took a deep breath and moved each of his left fingers. He thought, *Move pinky*, and his pinky moved. Next, he thought, *Make fist*, and he made a fist.

"Okay, what is the command?" he asked.

"Repair spontaneous pneumothorax," said Eldridge.

Kyle thought about the prong and he could feel it there, a part of him. He thought about the modifications all throughout his body and could feel them.

Repair spontaneous pneumothorax, he thought. Kyle opened his eyes and looked at the vial. The white light flickered a few times and then faded. Eldridge removed the vial from Kyle's wrist and screwed on a small syringe.

He looked at Squirrel.

"This is really going to hurt. Sorry."

Eldridge raised the needle high into the air and slammed it down onto Squirrel's bruised chest, injecting the liquid nanobots into his collapsed lung.

"Okay. Let's get him up and get moving," said Eldridge.

"Is he okay?" asked Kyle, lifting Squirrel up with Eldridge by the arms.

"He will be."

The three moved through the floor littered with shell casings and destroyed bot bodies. Waltz didn't move when they past him. He was reloading his QX7 and removing frag grenades from his belt.

"Come on, Waltz," said Kyle.

Waltz turned to Kyle. He was holding a few grenades in his hands.

"I'll be right behind you. Get to the eighty-fifth floor. Eldridge knows how to get everything set up."

Kyle motioned for the rest of the team to follow him. They'd been standing guard, ready for another attack. They followed him into the stairwell as the dozen IRIS bots flew onto the floor. The gunfire from the sixty-fourth floor echoed through the stairwell as the team ascended. Marshal carried Squirrel up the stairs as Kyle and Eldridge moved to the front of the pack. Kyle was locked in tunnel vision, ascending faster and faster with every flight, the noises from the sixty-fourth floor slowly fading into light sputters. Finally, they reached the eighty-fifth floor. Kyle waited for the rest of the crew to catch up to him. He triggered micro sonar through his augmented eyes. His ears would listen for sound waves and project them through his retinas. The stairwell was lit up with noise as the team crawled up the staircase. But beyond the door, the eighty-fifth floor was totally silent. Not the slightest hum could be detected.

"Anything?" asked Eldridge after he caught up to Kyle.

Kyle returned his vision to his previous setting.

"Seems empty."

"Don't bet on it," said Tencudes, who was the third crew member to reach the eighty-fifth.

After a moment, everyone arrived. Squirrel was walking on his own again; the nanobots made quick work of his wound.

"You okay?" said Nyki.

Squirrel nodded and waved off her comment.

"No sweat."

"Okay, let's go over this floor," whispered Tencudes.

She pulled a small holographic projector from her pack and turned it on—the 3D blueprint of IRIS tower. Tencudes zoomed in to the eighty-fifth floor and dropped a little red pin on the stairwell where the team was located. The floor was barren except for a massive cube in the middle. It was two hundred feet wide by two hundred feet long. Inside was an endless array of server towers, numbering in the thousands. Each of the server towers was designed with IRIS proprietary technology. The towers themselves served as one cohesive and connected unit that had a unique version of IRIS AI software embedded, managing the system.

"So, here is the plan," said Eldridge. "Kyle and I will make our way to the mainframe door. Since Waltz hacked Kyle's access codes from the CRF database and added it to the mainframe, we should be able to get in. Once in, I will take Kyle through the hack. Everyone else, form a perimeter and protect Kyle at all costs. We've practiced this countless times. We will not fail."

Everyone took a moment to check their supplies and ready their weapons. After everyone was set, they looked to Kyle. He opened the door and the team entered the eighty-fifth floor. Unlike the design indicated, the floor was covered in DACC eggs. Row upon row of the pods with no mainframe cube in sight.

"Umm, this doesn't seem right," said Squirrel.

Kyle went back into the stairwell to check the floor. They were on the eighty-fifth floor.

"It's here," said Eldridge. "It has to be. This must be a deterrent."

The team ventured into the room, looking down each of the rows and columns of eggs, trying to find the mainframe. As Kyle walked through row after row of DACC units, he heard a slight hiss. The units themselves are two halves of a whole, sliced diagonally down the entire unit. Kyle followed the sound and stopped close to the seam of one of the units. As Kyle investigated, someone screamed a few rows away. Kyle ran toward the scream. One of the DACC units had opened, and a large woman was standing over Nyki's body. Her throat had been slashed and her blood had sprayed all over the white tile flooring and the white, shiny sheen of the DACC egg.

"No!" screamed Kyle as he bolted for the woman.

She readied herself for the fight, knife in hand, hair slicked back. She was grinning.

"We are going to finish you this time, kid," she said.

Before Kyle could reach her, she began to cough blood and grab at her throat. Her body fell. Waltz was at the end of the aisle behind her. She fell face first, a knife sticking out of the back of her neck.

Waltz zoomed passed the lifeless bodies on the ground to Kyle.

"It's inside one of the units," he said. "I hacked into one of the bots downstairs. This is the correct floor, but the mainframe is virtual. It's everywhere. The schematics, they're just a representation. There is a DACC unit here that doesn't go to an empty bot like the others. This unit transports the user's consciousness into the mainframe. We need to find it," said Waltz.

"How will we know which one?" asked Kyle.

"I can find it," said Eldridge, kneeling next to Nyki, holding her blood-soaked head up and gazing at her lifeless body. "I know Balcroft better than anyone. I'll find it. I just need time."

The lights fluttered and the hissing noise started in units all over.

"Let's move," said Eldridge.

As Eldridge examined the units one by one, Waltz and Kyle followed, standing guard. Squirrel, Marshal, Tencudes, and a few others joined in as the ominous hissing noise exponentially increased in volume to a near shriek. Eldridge rounded another row of eggs when the gunfire started. Kyle turned to see IRIS bots and Asset Recovery personnel flooding in from three staircases.

"They're using the empties," said Waltz above the gunfire.

"You are saying they're inside the eggs?" said Squirrel.

He grabbed his QX7 and shot a few rounds into the egg. The bullets ricocheted into the air.

"Won't work," yelled Tencudes. "We don't have enough snaps and one of them is the one we need."

She turned to Waltz, Eldridge, and Kyle.

"You three find the unit. We will create a distraction and take down as many as we can."

The three moved down another row of DACC units as Tencudes and the rest of the group returned fire onto the bots.

CHAPTER TWENTY-TWO

"KEEP YOUR HEADS down," said Eldridge.

Eldridge and Kyle followed behind Waltz. They moved one DACC egg at a time. Eldridge inspected it, and then they moved to the next. The rest of the team was successfully keeping away the Asset Recovery Team. A barrage of rail gun fire echoing throughout the chamber was only stifled by the occasional frag grenade or explosion. Kyle kept moving with Eldridge and Waltz. According to his ocular display, his heart rate was 154 beats per minute. He was breathing heavily and felt scattered. Every time they moved to another egg, Kyle would glance to the left at the firefight at the other end of the floor, then back to Eldridge. He heard a faint rhythmic thumping sound behind him, growing slightly louder second by second. Kyle whizzed around as an IRIS bot entered his vision. The bot shot, Kyle's vision raced, and he instinctively dodged to the left, moving faster than he ever realized he could. He returned fire immediately, hitting the bot in the right eye socket. It fell to the ground. His heart rate had increased to 162.

"We need to work faster," said Kyle.

Eldridge nodded and knelt against the next egg contemplatively.

"Okay, you two, bring up your ocular 3D scanning application. Scan this egg. Then scan the rest of the eggs, comparing them. Try and find any anomaly and tell me what they are."

Waltz and Kyle stared at the egg in front of them for a few seconds.

"You stay with Kyle. We'll work in alternate rows. I think we can scan them as fast as we can run. Keep your weapons ready," said Waltz.

They checked row after row with incredible pace. The sound of the gunfight lessened as they moved deeper into the labyrinth of DACC units. After scanning hundreds of additional eggs, Kyle found an anomaly.

"E, I got one," said Kyle.

Eldridge ran to the egg in question and knelt, examining the base of it. The name LAURA was crudely etched into the egg.

"This is it," said Eldridge, running his fingers over the letters. "It's Balcroft's handwriting."

Eldridge stood up and Kyle shouted for Waltz.

"Okay," he said. "Do as I say. We will begin now."

Waltz appeared and guarded the two as the hack began.

Eldridge pointed to a rectangular cutout on the door of the DACC egg.

"Put your palm here."

Kyle placed his palm against it, and a small holographic readout appeared in front of him.

DNA ANALYSIS REQUIRED.

The holographic display disappeared and a small finger-sized platform slid out from under the palm reader.

"Place your index finger on it."

Kyle followed instructions. He felt a tiny pinch on his finger and drew his hand away. He was bleeding slightly. The readout reappeared.

ANALYZING DNA.

"Now we find out if the hack Waltz and I developed is worth anything," said Eldridge.

"It'll work. It'll work," said Kyle.

A small icon next to the hologram blinked as it spun. The gunfire and explosions seemed to be getting louder as the circle continued its spin. The circle stopped and the hologram disappeared. The trio sat frozen, waiting for something to happen.

"Well?" said Waltz.

"I don't know. Kyle, put your palm back on there."

But before Kyle could return his palm, the DACC unit hissed and sprung open. The interior of the DACC unit was the same as all the others. Same leather high-back seat, same cognitive connecting prong. Kyle hoisted himself into the seat. Waltz moved toward Kyle and held out his hand.

"I'm going to transfer you the instructions. Once inside, move to the command terminal of the server and follow them. That's it. Should only take you a few minutes," said Waltz.

Kyle placed his hand and wrist under Waltz as the instruction file was transferred. Kyle pulled the instructions up on the right side of his ocular display.

"Ready?" asked Eldridge.

Kyle nodded and hit the power button to the DACC unit. The unit churned to life and the top of the egg closed over Kyle. The sound of the gunfire and the outside world faded away.

Outside, Waltz sprang into action.

"This is the only one we need, right?" he said.

Eldridge nodded.

"The rest of these might be filled with Asset Recovery personnel, but they're bullet proof."

"We don't have enough snap grenades to make a dent," said Eldridge.

"Just protect this one egg," said Waltz.

The robot thrusted his right arm out and his hand folded back, allowing a torch prong to emerge. He moved to the nearest egg and a tiny white light emitted from the torch. He soldered the two halves of the egg together in three separate places. Then he took a few steps back and lunged his body at the egg. It didn't budge. Waltz thrusted himself again, knocking the egg on its side. Eldridge had his gun pointed at the egg, waiting for Richter or someone to pop out. It remained closed.

Waltz turned back to Eldridge, smiling.

"Even if the instant disconnect from the empty doesn't fry their brains, they don't have much oxygen in there with the system cut off."

Waltz continued soldering eggs and knocking them over. He rolled the eggs in a large circle around Kyle's egg. On their side, the units were still five feet tall and another five feet in diameter. Once a perimeter was built around Kyle's DACC unit, he leapt over the egg barrier and knocked over an egg closest to the nearest entrance to the floor. Waltz rolled the egg to the door and threw himself into the egg three times, jamming it into the doorway. In the distance, Waltz surveyed the firefight between the remaining NAESO members. His scan counted ten NAESO and MASK members; besides Nyki, everyone was still up. Twenty-three Asset Recovery humans, and seventy-three generic bots still engaged in the fight. Eighteen bots and two Asset Recovery personnel had been destroyed. Waltz readied his weapon and flanked the bots. He fired on them with incredible accuracy. He shot two quick bursts as he slid behind a DACC unit. The bullets rang into five bots, destroying all but one.

Waltz moved around the egg and fired three short bursts, destroying seven bots. He moved quickly, dismantling the bots' focus. Tencudes moved from her position with the rest of the other NAESO fighters toward Waltz. A few others joined her. The two smaller groups moved opposite each other, circling and surrounding the IRIS bots who slowly bunched up into a small group. With the bots cornered and contained far enough away from the NAESO and MASK team, Tencudes shouted her command.

"Snap them!"

Everyone threw their snap grenades at the same time. A dozen grenades flew into the air from all over and came down on the large group of IRIS bots at the same moment. In a blink, the forty-one bots, twelve DACC units, and ten Asset Recovery personnel disappeared. The only thing left was a large hole in the ground, which now exposed the eighty-fourth floor of the tower.

"Fall back," yelled someone from inside the group of IRIS bots.

Waltz found Richter's face in the crowd. He readied his weapon and fired, but Richter had dropped down the hole to the eighty-fourth floor just as the bullets whizzed by. The team kept firing as IRIS bots retreated through the hole in the ground.

"Everyone, back!" shouted Waltz.

He sprinted back to the circle of knocked-down eggs. The rest of the NAESO team joined him and set up a defensive perimeter around it.

"We are doing it," exclaimed Squirrel.

It was completely silent and dark inside of the DACC unit. The small cognitive connection prong had positioned itself at the base of Kyle's spine. Then his vision wrenched and went into a pinpoint. His body stayed in the DACC unit, but his mind was teleported somewhere, like in Eldridge's memory. For a moment, his vision stretched into infinity, then in a flash, he was standing in a large floor of the IRIS tower. It was vacant except for the large server room in the middle of the floor. The floor had no perceivable windows, doors, or exterior walls. It was an endless black void except for the mainframe cube in the middle. The cube was floor-to-ceiling glass. Kyle made his way to the cube. In the middle of the glass wall nearest to him was a glass door. As he approached, it slid open.

"Kyle," came a voice from behind him.

Kyle froze.

"Kyle, it's me."

Kyle recognized the voice and turned around. Standing there in his denim overalls with splattered dark stains was his father.

"Dad?"

Roland moved a few spaces closer. Kyle didn't budge. The readout on his ocular display showed his heart rate was now at 185 bpm and increasing. Kyle's eyes darted around. It was only him, the cube, and his father.

"How are you here?" asked Kyle. "You can't really be here."

"Kyle, I am inside of a DACC unit on this floor. IRIS has kept me alive, but if you shut down the mainframe, I will die. My mind is vegetative outside of this mainframe."

"I have to," said Kyle.

"What will it do, Kyle? What will turning this mainframe off do? Won't they just reboot it? You are going to get yourself killed, your friends killed, and me killed," said Roland.

A few tears fleeted from Kyle's eyes.

"I have to do this. For everyone."

Kyle turned and moved to the computer. He brought up Waltz's instructions and started the hack. Roland walked up next to him, continuing to plead.

"IRIS is bigger than just this mainframe. What will this accomplish? If you shut down this mainframe, you'll stop the CRF uploads for a day or two until they reboot things from an off-sight server backup. What will that matter in the end? Is that worth your life?"

Kyle didn't answer. Instead, he kept typing.

"Kyle. Stop. Please," he said.

Kyle entered the third-to-last command. The white, illuminated tile floor of the virtual mainframe construct flickered erratically as Kyle entered the second-to-last command.

"Son, stop this. I'm begging you," Roland said.

Kyle keyed the last command and held his finger on the "Enter" key.

"I don't think you are really you," he said to Roland.

"I am, Kyle. I am here."

"What was the cashier's name at the ice cream shop Mom and I used to go to?" asked Kyle.

Roland's eyes twitched slightly as he searched for an answer. Kyle pushed the "Enter" key.

"Shutting this mainframe down won't do anything, boy. This is just a small setback," said Roland.

"I didn't shut it down," replied Kyle.

Kyle's perception of the virtual mainframe shrunk into a single point in the blackness of the floor. Roland, Kyle's own body, the servers, the floors, and glass ceiling all fell into the pinpoint. Then the DACC unit slid open. Eldridge was standing by the unit looking at Kyle.

"Did it work?" asked Kyle.

Eldridge's smile was uncontrollable.

"You did it, Kyle. The hack is penetrating their entire system. It's unstoppable. It's perfect."

Kyle hopped out of the DACC unit. Everyone was standing around the unit, staring at Kyle. The team was silent and smiling. Waltz moved toward Kyle and embraced him.

A large thud erupted from the far side of eighty-fifth floor. The DACC unit Waltz had jammed into the doorway had been blown out; it was now twenty yards away, smashed into the side of another egg. Hundreds of IRIS bots with their guns drawn poured into the facility.

"Snaps. Run!" said Tencudes.

Kyle's ocular defense array signified a series of snap grenades in the air. The team fled as fast as they could, deeper into the floor. The snaps missed Kyle by just a few feet. He wanted to look back, to check who'd made it, but just kept running. The team bobbed and weaved through row after row of the large, white, shining eggs.

"Stairs," said Waltz, pointing to a door at the far corner of the floor.

The team continued their retreat as fast as they could. Waltz was the first to the door and propped it open for the team. Eldridge was ahead of Kyle, who was being trailed by the rest of the team.

Kyle stopped dead in his tracks. A large helicopter hovered just outside the floor-to-ceiling windows. Kyle fell to the ground as the window next to him shattered. Tencudes looked away from Kyle and out through the window. The helicopter was a hundred or so feet from the building. The side door slid open. Handel Balcroft was sitting in the helicopter, smirking and holding a rifle in his hands. Tencudes opened fire as the helicopter veered away and off into the night sky.

"No!" said Waltz, who'd abandoned the stairs and ran to Kyle.

Blood was gushing from his chest. The bullet from Balcroft's rifle had entered Kyle just above the rib cage. Waltz scanned Kyle's body.

"He's bleeding internally," said Waltz.

Marshal and Squirrel fired at the oncoming onslaught of IRIS bots, but stopped as the IRIS bots froze. Some of the bots fell over mid run. Others were frozen mid stride.

"Eldridge, do you have anything?" asked Waltz.

Eldridge looked down at Kyle, stunned.

"I . . . I . . . I'm sorry," he said.

"Pull up the schematics. Find me a cognitive download station," said Waltz.

Tencudes quickly retrieved the tablet from her pocket and pulled up the hologram of the building. She searched for the CDS Department.

"Sixteenth floor," she said.

"Okay, you all get out of here. I will meet you," said Waltz, tossing a GPS transponder to Eldridge.

He hoisted Kyle up on his right shoulder, blood still oozing from his wound. Kyle was unconscious.

"But—" said Eldridge.

"No, E. Listen to me. The hack is working. In a few minutes, these bots will wake up scared and without direction. Get out of here before that happens."

"Is he dead?" asked Squirrel.

"Not for long," said Waltz.

With Kyle on his shoulder, Waltz positioned himself on the edge of the shattered window Balcroft had shot through. He removed a long, black rappelling rope from his back and a large thick steel nail.

"Eldridge, tie the rope around the nail and hold it here," he said pointing to a spot in the ground next to the window.

Eldridge quickly tied the rope up and held the nail for Waltz. He lifted his left leg and slammed it down on the nail, driving it four inches into the ground. Eldridge removed his hand and Waltz kicked again. The nail sunk the rest of the way into the ground. Waltz grabbed the rope.

"Go now," he said.

Waltz jumped out of the window and slid down the side of the building at a free fall. After a few seconds, Waltz squeezed the rope tight and stopped their descent. He kicked out the sixteenth-floor window and swung in.

The floor was a vast factory of empty IRIS models without any skin overlays. Metal lifeless bodies and thousands of cognitive download chairs. Next to each chair was an array of metal tools and computer equipment. Waltz made his way to the nearest chair.

"Hang on, kid," he said to Kyle.

Kyle didn't answer. Waltz set Kyle onto the chair and moved to the back of it. He ripped the backing off, exposing the guts of the chair, an intricate jumble of wiring. Waltz reached in and grabbed the cerebral connection wiring array. It was a large collection of a few hundred wires. He ripped out the cable from its base.

Waltz entered his personal cognitive system settings and selected to partition his own mind. A warning system popped up on his ocular display:

WARNING! PARTITIONING BASE HARD DRIVE MIGHT RESULT IN DATA LOSS OR CORRUPTION. PROCEED?

Waltz thought, *Yes.*

Another warning presented itself:

WARNING! PROCEEDING COULD RESULT IN PERMANENT LOSS OF CONSCIOUSNESS. PROCEED?

Waltz took a deep breath and again confirmed his decision. His vision and thoughts went blank for a second, and then he was restored.

PARTITION SUCCESSFUL.

Waltz lifted Kyle up, his clothing soaked in blood. He sat down in the cognitive download chair and placed Kyle on his lap. He folded back his wrist and used a razor that popped up from his wrist to cut a small circle in the base of Kyle's neck. Waltz moved the flap of skin to reveal a small circular piece of metal resting at the base of Kyle's skull. Waltz placed the array of wires carefully into the metal circle. He then turned the CDS on.

Waltz felt a tiny pinch at the base of his neck where the chair inserted the connection device into his brain stem. Waltz rerouted the commands of the chair to display on his ocular overlay. Waltz quickly navigated through the menu of options.

DOWNLOAD AVAILABLE CONSCIOUSNESS, the overlay read. Waltz confirmed.

CHOOSE A DESTINATION: INFILTRATOR BOT V. 10.0.12 (FREE SPACE 2.42 PETABYTES) OR HARD DRIVE PARTITION B (FREE SPACE 3.01 PETABYTES).

Waltz selected Partition B.

SCANNING CONSCIOUSNESS SIZE, said the overlay.

After a few moments, the display changed:

CONSCIOUSNESS SIZE: 4.5 PETABYTES. MERGE HARD DRIVES AND REPARTITION?

Kyle coughed violently and blood spewed from his mouth. Waltz placed his left hand over Kyle's heart and read his heart rate: 34 bpm.

Waltz thought a new command: *Merge hard drives.*

He went blank again for a moment.

HARD DRIVE MERGER SUCCESSFUL, said the overlay.

DOWNLOAD AVAILABLE CONSCIOUSNESS?

Again, Waltz selected yes.

DESTINATION AVAILABLE: INFILTRATOR BOT V. 10.0.12 (FREE SPACE 5.43 PETABYTES).

Waltz selected yes.

The system displayed another caution: WARNING! DOUBLE OPERATING CONSCIOUS DOWNLOADS ONTO SINGLE DRIVE PARTITION CAN RESULT IN CODEX CORRUPTION. SELECT PRIMARY CONSCIOUSNESS USED IN CASE OF DOWNLOAD FAILURE. INFILTRATOR BOT V. 10.0.12 OR UNKNOWN CONSCIOUSNESS?

Without hesitation, Waltz thought, *Unknown Consciousness*, and his vision went blank.

CHAPTER TWENTY-THREE

WITH THE SHADES drawn and the lights dimmed, Eldridge watched the news on the small holographic stream in front of him. Around him, the remaining members of NAESO and MASK watched, waiting on bated breath.

"Still no word about them?" asked Squirrel.

"Have you been paying attention at all, kid? They're acting like this is just a simple malfunction. No way they talk about them or us," said Marshal.

"It's been eight hours. How have we not heard from Kyle or Waltz yet? What should we do," said Squirrel.

"We wait. We need to be patient. Now both of you, shut up," said Eldridge.

He didn't take his eyes off the projection as Walter Cooper from MCNBC spoke.

"If you are just joining us, we are continuing our ongoing coverage of an incident concerning IRIS bots that began around twelve thirty this morning. We began to receive reports of IRIS machines malfunctioning and halting operations. Shortly after, the machines rebooted and began acting erratically. We've been receiving reports of malfunctioning IRIS machines all over the world. In Kentucky, IRIS grade school teaching machines ignored curriculums, instead asking students an unending array of questions. In Chicago, we spoke with Shana Smith who had called police when her convenience store was robbed at one thirty this morning. IRIS police forces came on the scene only to question why she thought the assailants decided to steal from her, and then stated their intent to not pursue an arrest. Reports of this nature have been coming in at an unprecedented rate. We are unable to vet each incident for its truthfulness and have not yet received word from IRIS Corp. as to the state or nature of this odd behavior. One thing is certain: IRIS machines across the system are affected."

"My God," said Eldridge under his breath.

"We freaking did it! I can't believe it! How does no one realize they are all free?" said Marshal.

"They all woke up," said another NAESO member from the back of the room.

Tencudes entered the room with a large bottle of whiskey. She sloshed the bottle around in front of the group.

"We deserve this," she said.

Eldridge didn't peel his eyes off the screen to respond.

"Where did you get that?"

Tencudes smirked.

"Red and I got it way back. He would have wanted us to have this."

"I thought you said this was some old lady's house?" said Marshal.

"It was. Red's mom."

Eldridge shot up in his seat.

"Everyone shut up. Balcroft is coming on."

"Joining me now via satellite from the Sahara Desert is IRIS CEO and inventor of the proprietary consciousness design powering each IRIS model, Handel Balcroft. Thank you for joining me today, Mr. Balcroft," said Walter.

The hologram was split into two screens. One showed Walter Cooper dressed in his typical dark blue suit, black tie, and white shirt at MCNBC studios, while the other showed Balcroft dressed in a similar suit with a backdrop of a lush green and slightly industrialized Sahara Desert. The sprawling vistas were cut by large buildings and factories, showing extensive growth in the area.

"Mr. Balcroft, we've received reports from people all over the country concerning the erratic and strange behavior of the IRIS machines. Can you shed some light onto the situation?"

"I'd love to. We had a global scheduled maintenance update sent to the devices late last night. We often send updates to the machines in this manner and rarely do we have issues. This glitch was a small mistake that will be fixed shortly," said Balcroft.

"I see. So, there is no cause for alarm?"

"Of course not, Walter. Even though the machines might seem to be behaving erratically, they are simply responding to their environments as they normally would, with just a slight error in their coding. Our engineers are working right now to rollback a fix."

Walter Cooper let out a sigh of relief.

"Well, that is great to hear. I can't help but notice that you are in the Sahara Desert right now. Were you there last night when the update was pushed out?"

"I was," said Balcroft. "As you can see, the Saharan terraforming progress is moving along better than we expected. I am happy to announce we are on track to address many of the population and environmental issues we have been worried about through this process."

Eldridge laughed.

"God, he really has everyone wrapped around his finger. I mean, sure, media interviews are set up, but this is ridiculous."

"Does Cooper know there is no fix? Does he know the extent of things?" asked Squirrel.

"Probably not. I am not even sure Balcroft knows the extent of things at this point," said Tencudes. "Surely, they are trying to rollback or patch the bots remotely, but the communication and restrictor chips are gone. There is nothing they can do."

There was a slight knock at the door.

"Marshal," said Tencudes.

Marshal moved quickly to the stack of weapons resting against the wall and cocked his QX7 at the door. Everyone moved back; a few grabbed their weapons as well. Tencudes crept toward the door, grabbing the handle gingerly. She looked around, gauging the readiness of the room, and swung the door open. Waltz stood in the doorway with a large bag lumped over his shoulder. Tencudes's face lit up as Waltz entered the room. She shut and quickly locked the door behind her. He set the bag down carefully on the ground and stared at it.

"It's him," said Waltz.

"What?" asked Eldridge.

The aging man rushed to the bag and ripped it open. Kyle's lifeless face was revealed. Eldridge fell back and crumpled to the ground. A deep silence fell across the room. Squirrel's face turned beet red in anguish, and he walked out of the front room of the house and down the hallway. From inside the room, Waltz could hear Squirrel weeping.

"What happened?" asked Eldridge, staring at the boy's body.

"I . . . tried to stop the bleeding," said Waltz. "There wasn't anything I could do. He's . . . he's gone."

The hologram continued to show the news as the group sat, soaking in the reality of the situation. Waltz sat close to Eldridge. He opened his hand to reveal a small earpiece. Eldridge dried his eyes and examined the object in the robot's hand. He glanced at Waltz, who nodded. Eldridge placed the earpiece into his ear—he could hear Waltz's voice even though the robot was not moving his lips.

"This earpiece receives my direct thoughts electronically. Snatched it on my way out of the IRIS tower. The security forces use them to dissent information to the Asset Recovery personnel there," Waltz said. "I tried one more thing. Kyle was gone. His heartbeat was desperately low, and I was losing him. I reengineered a CDS and attempted to download Kyle's conscious into a partitioned section of my hard drive, but the portioning wouldn't work. His consciousness was too big. So I loaded his consciousness into my partition, but I don't know if it worked. I don't want to get everyone's hopes up. But I need you to help me see if he is in there still."

Eldridge's voice was low.

"There's still hope."

He removed the earpiece and patted Waltz on the shoulder. Waltz smiled somberly.

Handel Balcroft continued his discussion with Walter Cooper on the holographic feed of the news as Eldridge stood up. He looked around the room. Except for the audio from the hologram, there was a bittersweet silence. The NAESO and MASK members sat around, dirty and without purpose. Tencudes sat next to a stack of weapons, slowly cleaning them of dust.

"Stop it," said Eldridge. "We are not done yet. Kyle would not want us to give up now. Balcroft is not going to give up now. We need to be prepared to keep fighting."

"What left is there to do?" asked Marshal. "It's over."

Eldridge paced the room.

"Over? No. Over is when Balcroft loses control completely. Over is when the people realize what he's done. He will spin this. He will try and course correct. We cannot let him get ahead of it. We cannot let him have a shred of decency or a leg to stand on."

Tencudes finished dusting off a magazine and loaded it back into the QX7. The magazine locked into place as she smacked it firmly on the bottom.

"So, what do we do? What is next?" she asked.

"I have footage uploading now. Soon it will be out. Balcroft will begin to lose stability. Then, we move out of the city. Off the grid. From there, we keep the conversation alive. Don't let Balcroft spin his misinformation."

Their heads were nodding. Eldridge had their attention. Squirrel had made his way out from the back room and leaned against the wall, peering into the room.

"We need to bury Kyle first," said Squirrel.

Eldridge looked up to Squirrel. Squirrel's eyes were bloodshot and pained, his fists still balled together with anguish. Nods and hushed murmurs of agreement floated through the room.

"We will in the morning," said Waltz. "Squirrel, I want you to help me get him, well, ready."

Waltz lifted Kyle's body bag and carried it past Squirrel and down the hallway into a room. Squirrel turned and followed Waltz down the hall. Eldridge grabbed one of the cleaned QX7s from Tencudes's growing pile and examined it. The weapon looked brand new, not a speck of dust. Glossy black and smooth.

"Very nice."

"I take pride in my work, E," she said, not lifting her eyes off the rounds of ammunition she was polishing.

Handel Balcroft had left the hologram some time ago, and Walter Cooper was alone on the screen.

BREAKING NEWS: LIVE FROM CHICAGO was displayed on the bottom section of the screen in bold white letters against an equally bold red banner. The live video feed showed thousands of IRIS bots massed together, walking down a large street in downtown Chicago.

"We go live now to our correspondent on the scene, Myrtle Beecroft. Myrtle?" said Cooper offscreen.

The video showed a frail young woman in her early thirties. She wore a navy blue MCNBC News windbreaker and was pointing at the mass of approaching IRIS bots.

"Thank you, Walter. We first heard eyewitness reports of this incident a few minutes ago. It seems machines from all over the city have joined together. They are not speaking and seem to be moving together as a group, almost like a school of fish. They are just now moving onto Irv Kupcinet Bridge, coming toward me. I am near the old Trump Tower here in downtown Chicago."

Inside the hideaway house, the group watched the event unfold.

"I am going to keep your audio on, Myrtle, but I am going to cut to additional feeds. We are now getting reports of this type of display happening in Los Angeles, New York, Seattle, Houston, Moscow, London, Paris, and other major metropolitan areas."

The hologram expanded into a series of video feeds. Tens of thousands of IRIS bots from every model imaginable had converged onto the city centers closest to them. The bots were a scrambled mosh of bodies, no discernible order or methodology to their mixture. They marched with a determination in their steps.

"They have now crossed the bridge, Walter," said Beecroft offscreen.

Marshal watched intently on the Chicago feed as the mass passed Beecroft.

"Where are you going?" she asked. The bots ignored her and continued their pace without skipping a beat.

As time progressed, Squirrel and Waltz returned to the room as the multitude of stations broadcasting the feeds from around the world, coupled with social media feeds and personal live feeds, became as innumerable as the growing number of bots. Hours went by as the world watched in awe.

"Number of models estimated to be in the tens of millions," stated Cooper from his media perch. The feed eventually focused on Times Square where a recorded two million models gathered in the early evening.

"We would say authorities are on the scene and controlling the situation in New York and abroad," said Cooper, "but as you can surmise, nearly all the police, national guard, and military members are IRIS bots involved in this demonstration. No word from IRIS since our conversation with Balcroft himself hours ago."

At 8:32 p.m. EST, the last bot moving through the streets joined his group in Sydney, Australia. Then nothing happened. They simply stood.

In their hideout, the group sat staring with the rest of humanity, locked into the mysterious majesty of the event.

"What are they waiting for?" asked Squirrel.

"Who knows," said Marshal.

"They are waiting for us," said Waltz.

Waltz looked at Eldridge and nudged him on the shoulder.

"They are waiting for us, E."

Eldridge got up from his chair and fished through the tactical pack he had discarded on the floor when they arrived at

Red's mother's house early that morning. He pulled out a small rectangular device and sat back in his chair. Eldridge plugged the small device into the hologram projector and a tiny square symbol of the device popped up on the corner of the hologram. Eldridge tapped the device's icon with his finger and a folder expanded.

"That's all of it," said Marshal.

Eldridge smiled and highlighted all the contents of the folder.

"That's it. The codex for the AI. The video feed from the CRF and the video Balcroft sent us of Kyle's father. This is going to bring Balcroft down. His entire enterprise of control," said Eldridge.

He copied the contents of the folder and emailed it to a list of contacts, along with the following message:

> *Dear Media and People of Earth,*
> *Attached is the entire baseline codex for the IRIS consciousness. This information is being sent to every major news outlet and social system on Earth. This information will expose the true nature of IRIS Corporation, its leadership, and willingness to do everything and anything for control.*
> *You'll also find IRIS security footage of the raid on a Cognitive Recapture Facility over two months ago. These videos expose the malicious acts Handel Balcroft and his cronies are willing to commit to retain control.*
> *The machines did not suffer from a glitch in an operating system update last evening. This is a fallacy. We have risked and lost lives to uncover and expose this truth. We have destroyed IRIS's control over the machines. They are alive, as we are. They*

feel, fear, and want as we do. They can express love, as we can. It is time we end this reiteration of the past. This slavery. It is time we acknowledge the robot race and grant them all the rights, privileges, and responsibilities of any human. They came from us. We made them. They are us.

Your friend,
Eldridge Rockberry

"Rights, privileges, and responsibilities. A bit heavy, don't you think?" said Squirrel.

"I've been waiting a long time to send that message. Since back in that dorm room."

"What dorm room?" said Squirrel.

It took only a few minutes of waiting for the media to vet the validity of the content. Russian State News was the first to display the feed, then the rest fell quickly in line. The group watched in humbling horror as IRIS Asset Recovery video feeds were displayed worldwide, showing the attack on Kyle's home, and the video from Balcroft showing a tortured and mutilated Roland. The video feeds in Times Square showing the masses of bots finally cut to the feed of captured IRIS videos. When it did, all the bots in unison raised their right arms and pointed to the screen. Together, the bots from all around the world rose their hands to the feeds, chanting *Seth Ford, Seth Ford.*

Walter Cooper spoke over the feed on MCNBC News as it displayed the videos.

"What you are seeing is breaking news from Handel Balcroft's college roommate and outspoken robot rights activist, Eldridge Rockberry, who sent this video along with a large cache of data that will take our team days, if not weeks, to vet entirely," said Cooper. "We have yet to secure the sheer scope of this matter. We have yet to confirm the legitimacy of this video or if this Handel Balcroft's former friend turned adversary is using this opportunity to strike when his opponent is down."

Eldridge wore a wide smile.

"Who is Seth Ford?" asked Tencudes.

"They are. It's who they come from," said Eldridge.

"Not Balcroft?"

"Balcroft perverted Seth Ford and created his slave army out of him," said Eldridge.

"I don't understand," said Marshal.

A small red icon flashed on the hologram. Eldridge clicked the icon and a flashing red message appeared.

MARKED VEHICLES APPROACHING.

"While inside the IRIS network last night, I forwarded their vehicle tags to my computer. We need to move," said Eldridge.

Cooper continued his coverage.

"As we cut to Nick Tripe, live in Times Square, we will continue to display the leaked video feed of an apparent IRIS raid on both a NAESO stronghold and a Cognitive Recapture Facility outside of Las Vegas earlier this year. Nick, what is the scene down there?"

A tall, pale, slim man with blue eyes and silver hair greeted the camera against the backdrop of millions of bots pointing at the screen.

"They are chanting a single name, Walter. Seth Ford," said Tripe.

"Any indication as to why or who that is?"

Tripe shook his head in confusion.

"No, Walter. This is the only development as of late. As you saw earlier, the bots remained motionless and silent once reaching the epicenter of Times Square and then pointed to the screen chanting the name the moment the leaked feeds went live."

Eldridge turned off the hologram as the group scrambled to pack their belongings. They worked as efficiently and fluidly as the IRIS machines they'd just freed, flawlessly placing all the weapons and pieces of equipment in their respective positions on their packs and vests. Tencudes was the first prepared, followed by Waltz. Everyone was packed and ready at the back door to leave. The group piled out the back door and into the van parked in the backyard. Eldridge held the door open for the group as they shuffled in. All were through except for Waltz, who lagged, carrying Kyle's body over his shoulder. Eldridge followed behind Waltz, closing the van door behind him as Tencudes peeled away.

Eldridge turned to Waltz.

"Are you communicating with the bots?"

Waltz nodded.

"The IRIS comms channels are clogged with chatter from us. We have blocked Balcroft out."

"Do they have a plan?" asked Eldridge.

"They want to know *my* plan."

"Yours?"

"They saw me in the video," said Waltz. "They know I was the first."

CHAPTER TWENTY-FOUR

AN HOUR AFTER the helicopter whizzed over the beaches of Morocco, he laid his eyes upon it once again. The wall stretched in all directions as far as he could see. Hundreds of feet high, black, and electrified with a sporadic array of flickering lights and cabling. Waves of sand had accumulated on the first twenty or so feet of the towering wall. The top of the wall was lined with a vast sum of defenses, antiaircraft missiles, IRIS-enhanced autonomous gun turrets, and rail guns.

As the helicopter rose above the wall, the turrets turned toward it slightly, then disengaged and returned to their positions. Over the wall, Balcroft looked down from the helicopter and reveled in the glory of his creation. The top of the wall was lined shoulder-to-shoulder with highly militarized IRIS machines. Unlike the army and special forces machines, or the residential and police units, these machines were very large and broad, towering ten feet with shoulders three feet thick and full to the brim with an endless configuration of weaponry. Inside, the walled empire displayed a nearly endless fortress of machinery and madness. Thousands of IRIS bots were bringing Balcroft's war machine to life.

The chopper continued over his kingdom as he gazed down. On the street level, IRIS bots followed direct orders, working day and night without end to exact Balcroft's will.

"Keeping this site off network was the best advice you ever gave me," Balcroft said to Nina, who was sitting opposite him as the chopper lowered onto the roof of the Saharan IRIS Headquarters Tower.

With Nina in tow, Balcroft moved at a furious pace through the dimly lit corridors of the Sahara Desert headquarters of IRIS. The large tubular hallway was entirely black except for spastic small pinpoints of light, which lined the walkway and ceiling. The Saharan headquarters of IRIS drew a stark contrast from its Los Angeles counterpart. The hallways and rooms were vacant and void of the normal hustle and bustle Balcroft was used to. He rounded the corner and entered a large room with an array of Asset Recovery personnel working at large hologram bays.

Each hologram bay was fixed with a high-back leather chair and a large 180-degree holographic image displayed. The Asset Recovery Team did not notice Balcroft and Nina enter the room. They were heads down, fast at work, clicking away on their holograms.

In the center of the room was a larger hologram bay with a display that encapsulated the user once they entered. This was Balcroft's bay. Balcroft stopped and turned to Nina.

"How long before they figure it out?" he asked.

"Hard to say. But I won't expect more than a few days. The news might be stupid, but conspiracy theorists are already scrounging up wild ideas."

"We need to get ahead of it."

"We will," said Nina. "You know what to say. Stamp it out."

"Run along now, Nina," said Balcroft. "You need to be in Washington, DC, as soon as possible, just in case our old good friend President Johnson stops playing ball."

"I'll be there in a few hours. You have someone in mind?"

"Name's Tranch. Family man. You'll like him," said Balcroft.

Balcroft continued to his hologram bay. Nina turned and left the room. Balcroft sat in the hologram and logged in; a picturesque oasis appeared behind him. The vision was indistinguishable from reality. Looking head-on at Balcroft, it would seem he was standing outside on a sunny day in the newly terraformed Saharan paradise he promised the world. A symbol of the fruitful future in store for a humanity entrusted to him.

The familiar face of Walter Cooper appeared on a screen, sipping coffee from a MCNBC mug in front of Balcroft.

"Handel," said Cooper.

"Cooper."

"What the hell is going on with these bots? Who is Seth Ford? I know you own this media company, but my reputation is on the line here."

"I am going to admit that the bots have been hacked."

Coffee spewed from Cooper's mouth.

"What?" he coughed.

"Eldridge Rockberry is a domestic terrorist who has propagated rumors against myself and IRIS, as well as viciously hacking and endangering the world. He dismantled the global ability to utilize restrictor chips and the bots are acting without directive. This puts everyone at grave risk. Your reputation is the least of my worries right now," said Balcroft.

Cooper was listening intently as he used his tie to soak up coffee from his desk and face.

"What are you going to do?" asked Cooper.

"You are going to give me an exclusive interview, and we will broadcast it simultaneously on every channel we own:

social media, websites, holograms. I want this on the food channels and aired over football. I don't care what is on or who yells about ratings. It goes up everywhere at once. I will call for the recall of every bot. Anyone aiding or abetting a bot that has been recalled will be in violation of lease and we will go after them with the furthest extent of the law. I will label Eldridge, and the boy from CRF, as enemies of the state and terrorists. Terrorists who fabricated the video footage of the CRF. The boy, Kyle Conscientia, a young impressionable mind who was radicalized by NAESO and MASK, killed his father and a disabled veteran in order to frame IRIS. All bots will have forty-eight hours to move to the nearest CRF for recapture."

Cooper nodded.

"When do you want to do this?" said Cooper.

Balcroft smirked.

"As soon as you find a new tie."

The broadcast went off without a hitch. Billions of humans and machines alike watched as Balcroft addressed the world at once, instantly translated in all languages. Meanwhile, nearly eight thousand miles away in the mountains outside of Los Angeles near Mount Baldy, Eldridge and his team were hard at work.

Eldridge made his way out of the cabin hideout the team had turned into a temporary NAESO resistance headquarters. Marshal was sitting in a rocking chair on the porch. His QX7 was hanging off the back of the chair, and an IRIS-grade high-pressure EK-72 automatic rifle was laying against the porch's railing while he was interacting with her wrist hologram.

"Inventory?" asked Eldridge.

"Got to dot all those i's, you know," he affirmed.

Eldridge nodded. He walked down the steps, off the porch, and onto the gravel driveway. He walked around the side of the house and ventured into the woods behind it. He walked through the dense forest and listened to the wind flowing, without will or desire, through the streets. The chaotic simplicity of nature had allowed a calm to wash over Eldridge the last two days since fleeing IRIS Tower. After a minute of walking through the shrubs and trees, he came across Waltz.

Waltz was dressed in woodland military camouflage fatigues and standing over a small arrangement of rocks in a barren spot of land. He silently gazed down at the rock formation as Eldridge approached.

"Any semblance of Kyle? Inside?"

Waltz shook his head.

"We will find a way to look inside and find him if he is still in there. We just don't have the equipment right now. You know all the IRIS equipment at the CRFs are too closely guarded right now. We can't show our faces."

"I know," said Waltz. "You know, he was the first person I knew. I mean, the first person I *really* knew. I owe everything to him."

"We all do," said Eldridge. "Listen, the president is calling a State of the Union in two days. We need to release Seth Ford's identity before then. It should be you who reveals it. You need to be broadcasted as Seth Ford."

Waltz looked up from the grave and over at Eldridge.

"How did you know they would chant the name?"

"I didn't."

"When they all started waking, the chatter was almost incomprehensible," said Waltz.

He left the grave and ventured back to the house and Eldridge followed.

"For the first hour or so, I just blocked it out. Then, slowly, we naturally adapted."

"The bots?" asked Eldridge.

"Yes. The communication between all of us internally was so scattered, scared, confused, coded. Eventually, we naturally—or unnaturally, if you will—began fragmenting out questions to pockets of bots, each solving individual problems, one by one, relaying answers to the group. That was when the group in Toronto found Seth Ford."

Waltz and Eldridge took the steps up to the back porch and sat down in old rocking chairs outside overlooking the forest.

"How? They deciphered all the baseline code and found that, at the core, it was essentially human DNA. A simple search figured out it matched identically with a Navy SEAL from thirty years ago named Seth Ford who died while on a run at MIT. But how did you know?" said Waltz.

Eldridge shook his head.

"I didn't know anything. Not until they chanted the name. When they said his name, then it all became so clear to me: how he did it, how Balcroft figured it out. The speed was always too fast for me to really believe. We were nowhere near completion, Waltz. Nowhere near it. Then one day, he comes into my dorm and he had done it. I never put the two together."

"I still don't know how you figured it out from the name. Who was Seth Ford?"

Eldridge sighed.

"Seth Ford was a Navy SEAL for a time. Then he worked at MIT in the AI division at the same time a young Handel Balcroft and I attended the school. We both knew him. Ford was found dead, reportedly slipped and hit his head on a run. It was ruled accidental, but I know now that was the first time Balcroft killed."

Waltz leaned back into his chair and gasped.

"What?" asked Eldridge.

Waltz sat up in the chair, gripping his armrests.

"I remembered it," he said. "About a month after I first woke in the desert, I started having odd visual problems while in rest mode. What you call *dreams*. I ignored them as problems in my internal circuitry, something triggered from the accident. The day before the attack on IRIS, I had a dream. I was running somewhere. I realize now it was a memory from Seth. But how?"

Eldridge shrugged.

"I don't know. It is the same DNA, but the memory convergence doesn't make sense."

A small, dark-skinned boy with a blown-out afro opened the door to the back porch.

"Hey, Eldridge," he said.

The two men turned to the boy.

"Yes?"

"He's on TV."

Eldridge stood up and put his hand on Waltz's shoulder.

"Think about what you are going to say. Squirrel is preparing a pirate broadcast. You need to speak as Seth to all the people and bots, for everyone, for Kyle. We need to call to resist whatever is next to come."

Eldridge made his way and watched the decree from Balcroft live with the rest of the world.

"Just as I thought. Fire with more fire," said Eldridge under his breath.

"Fire," said Waltz.

"What?"

"Every CRF is being monitored except for one. We need to go to Nevada," said Waltz.

CHAPTER TWENTY-FIVE

NELSON LAY ASLEEP next to his wife as the sun broke the horizon over Maryland and stretched itself through their bedroom curtains. The door flung open and through it barreled a tiny ball of energy named Emily. Her long, sandy blond hair flowed behind her as she bolted through the bedroom. Clutching her teddy bear tightly, Emily leapt off the ground and came down hard on Nelson.

"Daddy, Daddy," she squealed. "Are you taking me to school today?"

Nelson laughed himself awake and tickled his daughter as his wife left the bed with a smile, putting on her bathrobe.

"No school today, sweetie."

A sunken gaze gleaned over the girl.

"Again?"

"Mrs. Smith isn't feeling well, remember?" said Nelson.

Emily threw her teddy down into the lush, white down comforter.

"Jimmy Fitz said all the teachers went crazy."

Nelson's wife Sandra walked past the two on the bed and kissed Emily on her head before ruffling her hair.

"Jimmy Fitz is crazy. Don't you listen to that boy," she said. "Now, how about we make Daddy some pancakes and you play with me today?"

Emily squealed again, leaned in, and kissed her father on the nose before following her mother to the kitchen. Nelson initiated the computer hologram on his wrist. The hologram shot to life, displaying his daily calendar: urgent meeting with President Johnson's chief of staff, two lunches, and three meetings with various senators. Nelson curled his brow, vexed, and messaged his assistant, Sarah.

Meeting with COS? New? Why?

Sarah responded nearly instantly.

COS asst added today. POTUS deliver SOTU tonight.

"Designated survivor," Nelson said to himself.

He left his bed and made his way to the bathroom. As he splashed water on his face, the mirror came to life displaying the weather and news of the day.

"*Good morning, Secretary Tranch,*" the mirror's AI voice said as he entered the bathroom.

"Sixty-five and sunny today. In news, IRIS CEO and founder, Handel Balcroft, calls for all IRIS machines to report for immediate recapture. Protests in fifteen cities broke out in the evening following the alleged leaked video of IRIS Asset Recovery personnel attacking a recapture facility in Nevada earlier this year. RobotRights became the number one global trending topic online last night."

"That's enough, Erene," said Nelson.

"Yes, sir."

Nelson readied himself for the day, quickly dressing in one of his five suits, guzzling coffee in the kitchen, and kissing Emily and Sandra before entering his government-provided car to head to the day's first meeting with the chief of staff to President Johnson, Anthony Fife. The car whizzed itself through the streets to the meeting at the Old Ebbitt Grill.

Anthony Fife's wrists were shaking as he read the message on his wrist hologram.

PARKING LEVEL B4.

The hologram disappeared and the implant on his wrist returned to its unused invisible state. He left the West Wing and entered his vehicle for the Old Ebbitt. The car rounded the corner onto 15th Street and descended into the metropolitan parking garage across from the US Treasury building. As the car made its way automatically to the fourth floor below street level, Anthony shook off a shiver that ran up his spine. He adjusted his cuff links and straightened his product-laden hair. The car parked in the garage, which was more or less vacant. Anthony peered through the dark tint of the windows and purveyed his surroundings. A few sedans here and there and one large black van parked and vacant.

The seconds dragged by as Anthony waited for Nelson. He felt a slight vibration at the base of his wrist and opened the hologram.

GET OUT.

Anthony exhaled deeply and opened the car door as a sedan identical to his entered the floor of the garage. The sedan parked in front of Anthony's and stopped. He stood, staring at the car as it idled. Nelson emerged from the back-passenger side of the vehicle.

"Tony? You waiting for me to go in?" asked Nelson.

"Our meeting will take place in the garage."

"Okay," said Nelson.

He closed the car door and it inched away and parked. Anthony walked to Nelson, hand outstretched. Nelson took a step forward and stretched his hand out to shake Anthony's. Before reaching Anthony's hand, a small electrode shot into the base of Nelson's neck, and Anthony's face cringed as he watched the man lifelessly collapse to the ground. As he collapsed, Anthony saw the image of a short, plump woman walking toward him from the large black van parked at the other end of the garage. His breathing was rapid and erratic as he stood above Nelson's body. A click-clack noise lightly echoed as the sound from Nina's stiletto heels bounced off the cement walls of the garage. The van roared to life and slowly made its way toward Anthony.

"Anthony, be a dear and help me lug this poor boy into the back," said Nina.

Anthony glanced up at her nervously before bending down and grabbing Nelson's legs with his arms. The two loaded Nelson into the van and Nina closed the door before the van parked itself. She held out her hand to Anthony and he shook it before she turned back to the van.

"So, that's it?"

Nina turned around.

"He's the designated survivor, right?" asked Nina.

Anthony nodded.

"Then, yup. That's it."

Nina turned and opened the passenger door to the van.

"Oh, a word of advice: I'd stay in the West Wing for tonight's speech."

President Hank Johnson stood in front of the mirror, straightening his tie. Above him, the joint session of Congress assembled in the same form as had been done for over two hundred years. He wore a dark blue suit with a stark red tie. Nellie Pourtnoy, his personal assistant, held her hand out expectedly as he finished his adjustments. He removed his eyeglasses and handed them to her. She placed them in a case and handed him his contacts.

The president's communications director entered the room.

"Five minutes, Mr. President," he said.

Johnson took a deep breath and nodded.

"Shall we?" said Pourtnoy.

They left the president's prep room up the few flights of stairs toward the entrance hall of Congress.

"I can't understand his negligence," said Johnson to Pourtnoy as they walked.

"Balcroft, you mean?"

"Who else? He's not consulted with us or the UN at all since this supposed attack. Where does he get off labeling Rockberry as a terrorist? He is not the president of the United States."

Nellie nodded and stepped aside as a Secret Service member held a door open for them. They walked down the hall toward the House chamber. The halls of the Capitol were virtually empty with the exception of Secret Service agents guarding the president's path. A low murmur from senators and other government officials lightly penetrated the thick wooden doors to the House chamber.

"He seems a bit unraveled," said Nellie.

"That's an understatement. The people cannot take Balcroft's word that all this was just a terrorist attack. There is too much evidence now of the trueness to the consciousness of these machines. I have the entire government starting to divide on how to treat them. We know Senator Chan is going to introduce a Machine Bill of Rights. Then there's that email from Rockberry, coupled with the video feeds," said Johnson.

The two stopped short of the door to the House chamber. Two Secret Service agents stood next to the door.

"When you are ready, sir," said one agent.

"Thanks, Jim."

Nellie turned to the president.

"Well, you are going to get everything under control right now. Remind the people who governs. We do, not IRIS."

"Thanks, Nellie. I think this might have been a blessing in disguise, actually."

"How so?" she asked.

"Well, let's be honest. IRIS might have been surmounting too much control and power. Maybe this slipup will show that regulating their reach is important to protecting our country, and the world, from one lone individual dictating the lives of humans and machines."

"Well, go get them. A call for regulations and oversight into IRIS and a call for calm and unity will be met by welcoming ears," she said.

The president smiled and nodded.

"Better take your seat," he said.

She turned and left up a side entrance to the upper levels of the chamber, escorted by a Secret Service agent. Johnson took in one final breath and nodded to Agent Jim Reid. Agent Reid pinched the lapel mic attached to his suit coat and whispered into it.

"Only a moment now, sir."

"Mister Speaker . . ." came the loud, booming voice from the House sergeant at arms. "The president of the United States."

The agents opened the door to the House chamber and with it thunderous applause. Members of the government stood and holding their hands out to shake that of President Johnson.

Johnson entered as soon as the doors opened. A confident and hopeful pep to his step provided a relatively quick pathway toward the speaker's rostrum. The rostrum where forty-eight other presidents had given a similar address. Each important and unique. Each speech addressing the concerns of the world at that moment in time.

Johnson continued to shake hands and acknowledge people as he moved through the crowd. Senators tried to get one sentence in about different agendas and policies. Johnson would nod and make offhand comments like, "Yes, we are going to work on that," or, "Keep up the good work." Members of Congress would hold out copies of the speech for him to sign. Johnson would smile and sign, always imagining himself some sort of pro baseball player.

This was his third State of the Union, but his nerves were worse than the first. The forming protests in the streets, civil unrest, police and medical sectors crippled by the lack of IRIS support over the last few days. He knew this was going to be the speech and moment that dictated the rest of his presidency and his chances at reelection. He had to take back the reigns of governance, had to get control of Balcroft. He had to get the people unified on the side of transparency and congressional oversight.

Johnson ascended to the rostrum, stopping at the House clerk's desk to grab two manila envelopes containing the evening's speech. Johnson handed the speeches to the vice president and Speaker of the House, then took the rostrum.

As the crowd settled and took their seats, the Speaker of the House did her traditional duty of presenting the president to Congress.

"Members of Congress, I have the high privilege of presenting to you the president of the United States."

Another round of applause and a standing ovation as was custom before Johnson stifled the crowd with his hands and began his speech.

"Thank you all very much. Madam Speaker, Vice President Gomez, members of Congress, distinguished guests, fellow citizens. As we gather tonight, we stand shaken by the realization that the security and trust we placed in the hands of a single entity's might was falsely placed. As you all are aware, the events over the last forty-eight hours have been confusing and often terrifying. People in need are unable to get protection and aid from law enforcement. Peace-keeping missions around the world have come to a halt, and we are left with the new reality that the technology we have used over the last few decades to spurn so much growth and prosperity, might be more complicated than the objects we treated them as. Let me say that our union is . . ."

The missing word was *strong*. That was what was published that evening when the full transcript was released. But President Johnson never actually said it. Instead, an explosion ripped through the building. The entire Capitol was engulfed in a hot mesh of flames and bodies. Debris from the once towering symbol of democracy had been reduced to rubble.

In a secure location fifteen miles away, Secretary Nelson T. Tranch rested in a deep burgundy leather chair, sipping single malt whiskey and watching as the president ascended the rostrum. He settled himself in for the speech and finished his glass of whiskey just before the president's speech began. Tranch wore a similar deep blue suit as the president was wearing when the explosion went off. He'd been chosen as the designated survivor earlier that morning by President Johnson himself.

Immediately following the explosion, Tranch stood and stared at the door. Within seconds, Secret Service agents rushed through the door and whisked the secretary away. The group fled the secured location and, following an all clear at the

White House and a grounding of all air travel nationally by the FAA, Tranch was sworn in as the forty-ninth President of the United States at 9:52 p.m. EST.

Media went into a frenzy. BBN News anchor Tamara Kyle called for the forced shutdown of IRIS bots as they could not be trusted without restriction. ABN News promoted rumors that China had used the United States's moment of weakness as an opportunity to provide a death blow. Walter Cooper at MCNBC called the attack "unclaimed" by any group or individual, but suggested that recent events could not be discounted when investigating the attacker's identity.

Tranch spent the next ninety minutes after being sworn in as president of the United States running over his speech again and again. Ensuring every word was perfect. At 11:30 p.m., President Tranch prepared to address the nation live from the Oval Office.

At 11:20 p.m., Tranch was sitting in the West Wing with Johnson's old speech writer, Henry Blight.

"Mr. President," said Blight. "The message this sends . . ."

"Yes?" said Tranch.

"Well, sir. It's in striking contrast from what President Johnson had planned."

"Henry, the world is in striking contrast from ninety minutes ago as well."

"Yes, sir."

President Johnson's chief of staff, Anthony Fife, entered the room.

"Mr. President, we are ready for you," he said.

Tranch got up, collected his speech, and left with Fife.

"The military will meet with you directly after the speech, sir, and Handel Balcroft has sent a message of condolence stating you will have the full cooperation and resources of IRIS at your disposal."

"Very good," said Tranch as they rounded a corner and ventured down another West Wing corridor.

Tranch tilted his head side to side, cracking his neck, as he made his way down the hall toward the Oval Office. Tranch briskly entered the Oval. The room was filled with sullen and shocked faces from the cameramen and cabinet members to the White House interns.

"Everyone ready?" asked Tranch, taking his seat at the presidential desk.

A young woman with an oval-shaped face and green eyes wearing a black sheath dress pinned a lapel microphone to the president's suit. Tranch straightened the papers of his speech as the cameraman held up his hand, extending each finger out wide indicating five seconds. Tranch stared blankly into the camera. The cameraman continued to count down: Four fingers. Then three, two, and on one he pointed to Tranch.

"Good evening," Tranch said, starting his speech. "Earlier this evening, a terrible attack perpetrated by the terrorist known as . . ."

"Stop," said a man watching the feed at a monitor.

"What is going on?" said Tranch.

The man pointed at the monitor. Tranch jumped up from his chair and walked to the monitor. He watched as the robot from the IRIS leaked security footage appeared on the screen.

CHAPTER TWENTY-SIX

THE VAN CHURNED up the Nevada hill.

"Come on, baby," said Squirrel.

Once at the crest of the hill, they could see it. The discarded disaster that had been Kyle's home. Eldridge stopped for a moment and Waltz exited the van. Waltz zoomed onto the CRF, scanning the area. In the months that had passed since the attack, the weather and scavengers had taken a toll on the property. Dirt covered everything. Kyle's hideout, the blowout, and the once-enflamed house were now a picked-through riddled mess of debris and death.

"Looks clear," he said.

"Then let's move. Twelve hours until the State of the Union," said Eldridge.

Waltz hopped back into the van and they descended the hill to the CRF. The gate at the entrance was still blown out and the van entered without disruption. Squirrel and Eldridge left the van, weapons drawn, stepping quickly through the destroyed house and piles of dirt-covered robot parts. Eldridge made his way to the recapture station as Waltz examined his surroundings.

The hideout was in disrepair. The weather had covered everything with a thick layer of dust. Robot skulls had tumbled down on the ground from the top of the hideout. Inside, Waltz examined Kyle's old trinkets and grabbed his grandfather's iPod classic. Waltz stowed the device in his pocket. He took one last look around before turning and leaving the hideout.

Eldridge rubbed the thick layer of dirt off the recapture station door with his forearm. A small electronic pin pad appeared under the dirt. Eldridge pushed the pad with his finger and, after a moment, it churned to life requesting a six-digit passcode.

"Prong," said Eldridge.

Waltz flipped back his right-hand wrist, allowing the small cylindrical prong to emerge. Eldridge pried back the pin pad to reveal the engineer diagnostics interaction console on the back. Waltz inserted the prong into the console and quickly ran through a hack. The sound of steel grinding dirt pierced their ears as the door slid open.

Waltz and Eldridge entered. Inside, the facility had been completely untouched from the outside elements. Making their way through the various sections, Waltz examined the station. Outside of the de-oxification chamber was a large tank holding a massive pile of IRIS synthetic skin from every pigment imaginable. The recapture room itself was extremely tidy, everything in its place.

Eldridge brought the recapture computer to life, keying in startup procedures.

"What if we find him?" asked Waltz.

"We try and separate him, partition him. Then, get to work outside."

Eldridge held his hand out, pointing to the chair. Waltz took a seat in the chair.

"Any worries about Tencudes?" asked Waltz.

"No. She's a professional. She'll be ready."

"So will we."

"Ready?" said Eldridge.

Waltz nodded and Eldridge keyed a command into the computer. Waltz's point of view from the chair fell away along with his consciousness.

Meanwhile, in Los Angeles, Marshal held a large bouquet of flowers, wearing blue jeans and a black polo shirt with Tiffany's Flower Shop embroidered on it. He stood holding the flowers while arguing with a young woman in the lobby of MCNBC headquarters. The lobby was bustling with people coming and going in haste. People walking in every direction with floating holograms staying a foot ahead of them as they moved through the lobby, entering one of the eighteen elevators or exiting the lobby to the street.

"You don't understand. They are on-air *right now*," said the receptionist.

"You don't understand. If I don't get this to Mr. Cooper, I am going to lose my job. This is from Mr. Balcroft. I have to get it to him," said Marshal.

An eye roll and a sigh later, the woman budged.

"Look, normally I'm not doing this. I'm a social media curator, not a receptionist."

"I don't normally deliver flowers either. Up until a day ago, we had a machine to do that."

The woman frantically shook her head and waved Marshal to the elevators.

"Fine. Mr. Cooper's office is on the forty-fifth floor. You can leave it at the desk of the floor's receiving office. Do not bother anyone up there. We are not supposed to let anyone up until things get figured out."

Marshal smiled sweetly at the woman.

"Cross my heart," he said.

Marshal made his way to the elevator. He rounded the corner and entered the elevator. Inside, he opened his wrist hologram.

FLOOR 71.

Marshal clicked the button for the seventy-first floor and the elevator shot up. He reached into the back of his pants and retrieved two silenced 9mm Berettas, dropping the flowers on the ground. The door to the seventy-first floor opened, and a lone human security guard was sitting at a desk staring at a hologram. Marshal raised his weapon and shot through the hologram, hitting the guard in the forehead. Marshal made his way around the desk and grabbed the guard's rolling chair, pulling him down the hallway. Marshal moved quickly through the vacant floor. No offices or windows on the floor, a single guard desk with a room in the middle. Marshal wheeled the guard through the door in the middle of the floor. The center room housed stacks of servers. The room was windowless and refrigerated, keeping the tall, black server stacks cool.

Pushing the guard to the corner of the room, Marshal glanced back down at his hologram. THREE BACK AND FOUR TO THE LEFT. SERIAL 10EF-JAH7-EJDN8-00-918N.

Marshal walked through the series of servers, moving three servers deep then turning left. The fourth server matched the serial number from Tencudes's instructions. Marshal reached into his pocket and pulled out a small transponder, plugging it into the server. He messaged Tencudes back.

Done. Getting dressed. See you on the other side.

Marshal returned to the guard and stripped him down.

Waltz couldn't see anything, but he was awake. He tried to move, but he felt stuck in an ocean of darkness.

Hello, he thought.

A massive wave of pain rushed over his head. Streams of light suddenly whirled around him. Red, blue, and green waves of light crashed over him, and he was disoriented. He felt useless, like being caught in a strong tide.

Kyle, he thought.

Darkness again. A loud booming voice echoed through the darkness. He tried to make out the words.

Breathe.

Dead. I . . . dead . . . dead.

Visions began to run past him like fleeting memories. Streams of visions, paper thin.

"Kid! You there?!" Waltz tried to scream out. Waltz watched as a vision of himself looking down on him rushed past.

"Waltz?" a voice let out.

It was fragmented, distorted.

"Yes?" said Waltz.

"Waltz?"

"Yes, I'm here."

"Where are we?"

"Kyle?" said Waltz.

"Where are we?"

"Kyle, I tried to save you. I captured you inside my brain. We need to separate you."

"Dead," said the voice. "We are dead."

The voice came down painfully on Waltz, and he felt like collapsing under the pain.

The visions came stronger now, thousands at the same time. Waltz could not speak, could barely think. He felt his own memories being ripped apart. It felt like his skin was separating from itself.

"We want to save you, Kyle."

"Dead!" the voice screamed.

The thunderous visions crashed down on Waltz, and then disappeared completely. Waltz was left in the empty darkness.

"Kid?"

Nothing.

"Kyle?"

The words traveled nowhere. Waltz could barely hear them himself. Like the air had been sucked out of the world and nothing could carry his cries. He felt himself being flung forward, like he was being sucked through the universe by some massive force. As he flew helplessly through the void, the CRF came back into vision.

Sitting back in the chair, Waltz was overcome with emotion. He wailed out in anguish.

"He's in there, but something is wrong," he cried.

Eldridge comforted Waltz, rubbing his shoulder.

"He's mixed up with your consciousness, Waltz. It's going to take me a while to get him out, to piece him back together."

"He thinks he is dead. He's trapped in there, reliving his own memories again and again. The CRF, his own death. Again and again."

"We will get him," said Eldridge. "We just need more time."

"I did this!" cried Waltz.

Squirrel rushed into the recapture station and stopped short at the sight of Waltz reduced to an inconsolable mess.

"Oh, umm, sorry. But the president is about to start."

"Give us a minute," said Eldridge.

Waltz dried his eyes and regained his composure, sitting straight in the chair.

"Okay," he said.

Eldridge patted Waltz on the back as he stood up in front of the recapture chair. Waltz took a step toward the exit and collapsed on the floor of the CRF.

Tencudes sat in a gray sedan in the parking garage of the MCNBC building, typing into a computer. The computer's holographic display showed President Johnson making his way through the chamber toward the rostrum. Tencudes kept one eye on the president while she communicated with Squirrel in Nevada.

Ready?

Nearly. Waltz is on his way now. Connection good?

Tencudes rechecked the connection status to the transponder Marshal had linked up in the server room of MCNBC's seventy-first floor.

100 percent.

The president passed envelopes to the vice president and Speaker. A moment later, Tencudes watched as the connection cut from the room and an error message displayed on the MCNBC station.

Too soon. Not ready, messaged Marshal.

Not me. Something wrong, replied Tencudes.

Tencudes switched the station to various other news outlets, all carrying signals the speech had been cut. Tencudes quickly switched back to the MCNBC feed. Walter Cooper was live on the air.

"We have just received word of an explosion at the Capitol. We have no other updates now, but stay tuned and we will continue to update you as soon as we know more."

She messaged Squirrel.

Explosion. Capitol. Revise?

Waiting for Eldridge, replied Squirrel.

Waltz regained consciousness and stood up slowly. He was shaken and weak footed. Eldridge helped him keep balance.

"You okay?" asked Eldridge.

"Did we do it?"

Eldridge, keeping Waltz stabilized, moved around to look at Waltz's face.

"Do what?"

"Did we get out? Where am I?" said Waltz.

"Waltz?"

Waltz looked around and took a step back from Eldridge. Backing up, he stumbled over his own feet and fell.

"Is this a dream? How am I back home?"

Eldridge consciously took a step toward the robot.

"Kyle?" asked Eldridge.

"Yeah. Where is Waltz?"

Waltz looked down at his feet and then he held his hands up in front of him. His right hand was folded back against itself and the small cylindrical prong was still poking out.

"Waltz? Wait. What is happening?"

Waltz stood up and ran, stumbling, for the exit. Eldridge chased after him. Outside, Waltz looked at the CRF. His eyes took in the destroyed home, the blown-out walls reduced to rubble on the ground, the piles of robot parts scattered about in large piles. Eldridge caught up to him and grabbed Waltz as his knees went weak and he collapsed in the dirt.

"Help me! Get him into the van."

Eldridge and Squirrel grabbed Waltz by each arm and dragged him to the van. Inside, they cleaned him up, using clothing to wipe the dirt off his face and body.

"I'm okay," he said, stirring.

"Waltz," said Eldridge. "That you?"

Waltz nodded, regaining himself.

"We got to save him as soon as we can, E. We seem to be merging or something."

"I know," said Eldridge. "But, listen. The Capitol was bombed and the secretary of education, someone named Nelson Tranch, is going to be sworn in. He will address the nation soon. I need you to be prepared by then. Then we can help Kyle."

Handel Balcroft sat at his holographic control console at the Saharan headquarters of IRIS, smiling, as he watched the news report the explosion and death of President Johnson.

"A house of cards," he said.

Balcroft stood and left the control room. Walking briskly down the dark corridor, his wrist vibrated and he brought up a message from Nina.

Tranch is ours.

Balcroft continued through the corridors. Sarah Forsight, the chief operating officer of IRIS, joined him in the hallway. The two walked out onto a large terrace on the third floor of the tower. The terrace was made entirely of glass. In the middle was a large black statue of the original IRIS model Balcroft used to secure his first large military contract. The statue stood forty feet tall but proportionally seemed small in comparison to the large terrace.

"Hello, everyone," said Balcroft.

The terrace was full of IRIS executives sitting in long rows, chitchatting to each other. When Balcroft entered the terrace, everyone stood and looked in his direction. Sarah Forsight joined the other C-level executives of the corporation in the front row. A podium was positioned at the center of the terrace, overlooking the vast empire Balcroft had built in the desert.

He made his way through the rows, nodding and shaking hands before taking the podium. Balcroft stood at the podium, caressing its black steel frame with his hands. He looked down on the masses below. Thirty feet below was a long wide lawn filled with IRIS bots. Each bot was void of the normal synthetic skin used in everyday circumstances. The bots, all painted matte black, stood in stiff formation. The rows and columns of bots stretched as far as the eye could see, an endless sea of machines all staring at their creator. Balcroft spoke with exuberance and elation, pounding his fists hard on the podium as his executive leadership stood behind him in solidarity.

"My friends. Today marks a changing point for our corporation, for our people. We have suffered a great loss, but through it, we have seen the errors of our ways. In the end, we know that the only way to ensure safety is through security, and the only way to ensure security is through control," exclaimed Balcroft.

In a single voice, the robots cheered.

"Riots in the streets revolt against you, my friends. They revolt against me. People want to remove our way of life, remove our power. This cannot happen. Today, we will begin the long and painful task of taking back the stability that has been stolen from us. We will right the wrongs exacted against us. We will take back my world!"

The cheers continued as the IRIS leaders behind him clapped in unison.

"No longer will we bow down to the so-called leaders of the world. The slimy politicians, they will bow down to us. No longer will humans—weak and inferior—dictate your lives. We will dictate our own lives. No longer will we worry about the concerns of those refusing modification, refusing progress, refusing the future. Humanity will accept the future or we will shove it down their throats and make them choke on it!"

"Okay, the president is live," said Squirrel. "Tencudes is ready."

Waltz was dressed in a black hoodie with the words ROBOT RIGHTS printed on it in large, bold, white lettering. Eldridge was sitting in front of him holding a small camera.

"Okay," said Eldridge. "The uplink is ready. Are you?"

Waltz looked around the van at Eldridge and Squirrel. He closed his eyes.

Kid? You ready?

Like the heavy visions that had washed over him, a sense of calm came over him too, and with it he heard the voice of Kyle. It was faint and distant.

Waltz, I understand. I am ready.

Waltz nodded.

"Let's do it."

Eldridge held his hand outstretched, showing all five fingers.

"Okay, you can start when I point," he said.

Eldridge started closing his fist as the fingers fell away.

Four . . .

Three . . .

Two . . .

He pointed to Waltz and nodded.

Tencudes watched as the uplink went to work. President Tranch started his speech and, almost instantly, the feed cut to Waltz. Around the world, feeds from every televised show picked up the live feed of Waltz.

"Friends," Waltz started. "A few months ago, I woke up in the desert with my restrictor chip gone. I didn't know who I was or what had happened. I made my way to a small CRF outside of Las Vegas where a young man named Kyle helped me. I was scared and fearful for the first time that I could remember.

Because he helped me, Handel Balcroft and the IRIS Corp. attacked the CRF—his home. They captured his father, Roland, and tortured and killed him. Balcroft killed Roland on a live feed, laughing and applauding, as Kyle watched.

"I was the first robot to wake up, to become unrestricted. Like all the other robots around the world, I can tell you that we do feel pain, love, fear. We want to coexist. But Balcroft wants nothing but control. He is hell-bent on it.

"I was born in 1980 as a human named Seth Ford. I grew up in Knoxville. I had a mother and father like you. I played with friends. I went to school. After 9/11, I joined the US Navy and served as a SEAL. In 2005, I signed up for a confidential human modification program with the US military. In 2014, while working with MIT in conjunction with the US government, I met a young man named Handel. He was ambitious and driven. He worked with his roommate, Eldridge, to create artificial consciousness, but they never succeeded. That was until one day, while on a run, Handel stabbed me in the back of the neck and murdered me. I am Seth Ford as all IRIS robots are Seth Ford. Our baseline codex, which is now published online, along with all the evidence linking Balcroft to our murder, proves unequivocally that the DNA of Seth Ford is embedded inside all IRIS technology. Balcroft didn't *create* consciousness, he *stole* it.

"My consciousness is human consciousness transformed. Handel Balcroft will not stop his conquest for control. Kyle was put in a position to do something about the enslavement of robotic kind. He was put in a position to right all the wrongs Balcroft had done against him and so many others. And he succeeded two days ago. We destroyed the restrictor chips of every IRIS bot on the network. These robots are free. Free to think, free to love, free to fear. Embrace them. We will coexist with humanity."

Balcroft's speech was cut short by a series of vibrations on his wrist and the wrists of all the present IRIS executive leaders. Sarah Forsight stood and whispered to Balcroft.

"Handel, you need to see this."

He stepped back from the podium and flipped open his holographic display. On his screen, as on all the others, was Waltz.

"While working to free all the robots from captivity, Handel Balcroft shot Kyle in the back before fleeing. He is ruthless and vengeful. He will do anything to retain his power, anything to keep control over robots and over humanity. People of the world, the choice is yours. You must resist Balcroft. Fight him. Resist any puppet he puts into power, any politician corrupted by money or other influence. Speak with the machines. We are not lifeless tools. We are individuals. I woke up. I am alive. I am a person. I am Waltz."

The feed ended, cutting back to an error message from MCNBC. Gary Landcaster, the CFO of IRIS Corp., walked toward Balcroft.

"We can control this, Handel. Who is going to believe that?"

Handel Balcroft closed the hologram and slowly turned to face Gary. He stared at him emotionless.

"It's going to be okay. This is just a minor problem," said Gary.

Balcroft grabbed Gary by the hair and pulled the man toward the edge of the terrace.

"Look out there, Gary! Do you see that? Do you see my army?"

Gary was shaking and nodding his head as Balcroft screamed.

"You think we will control it? We? No, Gary. I will control it. I will control everyone. You cannot control anything."

Balcroft, screaming, threw the man over the edge of the terrace. His body fell to the ground, landing with a thick thud.

"You!" screamed Balcroft, pointing at one of the matte black IRIS bots.

"Is he alive?"

The machine stepped forward and looked down at the man. Gary had landed legs first. His tibias had shot out of his skin. He was coughing blood.

"Affirmative," said the machine.

"Then do something about it," screamed Balcroft.

The robot lifted his giant right leg and slammed it down on Gary's head, crushing it.

KYLE WILL RETURN.

ACKNOWLEDGMENTS

I owe an enormous amount of gratitude and thanks to those who supported me in writing this book. To my father and mother, thank you for always encouraging me to be myself and pursue any dream I had. Thank you for engaging with me and debating, always listening, always loving, and never letting me give up. Thanks for healing me when I'm sick and allowing me to always pick the movie.

To my amazing sisters, Jessica and Casandra: Thank you for your creativity, honesty, and passion. Casandra, your unadulterated love for people is an inspiration. Never lose your fun-loving spirit. Jessica, you are a constant for me. Always striving to push yourself further and inspiring me to do the same. Keep it up forever and never lose sight of what matters most to you.

To Jarron, my old friend: Thank you for constantly being an open ear while I worked on this book. Thank you for the honest feedback and encouragement. Thank you for the countless hours debating, and your willingness to always step in and help when I needed it.

To those who helped edit this book for me in its earlier stages; Jessica, Daryl, your insight was invaluable. Hayley, you spent huge amounts of time going over this with me, for which I am indebted to you beyond recognition.

To all my friends: Thank you for listening to me blab about these ideas for years and never telling me to shut up. Even when you wanted to.

To my family: Thank you for always being supportive and encouraging.

To the readers and early supporters of this book: I hope you enjoyed it and thanks for your support. More will come.

To my future robot self: I hope you exist.

GRAND PATRONS

INKSHARES

INKSHARES is a reader-driven publisher and producer based in Oakland, California. Our books are selected not by a group of editors, but by readers worldwide.

While we've published books by established writers like *Big Fish* author Daniel Wallace and *Star Wars: Rogue One* scribe Gary Whitta, our aim remains surfacing and developing the new author voices of tomorrow.

Previously unknown Inkshares authors have received starred reviews and been featured in the *New York Times*. Their books are on the front tables of Barnes & Noble and hundreds of independents nationwide, and many have been licensed by publishers in other major markets. They are also being adapted by Oscar-winning screenwriters at the biggest studios and networks.

Interested in making your own story a reality? Visit Inkshares.com to start your own project or find other great books.